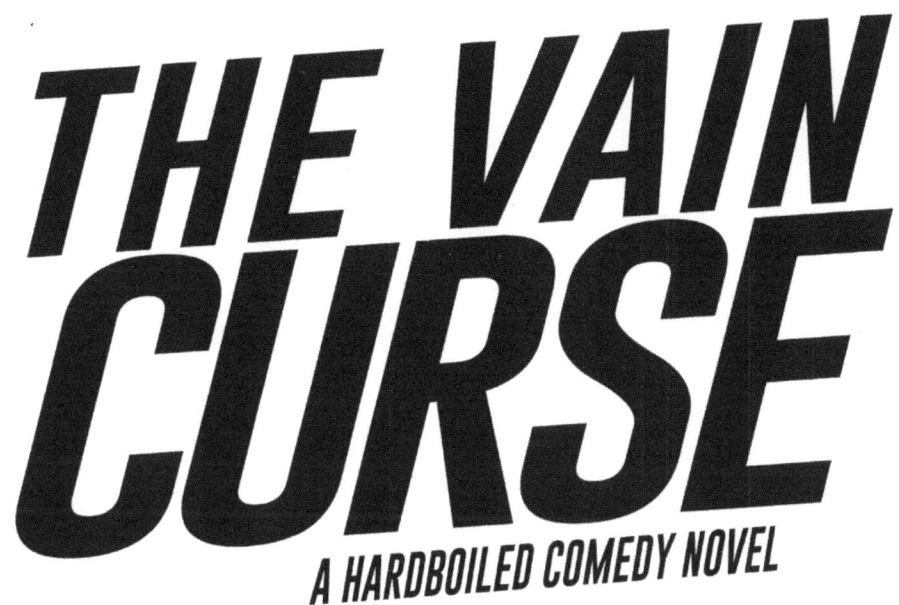

THE VAIN CURSE

A HARDBOILED COMEDY NOVEL

RYAN MORGAN MILLER

Black Rose Writing | Texas

The author grants the final approval for this literary material.

First printing

This is a work of fiction. Names, characters, businesses, places, events, and incidents are either the products of the author's imagination or used in a fictitious manner. Any resemblance to actual persons, living or dead, or actual events is purely coincidental.

ISBN: 978-1-68513-232-3
PUBLISHED BY BLACK ROSE WRITING
www.blackrosewriting.com

Printed in the United States of America
Suggested Retail Price (SRP) $21.95

The Vain Curse is printed in Minion Pro

*As a planet-friendly publisher, Black Rose Writing does its best to eliminate unnecessary waste to reduce paper usage and energy costs, while never compromising the reading experience. As a result, the final word count vs. page count may not meet common expectations.

To Meg

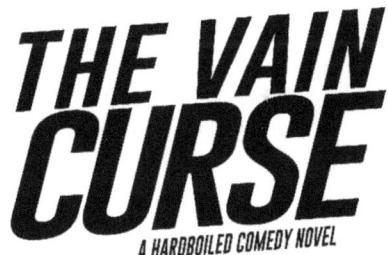

**THE VAIN
CURSE**

A HARDBOILED COMEDY NOVEL

1

Carly Simon is a cruel-hearted shrew. As I drink myself into the sweet, sweet embrace of oblivion, this is the only thing I know for certain.

The name's Tracer. Tracer Spence, Private Eye. P.I. for short, I guess, though I know "eye" starts with an "E." Just one of the many Sherlockian observations that average people hire me for. Because detecting is my business. Though my landlord calls it my hobby since it doesn't pay the rent. I tell him he should do some stand-up with funny lines like that. He always responds the same way, "Back-pay is due by the end of the week, you idiot. Pay me or I'm evicting you." We're a regular Dean Martin and Jerry Lewis with our repartee.

I've got my own office. Name's embossed on the opaque window and door. I've even got a wooden desk with drawers. That's how you can tell I'm a real detective—drawers in my desk. My prospective clients walk in and think, "Huh, I bet he's got all kinds of case files stashed in those things. So professional. I'm sure he solves all the cases and gets all the ladies." They'd be surprised that I mainly keep crackers in there. I get munchy during the day. But I'll never let them know that. I'd rather they think I'm a regular Lothario and successful detective. And even if I did tell them I don't keep files in those drawers, I'd imply that's because all the facts are up here, up in ol' Spence's noggin.

Yep, I'm a real private investigator—huh. That's where the "I" comes from. That's one mystery solved already.

But the Carly Simon story starts the same way all of my stories start, with a man walking through my office door. Did I mention the door's embossed with my name?

Marvin Hartley didn't seem like he'd be bringing in trouble from moment one. He was kind of on the shy, nerdy side. Buttoned-up collared shirt, khakis, glasses. The kind of man who probably never envisioned himself hiring a detective.

"I can't believe private investigators even exist anymore," he said, swiveling his head around the room like his head was on some kind of swivel mechanism.

I stayed silent. Most people I meet in this line of work make me turn to one of my best friends for help. I wondered which one Marvin would make me turn to. You see, I've got three best friends, and they're all slugs. One I keep locked and loaded in my revolver to give out to my enemies. One keeps me loaded, which I keep in my hip-flask. And one I keep locked in its terrarium on my desk. I named him Moby the Mollusk, and he keeps me company in this lonely business.

"What's with the snail?" Marvin asked.

"He's a slug."

"But he's got a shell."

"He's antisocial."

Marvin shook his head. "Are you Tracer Spence?"

"Who wants to know?" I like asking this because it's a good example of how I uncover facts. I figure any would-be clients might like to see how I work.

"I'm Marvin Hartley, and I'm hoping I can use your services."

"Hoping's free, pal, but the actual employing ain't."

I picked up a clip board off my desk. "Now, before I accept any case, I've got a form to fill out. Just some standard questions for me to ask you. Keeps me organized."

According to a book I skimmed the back cover of, organization is one of seven effective habits of a successful man. I was one-seventh of the way there.

"Okay Marvin," I said, "first question. Name?"

"Are you serious?"

"Not a good start lying to your P.I. I thought you said your name was Marvin. But I get it. You want to use an alternate moniker? It's a little outside-the-box, but I'll allow it this time."

"No, no, just...fine, put down Marvin Hartley. My name is definitely, definitely Marvin Hartley."

"Moving on, then." I said. "Do you have an attorney?"

"Yes."

"Hmmm...How about a girlfriend? If yes, where did you meet her? I've tried online dating apps, but you'd be surprised how ban-happy they are these days."

"Is...is that important?" Marvin asked, straightening his tie. "Look, I just want to say that I think I'm cursed. I need help."

"Cursed? Okay, let's skip down a little bit. What kind of curse? Witch doctor, gypsy, or obscenity?"

"What? None, I guess."

"None? The questionnaire doesn't allow for that. I'll check the box for 'witch doctor' so the form looks better."

"Check what down? You're not even using a pen!"

He had caught me, that Marvin. To be fair, I had lost my pen a few days ago, trying to fish my retainer out from my office's heating vent. How'd it get back there? That was a mystery for another day. There's one thing I knew though, and that's that my childhood orthodontist wouldn't have been happy with me if he were still alive.

"Alright, alright, we'll skip with the formalities. Why don't you just tell me your story?" I motioned for him to begin.

"This is a strange request...but I heard 'You're So Vain,'—you know, the song from Carly Simon—every day for the past two months and need you to find out who the song is about."

I leapt out of my chair and grabbed Marvin by the tie. I pulled him in close to me, all intimidating-like. This wasn't as easy as it sounds, as he was wearing a clip-on bow tie. Nonetheless, I think I got my menace across.

"Who sent you? Is this a joke? Are you mocking me?" I lowered my voice to a gravelly rumble, my face an inch away from his. I could feel his hot breath on my cheeks. The sensation of another man's breath on my face wasn't as uncomfortable as I had thought it would be, to be honest.

"What? I couldn't understand you."

I repeated myself, this time slower and with much less gravel in my voice. I wish he understood me the first time.

"No one sent me! You're crazy!"

I knew he was lying because his lips were moving. Oh, that was a good saying. I decided to tell him that.

"I know you're lying because your lips are moving."

Marvin didn't appreciate my turn-of-phrase. Maybe he wasn't a fan of the English language like I was. Or maybe it was because my breath smelled faintly of whiskey.

"Really! No one sent me. I just had the urge to know about the song and didn't know where else to turn! I can't live like this anymore."

My calloused hands let go of his tie and brushed his shirt off. I motioned for him to have a seat.

"Sorry," I said. "You could say I'm a little on edge. The same thing has happened to me, only I've heard that same song going on for almost a full year now." I slumped in my patched-leather chair behind my desk again, which gave a little THHHHBBP sound as my sturdy frame hit the cushion.

"That was the chair," I said. I still giggled because it was a funny noise, but I kept my eyes on Marvin the whole time.

I took a pull from my flask, needing to steady my nerves. "It started a little over a year ago for me," I continued. "I woke up every morning to my alarm clock, set to the radio, you know, one of them old digital alarms? And it just so happened that damned song would wake me up every day, *Groundhog Day* style. I felt like Bill Murray, except it wasn't funny. So I changed the station after a few weeks. And I thought that helped, until later that same day I heard it walking into the local coffee shop. Who would've thought it to start up as soon as I entered those blasted doors? It just took off from there. I go out to dinner, blam, it's playing in the diner. I walk down the street? Some numbskull's blasting it out of their car as they're stuck in traffic next to me. I even tried staying home, watching TV on mute with captions on. But no, my neighbors decide to play Simon's greatest hits through our incredibly thin walls."

"Look, maybe the song's just having a resurgence or something," Marvin said, taking the seat across from my desk. "Like 'Africa' by Toto, how that seemed to pop up out of nowhere a few years ago. Either way, I'm also hearing 'You're So Vain' at least once a day now, and I need to know. I need to know who it's about. It's driving me crazy, Mr. Spence."

"I've had the same thoughts, Marv—mind if I call you Marv?—and no, it's not having a resurgence. I've scoured the charts for any sign of one, but nothing. We're in the same godforsaken boat, but I never thought to hire a P.I. to investigate it for me. That would be crazy! I am a P.I. What kind of world would we live in if one P.I. hired another P.I.? That would be like cats and dogs becoming friends. Or peanut butter and mayonnaise on a sandwich. Or two other things that don't go together going together. Absolute chaos."

Marvin looked at me like I was bonkers. I get that look a lot.

I could feel Marvin pulling away from me, so I decided to reel him back in like a fish. Except Marvin didn't have a hook stuck in his mouth. Nor gills. Though, to be honest, I didn't look that closely at his neck. Either way, I decided to play what we in the P.I. biz call "the old fruity tooty."

Reaching into my pocket, I pretended my phone was ringing. I may or may not have made the vibration noise with my lips.

"Excuse me, Marv, I've got to take this real quick. Probably just one of the *many* esteemed clients I have."

"Sure, go ahead, Mr. Spence."

I put the cell phone up to my ear, no one on the other end of course. But I didn't audit two semesters of *Drama Appreciation* at the local community college for nothing.

"Hello? Mr. President of the United States?" I shot a glance at Marvin, trying to convey that yes, this was really happening and yes, I'm taking that tone of annoyance with the most powerful man in the world. "Yes sir, just calm down. Of course, I'm still looking into your case of the missing diplomat. But I do have another client in the room right now, so I really must go, your excellency. Oh, you'll let me use the Oval Office for a weekend? How kind of—"

That's the moment where my phone began ringing, cutting me off from my fake conversation. The *Inspector Gadget* theme song began blaring from my phone's speakers.

"My niece put this as my ringtone," I said to Marvin. A white lie between private eye and prospective client. "Haven't figured out how to switch it back yet."

Marvin rolled his eyes, like two spotlights in the dark signaling opening night of the next Best Picture runner-up.

"Hello, this is Spence."

"I know who it is, you idiot. Don't you have this number saved in your phone yet? You can see who's calling if you just look at the screen before picking up," the voice on the other line said.

"Ah, Detective Hardholm. What's up?"

Hardholm was a cop down at the precinct a few blocks away. You could say he was the closest thing I had to a friend in this town.

"Don't talk to me like we're pals, Spence. For the last time, we're not, and no, I don't want to get some ice cream with you. Not even if you're paying."

"What? What about all those poker nights you invite me to with the rest of your cop buddies?"

"You know I only invite you because you can never remember what hand beats what hand. I've told you that, on multiple occasions," Hardholm said.

He was right. How can anyone remember if a Straight beats Two-of-a-kind or a Flush beats an Old Maid?

"Listen," he said, "I just sent this broad over to your office. It's a case. Got it? I'm doing you a favor. I—the big time police man—am sending you—the teensy-weensy private detective—an actual case. I'm doing you a favor, got it?"

"…why?" I asked.

"Honestly? Me and the guys down here at the precinct have a couple bets on if you can actually solve a case or not. And so I can win my money, you actually need to have a case."

"Thanks. Goodbye, Detective," I said, even though he had already hung up on me.

I pointed to my phone and shoved it into my pocket. "My contact down at the cop shop," I said to Marvin.

"Do all cops treat you like that?" he asked.

"How…how much of that did you hear?"

"Well," Marvin said, "you had it on speaker phone the whole time."

"Right. Gotcha."

"Look, can you do this or not?" Marvin asked.

"Why come to me, though?"

"I said, I've got nowhere else to turn to. The cops would think I'm insane. I can't just ask Carly Simon. The internet's no help. Don't you think I've tried Googling the answer before? I've got this inkling that I'll go crazy if I don't find the answer. I'm obsessing about it. I've never been someone like that, someone who's that neurotic about something so trivial. So I came to you. You're literally the only private detective listed in the phone book. Which I didn't even know they made anymore. I had to ask my grandma to borrow hers. Why don't you advertise online?"

"I'll ask the questions here, bub," I said. Though I had to admit that advertising online seemed like a good idea. I made a mental note to look into this internet craze later. "You don't think this is too contrived a coincidence, though? Same song, same thing, day in, day out?"

"I think it's absolutely a coincidence, yes."

Marvin was pretty convincing with his answer. I dropped that line of questioning.

I got up out of my chair and looked out the window behind my desk, pretending I was deep in thought. A dark storm cloud blanketed half of New York City, draping it in overcast gloom. The other half was still bright and sunny. Some people would call the weather phenomenon portentous, a bad omen. But I wasn't some superstitious meteorologist. The only thing I knew these clouds warned of was rain.

"Look, I believe I can take your case, but it's going to cost you."

"How much?"

"You got a pen?" I asked him. Marvin handed one over to me from his breast pocket. It was fancy. A sleek black fountain pen, with three platinum-coated rings and the letters "W.B." etched into the side. Or "8.M." depending on which way I held it.

I scribbled something on to the back of an unpaid bill I had lying around and pushed it over toward him. He picked it up and read aloud.

"This just says 'how much you got.'"

I nodded. Good. Marvin could read, the little trickster. I still didn't trust him. I'm not paid to trust people—I'm paid to find answers. And in this case, I wasn't even paid yet.

"Look," Marvin said, "maybe this was a mistake. I better go. I don't think you're the right man for this." Marvin got up, his shoes scuffing the hardwood floor.

In my business, you gotta let people walk away sometimes if you want to hook them. Know when to hold 'em, know when to fold 'em. Reminds me of that Kenny Rogers song. "Islands in the Stream," I think. The one with Dolly Parton. What a babe she was. I'd let her sail away on my other world. One way or the other though, Marvin Hartley would never leave this room without hiring me for his job.

Next thing I knew I was kneeling in front of him, tears running down my face, sobbing. "Don't go, I n-n-need this, I can't afford my r-rent, p-p-please." Had 'im right where I wanted 'im.

Marvin put his hand on my shoulder. "There, there. Pull yourself together, man."

I pulled him in close and audibly blew my nose on his shirt. Finally, I stood up, lumbering over him by half an inch and wiped my eyes. "Thank you," I said, again in a gravelly, low voice to keep my dignity. I didn't care if he didn't hear me, I wasn't going to change my tone again.

Negotiations continued from there. He told me at first that money was no limit and he could spare no expense. I responded with telling him my normal hourly fee. He agreed to it, and then I lowered it. In retrospect, I should've listened to his side of the debate instead of following my normal script on auto-pilot. But Marv here was excellent at hard-ball. I swore I would never let him get the upper hand again.

I said I'd start right away on his case, and we shook hands. He pulled away almost immediately and wiped his hand off on his shirt. My hand was a little sticky, admittedly—another drawer in my desk is just full of sea-salt taffy—but it's not like his hand was the Queen of England's either. And I bet she'd have the good grace to not be so gosh-dang rude about it either. I heard them British royalties have to take classes on that sort of thing, social cues and all. Maybe that's how she got to be Queen, had the highest scores. I'd have to remind myself to research how to become a queen.

"Thank you, Mr. Spence," Marvin said. "I know it's such a strange case, but I'm desperate."

"Ain't we all?"

After that, I showed him the door. I'm quite proud of that door, but he wasn't impressed. Did I mention I got its window embossed with my name? It's not every day you see that. Still though, he left without commenting on it. I'd have to sign Marvin up for those British manners classes next time he came around.

2

Serena Dayton came in to my office like a storm. That is to say the waterworks started right away, she was full of rage, and she smelled a lot like what I imagine hurricanes to smell like. Toasted almond and a hint of lime.

I asked her to have a seat, gesturing to the stack of milk crates in front of my desk. I "rescued" them from an alley one night and never looked back.

She looked at me and the crates, sighed, and sat down. She pulled a tissue out of her oversized purse and dried her eyes with it.

"So, Ms…"

"Dayton. Serena Dayton." Her voice wavered like a drunk teenager playing the saxophone.

"Ms. Dayton. I understand you may have a case for me? My friend down at the precinct sent you?"

"You mean Officer Hardholm? He specifically told me to tell you that you're not friends."

"Yeah, that's just an inside joke between me and him," I said.

"He said you'd say that and that I should reply with, 'no, it's not just an inside joke. Stop telling clients that we're friends, and stop then saying that it's an inside joke.' I thought that was a really strange thing for a cop to tell me, honestly."

I took this awkward moment to get a sense of who Serena Dayton was. Her brown hair was pulled up in a bun, like a stereotypical librarian. She had those pointy cat eyeglasses, also like a stereotypical librarian. She wore a conservative beige jacket over a white blouse, again, just like a stereotypical librarian.

"Why are you looking at me like that?" She asked. "Stop it. It's freaking me out."

"Are you a librarian?"

"What? No. I'm a mechanic. Have a shop over in Bridgeport."

Likely story, I thought to myself. Turns out, it was a likely story because it was the truth. The likeliest of stories.

"So how can I help you?"

"It's…" Serena started, sobbing and wiping her eyes again, her tissue too damp to make any difference. Those eyes were gorgeous, bright blue, like the tip of a gas flame. "It's my sister, Ellie. She's gone missing. I'm worried she's been kidnapped. Or worse."

"Why do you think that?" I pulled out my small leather-bound journal which I use to take notes for cases and started using Marvin's pen to take notes.

"We normally talk once a week or so, and she hasn't answered my calls for a couple of weeks now. Hasn't called me back. I thought I would surprise her this morning, but no one was in her apartment, which was a complete wreck. She's a neat freak, you know? And she also has this…this fish, Wanda, like after the movie? Ellie loves that fish. Talks about her all the time. But when I showed up this morning, the fish was dead, just floating there in its tank."

Serena broke down, weeping. She blew her nose with her tissue loudly. It was very unattractive. That has nothing to do with her, but have you seen someone crying? All those muscles moving in not normal ways and all that yucky body fluid stuff going on? Just kind of gross.

"Do you…do you have any tissues?" she asked.

I opened one of my desk drawers and passed over a roll of toilet paper, like any normal adult man would use to blow their nose. She took it with only a minimum of eye rolling.

"It definitely sounds like something happened," I said. "But why jump to the conclusion that she was kidnapped?"

"Last time we talked she said to me, 'Serena,' she said, 'if you don't hear from me for a while, it means I was kidnapped.'"

"Huh." I massaged the palm of my hand. Scribbling in my journal was giving me a cramp. I looked at my notes. Just a drawing of me as Superman.

I looked back up at Serena. "So, Ms. Dayton, I'm only going to ask you this once. I want you to be completely honest with me, now." I paused for dramatic effect. "Did you do it? Did you kidnap your own sister?"

"Of course not! How could you even ask me that?"

"It's a little-known statistic, but 85% of clients are actually the offenders." I didn't know if that was actually true or not. I read that off of a Snapple bottle cap once years ago.

"That sounds made up."

"You sound made up," I mumbled.

"What?"

"Why come to me? Why not just let the police handle this? I know Hardholm sent you here, but if it's that dire, I don't get why," I said, redirecting the conversation.

"They blew me off," Serena said. She smoothed her blouse out, tugging at the bottom of its seams. "Said that they'd look into it, but that these sorts of cases rarely get solved. There was no blackmail note left behind, she's a grown adult, all of that stuff. So, I figured hiring a private detective might be the best way.

She's my sister. I would do anything for her."

The jingle for Klondike bars popped into my head. I thought it best not to mention that though.

"Ms. Dayton, do you know who would want to harm your sister? Any enemies? Anyone that would want to kidnap her?" I asked.

"No, nothing that pops into mind. She's well-liked at work. It's not as if she's filthy rich or anything. I can't imagine anyone that would want to hurt her." She rolled off a section of toilet paper and blew her nose again. "I did find this in Ellie's apartment though."

Serena reached into her oversized purse and pulled out a strange piece of jewelry. It was a golden arm bracelet—a thin band at the top with an arc and a star connected by chain links. The chains ran through the middle of the star design and towards the bottom, curving outwards at both ends. They connected to the band on the back-end of the bracelet. Diamond studs were also inlayed at each point of the star.

She placed it on my desk, halfway between me and her.

"I found it under Ellie's bed. I was straightening the mess up and saw something glinting in a mirror. I reached under and…well, this isn't hers. It's too—it's gaudy. Ellie didn't even like wearing earrings."

I referred to my notes. Superman was now holding a balloon while flying through space. Yep, this case was certainly shaping up to be interesting.

Serena continued, "Whoever took her must have left this at her place and forgot about it. Please, Mr. Spence, take it. Use it to find out what happened."

I looked at the ugly piece of jewelry. I wondered how much I could hock it for. Then I remembered I had a lifetime ban at the local pawn-store. The owner had an issue with me for buying my own microwave back using only loose change. It took me weeks to scoop 32 bucks worth of nickels and quarters out of wishing ponds, but no, some people want coins wrapped. Meaning I still had to eat my Hot Pockets cold, like a feral animal whose microwave was still sitting in a pawn shop's window.

Under the circumstances, I decided to do the noble thing and instead use the piece of jewelry in my investigation.

"Don't worry, Serena. I'll take good care of this. It'll go right in my hidden safe."

"Your hidden safe?" she asked. "You mean the one behind that *Little Giants* poster hanging up?" She pointed to the wall on my right.

"What? How—? No. There's no safe there," I lied. Of course I had a safe hidden there, protected by Rick Moranis' bespectacled face.

"It's not like it's in the wall all the way. I can see the outline of the handle and the combination knob through the poster."

"What I meant was—that's my *decoy* safe. Yeah. Decoy safe."

She didn't look convinced, so I repeated the words *decoy safe* a handful more times under my breath as a subliminal message.

"Stop saying that."

From there, we discussed the contract and the terms of my payment. Maybe I was on a high from my conversation with Marvin an hour or so beforehand, because Serena and I hammered out the details more quickly.

"Can I wire you the fee?" she asked, as she was signing the contract. "I don't see a checking account routing number here for me to send you the money." She waved her hand over the paper, indicating the spot where that information would normally have been.

"Checking account? I don't have one."

"You don't have a checking account?"

"I don't use banks."

"You don't use banks."

"Nah, I don't do banks. They're nothing but a government-run pyramid scheme. Same with airplanes and cast iron skillets. Getting those fat cats richer. No, I like to keep my money where it can work for me—in an old sock hidden under my dresser. That's what we in the biz call 'passive income.'"

"I—what? No. No. No, fine. Whatever. The more you talk, the more stupid hiring you seems. I can't believe the police suggested you. But whatever. What other choice do I have?" Serena sobbed again, but no tears came. She waved her hand in front of my face and angled away from me so I wouldn't say anything.

I respected Serena's wishes and instead took a sip of whiskey from my flask.

After a few silent minutes, she stood up, collecting herself. Serena pushed a strand of her brunette hair out of her face and tucked it behind her ear. She reached into her purse, pulled out a ring of keys which jingled in her hands, and tossed them onto my desk. They made a thud and slid a couple inches, tapping the side of Moby's tank.

"What's this?" I asked, holding them up. "I didn't think we knew each other that well that you'd invite me over tonight."

Serena sighed in response. "Trust me, you're not my type, Mr. Spence. No, those are the keys to my sister's apartment. I thought you might like to start there. 'Cause I don't think you'll find anything at the bottom of your flask."

"Don't know unless I try," I said, taking another drink. "But good idea. I'll take a ride over later today."

And with that, Serena left my office, slamming the door on the way out.

I had two cases now. I don't think that had ever happened before. I had to remember to get a second notebook to keep my notes straight.

3

Unlike most cases, I already had a lead on the Carly Simon one. Me. Most times I have to do some work to even come up with a lead. And most times, I'm not even a suspect, let alone the number one suspect.

I had to be careful about how I approached myself. I knew I'd be a tough nut to crack. On a scale, I'd put myself between walnut and macadamia. Any of the ones with a hard, outer shell. I'd have to use one of those decorative soldier nutcrackers to get the job done—you know, the ones from that ballet that makes me fall asleep?

We private eyes learn most techniques in this business the normal way: by watching repeats of *Law and Order* or *CSI* or *NCIS* or *The Big Bang Theory*. You'd be surprised how many police procedures one can glean during these police procedural shows. But make no doubt about it, we private eyes are always on the lookout for new skills to add in our craft. Inspiration can strike from anywhere, just like a lightning bolt. Though I suppose those only strike from above. Which makes sense too. So, inspiration can strike from anywhere, as long as it's from above. Like from God or Valhalla or the Supreme Court, one of those higher powers.

I decided the best way to get information from me was the tried-and-true tested way of good cop/bad cop. That's when one cop pretends to be overly nice to a perp and the other is overly mean. Oh, sorry, perp…that stands for perpvert, I believe. I'll try to explain these terms as I go so as not to confuse you too much.

Setting up the interrogation was harder than I expected though. You see, if I were me—and to be fair, I am me—I'd know that I'd do good cop/bad cop on myself. And it's not like I could just talk to myself and expect me to answer. No way, no how, that would be crazier than a pack of Himalayan mountain llamas filing their tax returns in a timely manner.

So, I did what any logical person would do. I pulled out my old Deluxe Talkboy—as made famous by Kevin McCallister in *Home Alone 2: Lost in New York.*

Sure, this cassette recorder had been through rough times with me. It was my trusty sidekick, and I used it any time I had to record a confession. Or whenever I had to infiltrate some bad guys' hideout and "wear a wire"—more business slang, which I never fully understood since Talkboys don't even have any wires or cables. But fact of the matter is, this device came with me on almost every case. The problem with criminals these days is they're so used to modern technology like smart phones that they don't understand what these old machines are. Ask any Generation Zoomer what a floppy disc is and they'll call it a "save icon" not realizing they used to be actual things. The same principle applies here. You'd be shocked how many criminals are willing to speak their plans into this recorder just because I ask them to "talk clearly into the black sticky-outy thing here."

But I digress. My Deluxe Talkboy would be crucial in my interrogation of myself. I could record my good cop/bad cop questions beforehand, use the "Slow Playback" function to manipulate the sound of my voice, and make myself believe that someone else was asking the questions.

It was a solid plan, and I saw no flaws with it.

Next on my list for setting up my interrogation room was calling an electrician. My office was furnished with decent lighting. When I flipped on my light switch, the whole room would brighten with two rows of buzzing fluorescent lights. Not to mention the window behind my desk looked out upon the city and let tons of natural light bathe me like I was some toddler scared of using the shower. Dumb idiot toddlers.

Simply put, this would not do. I needed the right atmosphere. Something dark and intimidating.

The electrician showed up and was quite confused when I said I needed all the lighting to be replaced by a bare bulb swinging on a metal chain. He was even more confused when I said I would only need that set-up for two hours max. I tried explaining it was so I could interrogate myself and this was all part of my process, but he couldn't grasp that either. I thought electricians were supposed to have some sort of schooling or education, but maybe their vocation is easier than they let on and they're just scam artists.

Seeing a pretty penny in his future, the electrician picked it up off my floor. I was about to chastise him, since the coin was on MY office floor and therefore MY penny. But I let it go, knowing full well the Finders Keepers rule. Besides, I think the whole penny episode made the electrician realize he could make quite the profit on this for only a days' work. And I could list whatever expenses occurred on my bill to Marvin Hartley as "incidentals." This was a win-win for everyone involved.

Finally, everything was good to go. Recordings set up, window blacked out, bare bulb swinging above my desk. I stubbed my toe trying to walk across the room in the dark, but when you're on the job, danger lurks in every corner. Especially hard desk corners that jut out where you don't realize.

I sat myself down behind my desk, which I had cleared of everything normally on there (including Moby, whose terrarium comfortably rested on the floor on the far side of the room) Everything except for my Talkboy and a glass of apple juice with a paper straw.

I pushed play, forgetting about the Slow Playback function.

"So, Mr. Spence," my tinny voice resonated through the tiny speaker, "you're here because you may know some information. Information that could be helpful to our case."

I pressed the pause button. Is this what my voice sounded like? A Land of Oz Munchkin through a dog whistle? No wonder my father used to leave me at rest stops. This high-pitched voice was basically unlovable. I took a mental note to take vocal lessons.

After rewinding the cassette, I made sure to press the correct button to play back my recordings—this time with a palatable, slightly less than human pitch. "So, Mr. Spence, you're here because you may know some information. Information that could be helpful to our case," the Talkboy repeated. "Would you like some apple juice? It's chilled and hopefully to your liking," the recording offered.

Not wanting to offend the good cop voice, I pulled the cup of apple juice in and took a sip. I would've preferred some Jack Daniels, but I understand, you can't just offer a suspect alcohol. That goes against plenty of rules and regulations.

"Thank y—" I tried getting out.

"NO!" A new accent screamed from the cassette player's speakers. "Don't you dare drink that!" I had used a different voice when reading through my bad cop script. I tried going for a '30s Irish cop affectation, but in actual fact, it came across more like Jean-Claude Van Damme doing his best cowboy impersonation. I'm not great at accents.

The bad cop voice continued. "You piece of filth, you don't deserve no juice!" In keeping with the fantasy interrogation, I slapped the red Solo cup of apple juice across the room. It splattered on the tan-painted wall, a Rorschach test of fruit extract. I saw a cockroach juggling three watermelons. Not sure what that says about my personality, but there it is.

I couldn't be sure, but when the juice hit the wall, I thought I heard a small voice call out "EEEP!" Last I checked, when apple juice splatters against drywall, it doesn't make that sound. But, I also haven't experimented using the scientific method, so who's to say?

I didn't have much time to think about that anyway, as the bad cop recording went on.

"Now listen here, you little cretin, you're going to tell us what you know, and you'll be *happy* to tell us."

"Over my dead body," I replied.

"Oh, we can make that happen."

"What my—erhem—partner means to say," the good cop continued, "is that we just want what's best for everyone. We know you've been hearing 'You're So Vain' for about a year now. We need you to come out with what you know about Carly Simon and her song. Before it's too late."

"I don't know nothing. I'm innocent."

"Now, no one's saying you're guilty, Mr. Spence."

"I am, you indignant punk," Bad Cop said. With my right arm, I reached behind my head, grabbed onto my well-kept hair, and slammed my forehead down against my desk. I didn't care for the possible contusion that I gave myself, but I knew in the moment that roughing myself up felt convincing.

My ears ringing with the sounds of a hunchback playing trumpet in the bell tower of Notre-Dame Cathedral, I tried focusing on my recordings.

"I apologize," said Good Cop. "My partner's a little on edge today. He just found out his wife of twenty-two years is leaving him." It's important to have good backstory. Makes it believable.

"At least I had twenty-two good years. I bet this creep never felt love in his life. Ain't that why you're in this situation, Tracer? Ain't it? AIN'T IT?" Bad Cop was hitting a little close to home, to be honest.

"Now, Mr. Spence, let's try to be reasonable. Why don't you just tell us what you know, and we can make this all go away?"

"I'd like my lawyer," I said.

I'm not positive why I wrote this into my script. First thing, I don't have a lawyer. They're expensive to hold on retainer, and I can barely afford *The Complete Idiot's Guide to Private Investigating*, let alone an honest-to-God attorney.

Secondably, I now sat in a mostly dark room for five solid minutes of silence, as did my fictional good and bad cop counterparts who had no response. Only the swinging bare bulb above me gave me any light. I used this time to pluck hairs from my forearms.

Lastly, I'm only a private eye. And I'm certainly not two separate policemen. When I'm interrogating someone, I don't actually need to honor their request for a lawyer. This is because I'm not really legally allowed to hold someone for interrogation. It was this loophole that my cop recordings finally figured out after the full five minutes.

"Nah," Good Cop voice said.

Bad Cop said nothing. Instead, he kicked my chair back until it hit the wall and banged the back of my head against the window sill. Or he would've done that, if he had been tangible in any shape or form. So, I just wound up pushing as hard as I could with both of my legs to get the desired effect.

You shouldn't ever believe those films where someone passes out immediately after being hit on the head with the butt of a gun. No, head trauma feels more like your brain is trying to escape from your skull by using the flat side of an axe. I wish I could've passed out in that moment. But I had a job to do, and this job waits for no one. If only it was a little less impatient; I get a stitch in my side every time I run after some culprit for more than fifty feet.

All in all, Bad Cop represented police brutality at its worst. This is what the System in the Big City has come to. Corruption. Abuse of power. Sitting backwards in chairs during briefings. This is everything I stood against.

But I was also sitting down at the moment, and in a lot of pain, so I gave in.

"Alright! Alright! I'll talk, you bastards." I held my head in my hands, as I regaled them with everything I knew about the song's origins. "Simon herself says it's about three different people, though many believe her claim to be a red herring. People point mainly to Warren Beatty—who Simon herself claims is partially true—James Taylor, and Mick Jagger. Jagger sang uncredited back-up vocals on the song, and Taylor was married to her at the time of the song's release. Those are the places I would start! But the subject's identity has been speculated on for—"

"This half-wit still refuses to talk, huh?" Bad Cop asked Good Cop. Apparently, I didn't give myself enough time in the recording to answer back. Nor did I realize I'd sing this quickly. "Let me bash him around a bit more. I think his face could get even uglier than it is. Look at that schnozz, hanging over that lip rug he calls a mustache. I bet I could break it so it hooks at a right angle." I could feel his non-existent breath hot on my face. I cringed.

"No, I think he's had just about enough."

"No fun. I could get one more back-handed crack right across his unshaven cheek. It'll be red for a fortnight."

"You know what'll happen, Bad Cop. We'll have to face the chief, and you know how he feels about internal affairs. He already suffers from that bad case of sciatica. You're letting the job get to you."

"And you're letting your panties ride up too far!"

This is when I reached over and stopped the tape. They would've gone on like that for another fifteen minutes. Then the sound of me grunting would take over as they had a wrestling match on the floor. Just so unprofessional of them, in the middle of an interrogation.

I sat there in the darkened room, reflecting on everything I had learned from myself. This was my least favorite part of being a detective. If I had known this job required this much thinking, I would've gone with my second career choice of interior decorating. But instead of putting rooms together, I was putting clues together.

Not only did I now have three names to add to my list, but I also now realized the mystery behind "You're So Vain" and who the song was about had been around for a while. It had already been investigated heavily. This meant I wouldn't be the first on the case. What had happened to all those who came before me? This spelled out danger. D-A-N-G-E-R. Just like a profusely sweating kid at a spelling bee, not wanting to let down his father watching from the audience. You know what, Dad, sometimes the "juh" sound can be a J and not a G.

It felt like the walls were closing in on me, as my mind raced with all this knowledge. Not like in that trash compactor scene from that *Star Wars* movie. No, more like an angry mob advancing slowly toward me.

Looking around the room, I swore I saw figures in the shadows staring at me. But this was absurd, because I was the private eye, and eyes are the ones supposed to be doing the watching.

I decided—it was time to take action. To the streets to uncover this obvious conspiracy. Well, first to an urgent care for my self-inflicted contusion, and then to the streets. Maybe I'd hit up the local diner for a burger in between, but it was surely to the streets after I sated my hunger. And after the post-office because I was running out of stamps. They call 'em Forever stamps, but you can only use 'em once. What a misnomer.

4

The case finally seemed to be picking up steam. I decided, after my successful interrogation, that I needed a secret name for this assignment. I couldn't just go around calling it The Marvin Hartley File, for confidentiality reasons. Nor could I call it The Carly Simon's "You're So Vain" Mystery. That one was a mouthful. I also thought of calling it The Ellie Dayton Kidnapping case, as a red herring code, but decided against that since I'd be the only one to get confused between my two cases. So, I figured I'd try a different option tentatively.

Operation: Eagle Bomb needed more information to fill out its holes. And information was hard to come by in these parts. Not as hard to come by as, let's say, true love. Or a monkey playing jump rope. Both of those are near impossible to come by. But good intel is still more difficult to find than an overpriced coffee shop. Just walk in any direction in this city for two minutes, and you'll find yourself in line ready to drop a ten-spot on a mocha-hazelnut espresso drink. So let's meet somewhere in the middle: information was medium to come by in these parts.

Every great P.I. has a street informant. That's rule number one for us. Starsky had Huggy Bear. Hutch also had Huggy Bear. And those are the only two examples I can think of at the moment. But the point is, even I had a street informant, and I started with him on every case.

He was in his usual hideout, the strip club. Okay, actually he was playing in a local arcade, but strip club sounds edgier. You just pretend that there are women taking their clothes off, getting down to their skivvies, while I'm telling this next part, okay? In your head, whenever you see the word "arcade machine," just replace it with "stripper." Everything else sort of fits in, because both joints are similar: sticky floors, dollar bills all around, peep show machines, kids fighting over whose turn it is on the pinball machine.

I called him Harry Potter. He was a wizard at finding information for me. He was my Golden Snitch. Also, I called him that because his name was actually Harry Potter. It's only sort of a coincidence, because that's a common name if you think about it. He did sort of look like Daniel Radcliffe only with longer, straggly hair. Plus, he was black.

Harry was feeding a couple dollar bills into a sexy, sexy arcade machine. *Galaga*, I think. Exotic. Must be a foreign name. Maybe from down old Latin America way, wherever that was.

He spotted me, his lips curling into a frown. I get that facial response a lot whenever I enter a room. It comes with the territory, much like I expect igloos, dog sleds, and cold snaps come with the Yukon territory. This is just my own version of a cold snap.

"Tracer. What are you doing here?"

"Can't a guy just come and hang out with the dregs of society?" I asked as a twelve-year-old boy ran in between us carrying an endless ribbon of arcade tickets. Who brings someone so young to a strip cl— an arcade? What a sad world we live in.

"Look man, I'm just trying to have some peace on my day off. I don't want no trouble."

What a sentiment. None of us want no trouble, but when trouble comes running, we all enter the marathon. Except maybe those with serious heart conditions. They're exempt from marathons in my book. Unless, how do those prescription medications work? Are they like steroids? You can probably enter the Olympics with a medicated super-heart, and you wouldn't even be breaking the rules, I bet. Maybe trouble does come running towards them after all. I don't make the rules, that's the job of the Olympics Rules Committee. You don't like it, take it up with them.

"No trouble at all," I replied. "Just looking for some answers." I slid a quarter into the machine Harry was playing on, feeling dirty as I did so. "Next game's on me."

"It's a dollar," he said, pointing to the sign on the machine. Classic bribery move.

I put two more quarters in. Then I dug in my pockets, trying to find more loose change. I only came up with twenty-three more cents and a Canadian penny. Not even Canadians take them anymore. Worthless. But it would have to do, and I slammed the change down on arcade top.

"What's the word around town, HP?"

"Uh, well, uh…" he seemed hesitant. "Bird."

"Bird?"

"Bird."

"Bird is the word?" I asked.

"Don't you know about the bird? Everybody knows that the bird is the word."

I tried to decipher his code. All good private eyes have got to have a code with their shady street informants. Don't want them getting caught snitching by the seedy underbelly of the crime world. I didn't want some wet work hit man taking Harry Potter out. "Bird" could only be in reference to The Drunken Swallow, a local dive bar. A '70s cover band was playing there tonight, and Harry must've thought they'd know something about "You're So Vain." I decided to move that to the top of the list.

"Thanks," I said, starting to walk away. "But, Harry, one more thing."

"Alright, what is it, Columbo?"

I didn't understand his reference and decided to ignore it.

"You know this man?" I asked, unfurling a 58 by 40-inch poster of The Rolling Stones. This took a minute, as I first had to slide the tight rubber bands off the sides. They made a THWIP sound, snapping into the palm of my hand. It stung. A thin red line formed across my skin. Harry waited patiently.

He studied the picture, really took it all in. He may have been trying to come up with a cover or excuse to not give me more information. But he wouldn't be able to get away with that from me.

"Come on, Potter, no dilly-dallying. Pitter patter. What's the answer? You know him or not?"

"Which one? There's like five guys there."

This made sense. It was a poster of the entire band, after all. I pointed to the one with the pouty lips and the glazed-over eyes.

"Yeah," Harry said. "That's Mick Jagger. Who doesn't know him?"

"Alright, don't get smart. Know where I can find him?"

"Sure I do, but that's gonna cost you, Spence."

"How much?"

Harry Potter looked around the room and then whispered, "Three hundred and fourteen dollars. Plus handling, service, and convenience fees."

"You're really gouging me here, man," I said, opening my wallet.

"You planning on driving? 'Cause that's another twenty for parking."

I handed over the money. Looks like Marvin Hartley was getting more "incidentals" on his bill.

Harry reached into his jacket and pulled out a rectangular strip of paper. He gave it to me. It read "Rolling Stones / Madison Square Garden" and had a barcode printed on the side. This must have been some sort of underground criminal currency, like those gold coins in *John Wick*. They say cheaters never prosper, but if these delinquent villains have the technology to use bar codes, I'd say they're prospiring right through the armpit parts of their shirts.

"Now look, Tracer. Don't get me in trouble for scalping, okay? This was a fair deal."

"Scalping? Don't know the meaning of the word." Harry looked satisfied with my answer and stayed quiet, which upset me. I truly didn't know the meaning of the word and hoped he'd explain it to me. I sure hoped he didn't mean he was taking the skin off the head of his enemy with a tomahawk. Context clues told me otherwise, but you never know with these delinquents. That kind of thing might be back in style.

Either way, Harry Potter had turned back to his game. Just like a criminal, using arcades for their own enjoyment, to get their own kicks off. Remember this, kids, if nothing else: stay in school. Get a degree. Don't sell your body like these poor, poor Konami and Namco machines.

5

I had some time to kill before heading over to the Drunken Swallow, so I decided to work on Serena's case, looking for her lost sister.

How do you find a missing person? I started where one always should start—the back of a milk carton.

The cashier at the local bodega was none-too-happy with me after I dumped a bunch of milk cartons on to his floor. I had checked the back of each one for faces of abducted people with the details of where they were last seen, but all I found was nutritional facts. When I explained to the guy what I was looking for, he told me they stopped doing that in the mid-90s. Only he peppered in a lot more four-letter words and questioned my intelligence while doing so.

So, I decided to check out Ellie Dayton's apartment. Maybe I could fish around for some clues in her building, find some hidden secrets that might crack her sister's case wide open. Crack it like an egg getting ready for a beating. And it was me that was going to be doing the beating of the egg that was the case.

I made a mental note to work on my metaphors for any future memoir I was to write. Title idea: *Tracer Spence, Sexy Cowboy Time Cop.*

On the sidewalk outside of the bodega, I stuck my hand out to signal a cab over. After a couple of minutes, one pulled up. He looked young, with shoulder-length hair and prominent acne smattered across his cheeks. I motioned for him to roll down the passenger side window, mimicking the old cranking movement. He didn't understand what I was trying to mime. Dumb kids. They should pay attention to old technology like window cranks and wristwatches.

After a few minutes of doing charades out on the street, the kid finally got the hint. Leaning into his cab, I told him Ellie's address and told him to meet me there as fast as he could. He was confused but took off down the road.

I hailed another cab, hopped in the back, and said, "follow that car!" Yes, I did all this simply because I had always wanted to say that phrase and didn't think it would ever happen organically. That's one of the rules of being a private eye: adapt, overcome, and improvise when butt up against a problem.

Turns out, Ellie's apartment was only three blocks away from where I was. I had to pay the cab drivers $1.56 each, plus tip.

Ellie lived on the fourth floor of a posh apartment complex, doorman outside and everything. Well, there was a man standing outside of the entrance, and he was polite enough to hold the door open for me. He may not have actually been employed by the building as a doorman. But that politeness made the apartment more posh than my current living situation, where if I passed anyone in my hallway I'd have to wipe spit off my jacket. But that might have more to do with how many times I accidentally set off the fire alarms while making popcorn.

I knocked on the door, my knuckles rapping against the wood. My hand immediately cramped up. I guess those finger-strengthening exercises I've been doing in my down time weren't worth diddley.

No one answered, like I expected. If Ellie had been kidnapped, the kidnappers probably wouldn't kidnap the kidnappee and keep her kidnapped in her own apartment.

I pulled her keys out of my jacket pocket and opened her door. It was a medium-sized apartment but looked smaller because of the clutter. I guess Serena hadn't cleaned up that much. Or she was just bad at chores. Speaking as someone who hadn't washed dishes in two months, I understood and wouldn't judge her for her shortfallings.

The opening hallway had a small oak table on the right-hand side with a circular mirror hanging above it. Unopened junk mail, scattered loose change, and a half-empty water bottle all rested on the table. I flicked through the unopened junk mail. Credit card applications, charity solicitations, a Publishers Clearing House *you-may-have-already-won* envelope, and ooh! Coupons to White Castle. I pocketed these. There was a small bowl, darkly painted with a stylistic elephant, that also sat on the table with a few quarters and used gum wrappers hanging out in it, but it seemed the rest of the litter was haphazardly placed along the oak surface.

The mirror above the table was inlaid in one of those brass sun frames, with the sun rays curving softly this way and that. Shoved in between the mirror and the frame was a picture of Serena and who must be Ellie. They were definitely sisters, though Ellie's hair was worn straight down to her shoulders. Unlike Serena, Ellie didn't wear glasses. If she had as bad of eyesight as her sister, Ellie may have worn contacts. Behind the picture was an airline ticket. July 31, 2008 to Nova Scotia.

I made my way deeper into her apartment, which made me feel creepy. Sort of like a freshman in high school, sneaking into the girls' locker room while they weren't around. It was like I was prying into Ellie's private life without her knowledge. Which I was. But that was one feeling that always gave me the heebie-jeebies about being a private investigator. I never wanted to be paid to be a Peeping Tom. But I also wasn't being paid yet, so that sort of made the hair-raising feeling go away.

After the hallway on the right was the kitchen. The fridge was pulled out of the nook where it would normally be. The microwave was askew, its door open. All the cabinets and drawers were wide open, with pots, pans, bowls, utensils, and a lot of zip ties scattered around on the laminate counters. Like an extraordinary amount of zip ties. A comical amount. There were so many zip ties. It was weird. The only feasible reason for a human being to own this many zip ties was if they were a collector, but I can't imagine any reason to own a collection if zip ties. But who was I to judge?

On the opposite side of her apartment was her living room. There, a television sat crooked on the entertainment center. The cushions of

Ellie's sofa had been thrown to the floor, the brown corduroy collecting dust in the grooves. The oak end table placed next to the couch had been shifted as well. On it, the phone was turned upside-down. This was strange to me. Not the upside-down part, but who in their right mind still had a landline? That was just one more way for bill collectors to get in touch with you.

The drawer of the end table was open. In it were sticky notes with scribbled phone numbers and website passwords, a thin recipe book, and a 2017 ticket for the Diana Stakes horse race in Saratoga. The bet was for Lady Eli to win and was circled in red ink. I thought about pocketing the ticket to see if it was a winner, but after reading the fine print, I realized that all winning bets had to have been collected within a year. That's always where they get you—the fine print. I learned that the hard way after I sold my soul to who I thought was the devil but turned out to just be Crazy Maximilian from *Crazy Maximiliian's Discount Furniture Emporium*. Still, he gave me a good price on a lounge chair.

In the corner of Ellie's living room was her closet with white bifold doors. Like everything else in the apartment, these were wide open and the clothes in it were strewn about on the floor carelessly, as if someone had been searching for something.

I used my foot to push aside jackets and coats, to see if anything was buried underneath the mountain of girly clothes. No going, unless whoever was here before me was looking for some soft-looking scarves. Ellie seemed to be a fan, all of them a pastel orange-yellow color, like ripe apricots.

There was only one more room to check, and I was hesitant to enter it. Ellie's bedroom. Real gentleman never enter a woman's bedroom unless invited in. Or unless they're tunneling out of a prison cell with a plastic spoon, and they pop up unexpectedly because the woman's house is right across the street from the jail and the prisoner misjudged the length of their own tunnel.

Nonetheless, I had found no clues out in the rest of her apartment. Unless I had and just hadn't noticed them, which is how my cases normally went. Since I was hired to find Ellie, I hoped she would forgive me in the future for breaking her privacy. Why ask permission when you could ask for forgiveness?

Just like the rest of her apartment, Ellie's room was a catastrophe. Blankets were scattered on the floor, the contents of her dresser were dumped onto her bare mattress, and her pillows were torn to shreds. Polyester feathers clung to everything, and it looked like a knife had made the gashes in each pillow. On her dresser was a clear fish bowl, dark red rocks lining the bottom with a plastic bonsai tree sticking up in the middle. No fish though. I guess Serena had sent Wanda to her eternal resting place in the porcelain throne to Fish Heaven.

On her mattress, Ellie's laptop sat, charging as the cord ran from its side into an outlet behind her nightstand. I sat on the bed and opened it up. The lock screen popped up with a background of a peaceful picture of a spoon being stirred in a mug of coffee.

I hit the enter key and the computer prompted me to enter her password.

I typed in, *1 2 3 4 5* and then hit enter.

The screen told me, *The password is incorrect. Try again.*

I sighed. This was going to be more difficult than I thought. This is why everyone should just use the same password of *1 2 3 4 5*. It would make looking for clues that much easier.

I tried again. *Password.*

The password is incorrect. You have one more try before you will be locked out of your account.

I felt like the computer was just mocking me at this point. The insolent electronic bastard. *You're nothing more than an over expensive abacus,* I thought. I had one more guess and I had better get it right.

YachtLover84, I randomly typed in.

The computer welcomed me with open arms, except the computer didn't have any physical arms. That would be creepy.

I immediately went to the most incriminating place on everyone's personal computer. I opened up the internet browser and clicked on the most recent searches. Unfortunately, Ellie was either one step ahead of me or she was the most boring person on the planet. The only searches in her browser history were: *french dance steps, how to dance like parisians, gavotte dancing,* and *dance instructors near me.*

After searching for any other clues on Ellie's laptop, and getting sidetracked in a twenty-minute game of Minesweeper, I closed the computer. Nothing more to be found except some spreadsheets for her job.

On her dresser, I noticed a red Moleskine notebook. I picked it up. On the front *Ellie's SECRET Journal—Do Not READ* was written, neat, in black marker. That skeevy feeling came back to me, but despite my guilty misgivings, I opened it up, flipping a couple pages in. I didn't start at the beginning because in movies the necessary information was always on a random page.

Day 35: In the food court @ the mall. Over the mall's speakers. Quickly ate my pizza and left. Too greasy.

That meant nothing to me. I didn't even read any of the other entries on the page. Instead, I flipped forward to the middle of the book.

Day 1999: On my way to the race track. Random radio station. Considering it good luck.

I flipped through some more.

Day 3285: Been over 9 years. It'll make sense soon. Requested it at my sister's wedding last night. Might as well, you know?

Hmmm…Now it made sense why Serena had said I wasn't her type when I met her. She was married and being faithful. *Obviously, that's the only reason,* I thought to myself, but I even knew I was just telling myself that to make me feel better about the rejection.

However, I still couldn't make sense of any of these entries in the diary. It was almost as if reading accounts out of order made continuity hard to follow. Nonetheless, I turned towards the end of the journal. The last twenty or so pages were all blank. I thumbed backwards until I found one of the last entries.

Day 4749: Meeting with S.O. later tonight. I'm ashamed. I shouldnt be doing this but I have no other options. I NEED to end this—and this is the ONLY way. Watched How to Lose a Guy in 10 Days *this morning. Damn Matthew McCounaghy. Damn Kate Hudson.*

I closed the journal, placing it back on the dresser. Clearly reading the inner most thoughts of a kidnap victim and what actors she hated wasn't helping me.

This search was coming up empty, and I felt ashamed both as a man and as a detective. I pulled my flask out of my jacket pocket and tried taking a sip. Only a drop of whiskey hit my tongue. I needed to stop at the liquor store for a refill. I was low in spirits.

In my peripheral vision, I saw a blinking red light. I turned. It was coming from an answering machine on top of Ellie's nightstand. She had a landline in her apartment, so why wouldn't she also have an answering machine? Of course she would.

I pressed the play button. The first six messages were robo-spam calls asking to speak to the owner of a non-specific automobile and that this owner could be derelict in their insurance payment for the non-specific automobile. What a scam. I knew this because I had fallen for these same exact calls. On at least nine different occasions. I didn't even drive a vehicle! But those computer-generated voices sure could be convincing.

The next call was from Serena. Her sonorous voice filled the small bedroom as she said that she was planning on coming down this weekend and would Ellie be up for a visitor?

After Serena's message, a beep sounded on the machine, and the mechanical female voice said, "Last message."

Following this, another female voice spoke. It was hushed, an alarming whisper. "Ellie, this is Sadie Marie. I haven't stopped thinking about what you did the other day. To me. How could you…how could you do this? How could we do this? I'm going to end this one way or another. One way…" Here, Sadie Marie trailed off, and I could only hear her quiet breathing for about fifteen seconds. "I've made up my mind. I'm going to take you out. Soon."

At that point, the mysterious caller must've hung up the phone, because the answering machine beeped loudly, and the monotone female voice said, "End of messages."

I replayed the last message, looking at the answering machine's digital read-out. I didn't have any scrap paper, so I wrote Sadie Marie's phone number and her name on my hand. Her threatening message chilled me to my bones. But I finally had a lead to go on. Just as long as I didn't wash my hands and smudge out the information before I could write the clue down in a safe space.

6

I was well-acquainted with most dive bars around my neighborhood, having been thrown out of every one. You'd have thought small businesses would like their patrons to be inside the building spending money instead of outside in an alley, spilling the contents of their stomach onto the back door. But they always had some excuse to throw me out: "Tracer, your card was declined" or "Tracer, you can barely stand up" or "Tracer, how the hell did you even get a military-grade taser?"

Either way though, I wasn't familiar with the Drunken Swallow. Of course, I had heard of the place, but I stayed away from it, not wanting to associate myself with the type of scum found there. Only drunken riffraff find aviary-based puns funny, and I loathe bird humor. This is the thin line keeping me on the side of "friendly neighborhood drunk" and not "riffraff drunk" that I held myself accountable to. God forgive me the day I say things like, "I'm going quackers" or "It's time to ruffle a few feathers," for that will be a day to rue. A day to rue, I tell you.

The '70s cover band playing that night was called Rumors. I knew nothing about this band, but I took their name to be a hint. A hint that the musicians would possess inside information related to my Carly Simon case. In retrospect, this assumption was idiotic. I should have done even a modicum of research. Their band name was less about their wealth of criminal knowledge and more just a reference to Fleetwood Mac's most popular album.

What I did know was that walking into that dive-bar with the rumpots and hippies, I would immediately stand out. Even though I owned one suit, bought nearly a decade ago for 100 bucks, even though all of my socks were mismatched, even though my wallet was simply a bent out of shape paper clip, I'd still be seen as immaculately dressed by these imbecilic bohemian drop-outs.

Luckily, I was a classically trained, certified "Master of Deception and All Things Disguised-related." *Classically trained* meaning "self-taught." Which makes perfect sense because all the ancient classics were entirely self-taught. Just ask Plato or Socrates. And you could even see the certificate on my wall at the office. It wasn't certified FROM anywhere, but instead just printed out after I Photoshopped it. It still fooled most of my clients, so let's be honest, that's just proof that I was a Master of Deception and All Things Disguised-related.

There's a real art to disguises. The basic principle stands that you don't want anyone to notice that you're in a disguise. Keeping that in mind, the first thing I did was to put a fake mustache on over my real mustache. Obviously. The fake one was almost imperceptible to the one I grew myself. No one would ever have a hunch that my appearance was false.

As for my outfit, I figured a leisure suit would be the way to go. They were popular back in the 1970s. I checked out a thrift store over on Delancey Street. As it turns out, I couldn't afford a real leisure suit. Did you know vintage ones are going for thousands of dollars? Hippies have too much money these days. Between spending their cash on ugly clothing and poetry books and those tiny rock gardens that you use mini rakes to smooth out sand, it seems all those years of designer drugs have ruined their financial mindsets.

Anyway, instead of buying a full-fledged leisure suit, I had to change my normal suit into something that resembled a leisure suit. I simply tugged on the bottom of my pants for about an hour on each side. This gave them that bell bottom look. I also left the top buttons of my shirt wide open to show off my '70s era chest hair. Chest hair that I penciled in since my torso was not blessed with the ability to produce any. I blame a chemical accident from my childhood. I told my father that he should never have left me in that industrial plant overnight. But he said it would be a great "field trip" to see how rat poison was made. I always thought it was strange that no other students came with me. But nonetheless, the fallout was that my body skin was now as smooth as a seal covered in baby oil on satin sheets listening to Kenny G's *Greatest Hits.*

Most importantly, I put on the thing that would make my whole '70s drug-inspired outfit perfect. Roller skates. Not only were they integral to my deception, but damn were they fun.

The night descended upon the city, and with it came the rain. Being a detective in the city, I could only look upon the night as an apt metaphor for the dark soul of the city. Evil lurks on every street, whether that's murder or drugs or the exorbitant prices of hot dog stands. I wasn't surprised that the evening would be as dark as the city's spirit. Namely because that's the way our 24-hour cycle on Earth works, with its rotation and all that creating day and nighttime periods.

I also wasn't surprised because bands normally have gigs during the evening. Just once, I would prefer a band to open their set around noon, but for some reason only kids' performers go on around that time. And let me tell you, parents have a real suspicion problem when a thirty-something man in a trench coat shows up to a Wiggles' concert alone.

I skated my way to the bar, splashing through a multitude of puddles. Pedestrians moved out of my way for the entire trip, which I took to mean that my disguise was working. The Drunken Swallow welcomed me with a blinding sign above its door, neon refractions being engulfed by the black night. The bar's name was lit up above a crude picture of a neon bird, flapping its wings. Although this bird could've been drawn by any toddler with a dull crayon, I was impressed by the technology of the animation. Neon sign engineering has come a long way.

Slipping in to the bar unnoticed, I was immediately overtaken by the pungent stenches of coconut, lemon, and lavender. I took another whiff and cringed at how these scents punched into my nostrils like Joe

Louis during his Bum of the Month Club era. The Drunken Swallow was such a foul, crime-infested hole in the wall—such a run-down gin joint—that instead of the stink of vomit and stale whiskey of a real bar, this place's odor did a 180 turning in something almost pleasant. Makes me sick, it does.

The floors didn't appear to be sticky like other dives, but I chalked that up to the fact that my roller skate wheels wouldn't stick to even the most syrupy, viscous substance. Gleaming brushed nickel surfaces covered most of the tables—the place was so clean, that they must've been hiding something heinous. Even the stage in the back of the room appeared to be up to code. That's how you can tell someone's breaking the law: they throw off those on to their nefarious activities by being overly law-abiding. They were obviously trying to fool someone, but they didn't count on someone having as much experience in the fool game as I did. They say experience is the teacher of fools, and I had graduated in foolery summa cum laude. I was hardy in terms of fools. If my name wasn't Tracer, it'd be tom, because of all the Tomfoolery that I was used to. But my name is Tracer, not Tom. I'm Tracer friggen Spence, fool extraordinaire.

The next thing I noticed was the customers scattered around the room. They were sipping on their drinks served out of mason jars and stemless wine glasses. They all had the same idea as I did, to disguise themselves. Whereas I tried to dress up like their hippie personalities, these non-conformist flower children were now clothed like normal people. Men in button-up shirts with ties, pullover sweaters, and khakis. Khakis! How dare they besmirch the glorious khaki. And the women! I expected frizzled hair, suede fringed jackets, and gypsy dresses. Instead, I was greeted by elegant topknots, smart blouses, and full-length skirts. Ah, how they turned the tables on me. Both figuratively and literally, as most of the tables faced towards the stage away from the entrance of the bar.

The band had not yet started their gig, and so the jukebox was piping "You Make My Dreams" into the speakers sprinkled around the room. Just like those lowlifes, to be listening to Hall and Oates.

"Hey man, uhh, you in the right place?" The twenty-something bartender called out to me, looking me up and down. He had stylishly disheveled hair and perma-stubble on a jaw-line you could cut glass with. He wore red and black patterned flannel, like a handsome lumberjack. I hated him. It was an intrinsic, immediate hate. The kind of hate you reserve for distant family members.

"Just give me a scotch, neat. Wiseguy."

I was expecting something like Dewar's or Famous Grouse, some cheap scotch that tasted decent and got the job done. "Job" being to get me inebriated, if you understand my meaning. I was not expecting Mr. Pretty Boy Barkeep to reach below the bottom shelf and pick some bottle of off-brand swill called Famous Clover O'Mac's Blended "Scotch" Wizzkey. Yes, "scotch" was in quotes and yes, they literally spelled it w-i-z-z-k-e-y on the bottle.

He poured this alcohol into a glass mason jar and slid it over to me. I literally saw stench lines coming out the brim. Think Pig-Pen in the *Peanuts* Sunday comic strips. I think paint started peeling from the ceiling.

I took my turpentine in a glass and skated over to a back table. The jukebox music cut off abruptly. As the lights faded, showcasing the stage and the band members' silhouettes, I took a sip. Flavor-wise, the scotch wasn't half bad. It was full bad. It even burnt my nostril hairs clean off. Which did me a favor, because I'd been meaning to trim 'em. I'd drunk worse.

The audience started applauding as a brunette dame stepped up to the microphone. "Thank you, thank you. We are Rumors." Her sultry voice reverberated throughout the room.

She and the band kicked in to their rendition of "Crazy on You" by Heart. Lighting spread across the entire stage, like butter across a piece of toast, only at 299,792,458 meters per second and without the use of a knife.

My eyes were immediately drawn to the siren at the front of the stage now singing. Vanessa Buckingham. A stage name, no doubt, but it rolled off the tongue much like I'd like her tongue to be rolling off of mine. The spotlight enveloped her in a warm glow, circled by a veil of darkness. She was dressed like Stevie Nicks, a black shawl making her look like a witch. A sexy witch. Not an old crone with a bumpy nose, a crooked chin, and a predilection for turning overly curious children into mice. She had legs for days. Specifically 10,687 days, as I found out later she was 29 years old. I had essentially turned into that wolf from those old cartoons whose eyes pop out of his head with steam coming out of his ears. I even said "AWOOOGA" out loud. The closest patron looked at me then, and I just pointed to me drink and said, "good stuff." I think they bought my excuse.

The band ran through a professional set. Some Tom Petty thrown in, Queen, Cheap Trick, Pat Benatar, and of course Fleetwood Mac. I was entertained. The music washed over me, a wave of sensual nostalgia. With how good this band was, I started becoming nervous at the prospect of confronting them to get the information I needed. They always say to ease your nerves when performing to picture your audience in their underwear. I'm sure it works the other way around, too, for the audience—so I started envisioning the band in their unmentionables. Starting with Vanessa Buckingham. Ending with her. And middling with her. Basically, only her, as I wasn't interested in picturing the guys in the band in their long johns. I wondered what she wore. Maybe a black garter belt holding up fishnet stockings. Or she could wear a pair of granny panties. I'm not picky. Of course, this line of thought only made me more nervous. What a failure it was.

I shivered, shaking me out of my reverie. Taking a sip of my drink, I steeled myself. The whiskey went down turbulently.

As the band's set went on, I grew concerned. It didn't look as if they were going to play "You're So Vain," the entire reason I was here. I was working, damnit. And if this band couldn't just ease my case along by doing what I exactly needed, then they were going to face the consequences of my inactions.

In an instant, my thoughts of pre-revenge froze up in my head. I felt eyes burrowing into the back of my skull, and goosebumps ran down my back. I turned around, but only saw the bar's entrance darkened with flickering shadows. The shadows seemed too dark, but ain't that always the way it seems in the obscurity of dusk? With the creeping feeling of someone watching my every move, time seemed to slow down. The band's music hushed in my ears, like I was underwater. My heartbeat got louder, quickening with a maddening pace, quicker than the snare drum. It was all that I could hear during this brief panic attack. I could swear someone, something, was hiding in the darkness behind me.

"Thank you so much, New York," Vanessa's voice cut in, ushering me back to reality. "We've been Rumors, and this is our last song. Drink up, and enjoy your night, everyone!" She gripped her mic stand and swung it out on her last word, timing it perfectly with the band.

The guitarist strummed his instrument, the sound echoing like he was playing in the middle of the Grand Canyon. His power chords permeated the semi-drunken atmosphere here at the end of the night. It was the opening to The Who's "Won't Get Fooled Again." His fingers were spider-like on his fretboard. He was all flash and no substance, I figured, not knowing anything about playing a musical instrument. So, I wouldn't need to talk to him.

I looked over to the drummer, hiding behind his set. How convenient, the coward. Almost as if he wanted something between him and the truth. He twirled his sticks with the self-assurance of a con man and bashed away at his snare and toms like they deserved the beating. It takes a real evil to play such a violent instrument, and this guy seemed to be Satan incarnate. He was profusely sweating. Why was he sweating so much? His shirt was darkened with sweat. Gross. Only liars sweat that much. Someone so cultured in fibbing as he surely was certainly wouldn't break under my fourth degree. A full degree higher than those nerds in NYPD, I might add. No, I wouldn't get anything out of him. He wouldn't be my entry-way.

I completely ignored the bass player. Anyone dumb enough to be bullied into playing bass doesn't know anything anyway.

Nope, it was settled. After the show, I would *have* to talk to Aphrodite herself. Vanessa Buckingham. The Femme Fatale. My temptress. I smeared some of my chapstick onto my lips, the peppermint subtleties stinging. If she was going to try to seduce me, it was only right I try to seduce her first. I knew I'd have to squeeze her for information, but I'd have to act quick otherwise she'd end up being the one putting the squeeze on me, much like a Californian farmer getting juice out of an orange. The most sexual of fruits.

And though I was used to being beaten to a pulp, this time I'd be the one concentrating.

I think I lost myself in this extended metaphor, because the song was already over, and the audience was in a rapturous applause.

I couldn't help but feel some semblance of relief—this was shaping up to be the first day in over a year that I wouldn't hear that damned song. Maybe my curse was over. There were only 15 minutes left in the day, and I had yet to hear Carly Simon's contralto vocals serenade me to anger.

Of course, my relief was all for naught. This is when the lights kicked back on throughout the bar, a brief blaze of incandescence. As did the jukebox. Through the speakers, the all-too familiar bass line, acoustic guitar, and piano started. I wanted to bash the jukebox with a sledgehammer, and failing at that, bash my own skull in with it. Luckily, I left my sledgehammer at home since I couldn't carry it properly on my person. I always said pockets should be much bigger than they are. The fashion industry is years behind.

I looked up from my table and drink and saw the greatest thing I've ever witnessed in my life: I wasn't alone in this predicament. As soon as the song started, Vanessa Buckingham had a startled look on her angelic face which quickly turned to resignation. We made eye contact, her green eyes piercing mine like she was a drilling rig off the coast of Mexico trying to strike an oil well—she'd only find eye fluids in this case, though. I wasn't the Gulf of Mexico nor did I have any oil stored in my body. Except canola oil, but that's only because I had French fries for dinner.

Still, we registered that we were two of a kind, a pair of travelers on the same road in the night. The road being Carly Simon's awful, awful song. What a curse.

I ordered another drink while waiting for the dregs of society to clear out of the bar and for the band to break down their equipment. This scotch seemed to be an acquired taste. Acquired with my money. The taste was still burnt cat piss, but there was nothing like cheap alcohol to screw up some liquid courage. And I found my courage to be more liquid than most—in a constant state of evaporation.

I found Vanessa's dressing room with the door propped open with a metallic trash bin, a welcoming sign—if also a fire hazard. A girl like her is someone who's heard fire safety lectures her entire life and still throws caution to the wind. As if the wind enjoyed playing catch. It's my experience that the wind has a terrible arm and never oils their mitt.

I knocked on the door frame and waited. And waited and waited and waited. Three minutes went by, passing like a fifteen-year-old with a driver's permit. I apparently knocked too lightly, and she hadn't heard. I knocked again, way overdoing it, sounding like an angry woodpecker hell-bent on turning all wood into dust. I rapped so hard my knuckles bled. Which is the most embarrassing injury I've ever had in my life. What were the odds that she'd have a frozen bag of peas in her dressing room?

"Come in," her voice drifted through the air like a ghost. Only not an aggressive one, but a friendly one. Sort of like Casper. Except not a little boy. So her voice drifted through the air like a sexy, female, full-fledged adult ghost who was also friendly.

I entered her room and found her staring at a dimly lit mirror, doing something with her eyelashes. I've never been a guy who understood makeup at all, so I assume she was either applying fake eyelashes or taking them off. Maybe there was mascara involved, but I couldn't pick a mascara tube out of a lineup if it was standing with four actual humans all wearing handmade signs reading "I'm not a tube of mascara."

The walls in the room were painted a light beige color, except for an accent wall across from me which was washed-out distressed brick. Her mirror ran the full-length of one side of the room, clearly meant for an entire band as opposed to just one person. A bronzed ceiling fan with faux-wood blades and an LED light circled us overhead, like a buzzard in a desert. There were scuff marks on the tile floor, probably from heavy equipment like amplifiers and drums being moved in a hurry.

Something told me that the boys in the band had already left. That something was Vanessa.

"The other guys in the band already left," she said, swiveling in her chair to greet me.

Up close now, she had a face that could stop a freight train. Because the engineer would be so distracted by how beautiful Vanessa was. She sat with her legs crossed, her hands folded in her lap. It's said that when women wear too little, men are turned off because there's nothing left to the imagination. Well, Vanessa drove me wild because she had changed into baggy sweatpants, an oversized T-shirt, a hoodie, a puffy parka, an insanely long infinity scarf, a pair of wrap-around earmuffs, and a gray knit hat. Everything was left to my imagination, and boy was it lewd.

"The name's Spence. Tracer Spence," I shook her hand. Unfortunately, my knuckles bled all over her nice, wool mittens. To her credit, she took it in stride.

"Have a seat, Mr. Spence. I take it you're a connoisseur of '70s rock and roll?"

"More a connoisseur of '70s ladies," I said.

A perplexed look spread across her face like peanut butter on crackers. "Like, ladies dressed like the '70s," I explained. "Not like geriatrics. Their wrinkly hands give me the willies."

She laughed. I didn't understand why because old people's hands are gross and nothing to joke about. Maybe she was one of those people with a dark sense of humor though. I didn't want to lose my lead, so I laughed to play along.

"I haven't seen you in here before, Tracer. Most the time, it's the same faces every week. The regular crowd. You must be someone who enjoys new experiences."

"You could say that," I lied. I never really had enough money for new experiences, unless you take into consideration the countless ways I lost money as new. I continued, regaling her with the first new experience that popped into my head, "Like, I ate at a Thai place the other day. Top notch chicken tenders."

She continued her post-show makeup routine while she told me her history. The dame had a way of talking that would make a fish run out of breath. It was a long run-on, and one in which I thought I was given a life sentence. The highs of it were low and the lows were flat line sleep-inducing. Apparently, she had lived a boring life and was determined to pass it on to me as well. The only way I made it through the conversation was by playing chess in my head. Which was difficult because I've never understood the rules of the game.

During our time talking, she inched closer to me, her knees closed between mine. I got a whiff of her perfume—sandalwood and vanilla. She placed a mittened hand on top of my leg. Sexual tension was palpable in the atmosphere. You could taste it. It tasted like sandalwood and vanilla—mainly since the olfactory senses are so entwined with our sense of taste.

Now was my chance. I had charmed her with my alluring blank personality and my listening skills. And this was the first time in fifteen minutes she had taken a break in talking. "Vanessa, I've got to ask you. How do you feel about 'You're So Vain?'"

The look of alarm on her face said all that she needed to say. Her cheeks had turned bright red, flustered out of fear. Shocked at my question, her tongue flapped stupidly, hanging out of her mouth. In actual fact, she looked like a fire alarm that someone had just pulled. I was surprised that a loud, constant sound didn't start emanating from her—the first time in a quarter hour.

"The same thing happens to you?" she asked.

"Yeah, every day, the same—"

"Shhh," she said, placing her pointer finger against my lips, interrupting me. I fought against every instinct to wrap my lips around it and suck the wool off it, like a furry lollipop. "I need to think. This can't just be a coincidence. Me and you in the same predicament. Could it?"

"As a private detective, I've found that most things in life are just coincidences, actually. It makes wrapping up cases much easier."

We both sat in silence for a few seconds. It was long enough for us to hear footsteps creeping outside Vanessa's room.

A chill drifted through the room. The air conditioning had great dramatic timing.

As if we were in some idiotic novel where the plot moves when the writer wants it to, a giant goon burst through the dressing room door, like a hairy Italian Kool-Aid man.

7

Vanessa screamed.

I screamed.

The muscle-bound, thick-necked thug screamed as well, surprised at our reaction, which again, was screaming at the surprise of his presence.

It was only after we all stopped acting like some teenage coed in a B-movie slasher flick that the two other ruffians appeared from behind our new friend. Although they weren't as built as he was, they both displayed the same intimidation. Intimidation which they got across by smacking tire irons across their open palms. Both of them doing the same thing seemed redundant, but I'm not a hooligan mastermind, so what do I know?

"I think you boys have the wrong place," I said. "The mechanic shop's down the road."

At the same time as each other, the two smaller thugs said "No, but something in here needs to be fixed," and "Yeah, well, it's time to strip your lug nuts." The whole thing came out jumbled, them talking over each other.

The one on the right turned to the other and said, "I thought I was getting the witty one-liner this time?"

"No, Sal, you got it last time, remember? You said, 'Eat my shorts, pervert.'" He turned directly to Vanessa and said, "It was much funnier in context."

"Will you two idiots shut up?" the main guy said, his voice gruff. "I'm doing the talking from now on." He turned toward me, a flash of violence in his eyes. Or maybe that was just the room's lighting reflecting in his irises. "You Tracer Spence?" he asked.

This guy, this mook, was built like a dump truck: Tonka Tough. His legs had the circumference of an elephant's trunk. His arms were Popeye's post-spinach chugging. He stood damn near 7 feet tall. He also had a tattoo was on his right side, where his massive shoulder met his equally massive neck. I couldn't get a good look at it though as most of it was hidden underneath his black T-shirt.

"Maybe. Who wants to know?" This is my standard question in these situations, but I've been considering changing the wording. Maybe people think it's rhetorical because no one ever answers it. But really, I would genuinely like to know who's interested in me being me. If only I could get this across somehow.

"Don't you worry about it, pal," he said—see what I mean? Just brushing off my inquisitive nature. So annoying. "Just know my employer wants something that you've got. Seems you've taken something that's not yours. A real thorn in the side of my employer. They want it back, and they want you to stop your digging into a certain case. So, I'm here for you to stop your digging."

"The only digging I do is trying to get to the root of the problem. Mainly in my garden. And the problem is normally roots in that case." We had entered the first phase of fighting: repartee. Often, all-out brawls could be won based off of smarts, right up front.

"Your garden, huh? Well, I suggest you LEAF well enough alone."

"Or what? You gonna STALK me?"

"Buddy, you may be left in a vegetative state."

"Please. I photosyntheSIZED you up the moment you walked through those doors," I said.

"Still, you need to LEAF this alone," he repeated.

"Ha!" I said. I had won the battle of wits. "You already used that one. Now if you'll get out of here so me and the dame ca—" The goon cut me off with a sucker punch to my sucker. Seems like we had entered the second phase of fighting: fighting.

Pain radiated throughout my face, and blood leaked from my nostrils. The lug broke my nose. No big deal. It's been broken before, and he may have even straightened it out a bit.

"Funny way to do plastic surgery," I said. Only my face was already swollen, so it came out more like "Puggy way phoo phoo baspick phurggy." Everyone in the room looked at me confused.

"What?" he said.

"Did you just have a stroke?" Vanessa asked.

Now and then, good ideas seem to just come to me. The idea this time was to use their confusion to go on the offensive and attack. That would certainly be one of them good ideas. So I head-butted the guy. Why I didn't punch or kick or tackle or choke slam or literally any other thing is beyond me. Head-butting seemed right in the moment. Of course, I almost blacked out from the pain it caused my already sensitive face. And it barely registered to the goon—since he was a foot taller than me, I only smacked my forehead into his tank-sized chest.

He grabbed my hair, his fist tangled in my luscious locks. Turning to the other guys, he said "Get her out of here, and I'll take care of the dick."

"Okay, Stuart. You're the boss," the one named Sal said. Huh, I never would've guessed Stuart was the thug's name. But see? A good detective always gets his answer.

Vanessa screamed once more, as the two henchmen grabbed her by the arms and started carrying her out. I felt a ping of jealousy at their hands touching her. I then felt a ping of pain as Stuart the mug threw me into the large mirror. Shards of reflective glass sliced into the skin on my back like I was a block of cheese on a charcuterie board.

I got up and felt a long sliver poking out of my back. The perfect size to wield as a weapon against this hulk in front of me. Summoning all of my willpower, I grabbed the shard and pulled it out of my skin.

Turns out, all of my willpower wasn't enough because that was extremely painful. I crumpled back onto the floor, a bloody pile of laundry waiting to be cleaned. And I expected Stuart was about to take me to said cleaner.

The goon kicked me in the ribs with his steel-toed boot. This seemed unfair to me. Steel-toed boots? Were these allowed? Maybe kicking someone with them was against the Geneva Conventions, but I don't know enough about international law and basic wartime rights to know for sure. I reminded myself to do some research on the subject. It would be a good idea to know in the future: not just so I could report criminals for war crimes, but so I could know the loopholes for myself.

As I rolled onto my back, Stuart laughed. It was an ugly laugh. I'd rate it a three out of ten. If the laugh were a potential date, you'd say it "had a good personality." It sounded like a freight train rocking down its iron tracks. In that moment, I made it my life goal to derail it.

It was time to fight dirty.

I got up once more and reached into my pocket. I grabbed a handful of Fun Dip, that Willy Wonka Candy Company sweet powder—I always keep some on me just in case my blood sugar level drops—the package had torn open during the brawl. I flung it into my opponent's eyes, blinding him. The sugar must've stung, because he yelped and tried wiping the powder away from his face, which only smeared it more in.

I kicked him in the gonads, the front of my roller skates connecting. Who needs steel-toed boots when you've got a hunk of hard plastic from the '70s strapped to your feet? He dropped to his knees.

I got a good look at the hard number's face. He could've been a real leading man in a one-man show, off-Broadway. His steel-colored eyes showed no fear, and his crooked nose could've only gotten that way with a hard experience in fighting. Most striking however was the tattoo that was finally showing. His T-shirt had torn slightly, revealing a five-pointed star underneath an arc. It looked vaguely familiar. I wondered the meaning of it. Maybe it was a gang sign or something, an initiation that he went through. I shouldn't have been surprised by the tattoo, as all criminal scum had this cliché. I pegged him for the worst kind of scum. Soap scum. The kind that drips down on your shower walls that you scrub and scrub and scrub but still can't get off. Well, I was going to scrub him out no matter what.

"Oh, how the tables have turned," I said, smashing him with an end table. "Much like you'll be turning over in your grave." I thought this was pretty clever. I doubt Stuart heard it over his own screams and the smashing of wood against his skull. Another brilliant line wasted on an unforgiving audience.

Like a monstrosity, Stuart found his legs again, and he got to his feet. His eyes were as puffy as apple turnovers. Probably just as sweet too, with the candy dust dotting his crow's feet. The crash of the wooden table had cut and bruised up his face. A long splinter had dug itself into his left cheek, a glacier with most of it below the skin. That would certainly leave a scar. Dust from our dust-up patterned his dark clothes. He looked terrifying.

But I was never one to run away from a fight, or so I told myself as I tried running away. I tripped, forgetting the roller skates on my feet. My shins hit the tile floor, and my field of vision started to swim.

I turned to him, facing this man, this abomination who seemed more than human. Stuart took two steps toward me. Two steps toward my impending doom. And then he wobbled, and face first hit the ground.

"And take that," I said, to no one. Totally a power move. I even high-fived myself, since no one else was around to give me props.

I felt along the brute's neck, right above the tattoo pentagram's top point. He still had a pulse.

Then I remembered Vanessa, and I darted out the door.

At the end of an unlit hallway, a steel backdoor was wide open. I saw a silhouette standing in an alley. A sexy silhouette. Didn't know I could be attracted to a shapely outline. This was news to me, but I would have to process this information later.

I reached the alleyway, lit only by a floodlight above the door on the outside of the building. Vanessa stood there shaking, a maraca in a subpar mariachi band performing in the subway. She had tear tracks down her pale face but no longer appeared to be crying.

"Are you okay?" I asked, wrapping my arm around her shoulder. This was a smooth move on my part, one that I used over the years. It mainly worked better when I practiced on couch pillows than on real women, but practice makes perfect.

She said, "I don't...I didn't...I didn't see what happened." She pointed to shadows in the alleyway where a heap of something was piled.

I moved closer. Bones. Skulls and femurs and ulnas and all other types of bones. Clothing too, just ripped up with torn patches haphazardly strewn about. This mound of body parts must've been here a while, in the state of decomposition that it was in. It made me hungry for stew, if I'm being honest. Nothing like a good stew.

I huffed. "Where...where did they go? The guys?"

"That's them," she said and just continued pointing.

That's when I noticed two tire irons next to the pile of viscera. The two other goons were these bones. The skeletal remains of the henchmen littering the city. Just like bad guys, to just leave trash all over, even in their death. Haven't they heard of being eco-friendly?

I didn't understand how this had happened, but I felt my injuries catching up to me. The ringing in my ears played me a lullaby, a *hush little baby*. "You mean..." is all I got out before I fainted, crumpling onto the alleyway street.

8

I was out. Gone for lunch. Kaput.

For days, I was somewhere between reverie and reality, as I laid in a hospital bed recovering from my nightmarish beat down. My wounds had been so drastic that I was in a comatose state for the better part of a week—you read that right: better. Because who doesn't love a long nap? It's being awake that fills me with existential dread. I almost never get pulverized like a chicken breast while I'm sleeping.

But my mind drifted in a strange dream-state. Drifted like a kite on the wind, pulling on the arms of some frail boy, testing the tensile strength of his puny limbs. All he wants is his dad to look up, pull his nose out from between the pages of some inky newspaper, and be proud of his son for finally getting the kite up in the wind. But no, the stock market is way more interesting, ain't it? It isn't until the kite takes a sharp breeze and pulls me down into the dirt, smearing soil all along the front of my favorite shirt—Garfield kicking Odie off a nondescript table—and getting the bitterness of grass in my open mouth, that he looks up. And then he laughs! And points at me, calling other parents to stare! Anyway, yeah, that's how my mind drifted.

Honestly, you know those wavy lines that they use to signify flashbacks in soap operas? The ones they put on the frame of the screen? You could pretend that those were on the surroundings of my consciousness, and it would be pretty apt.

Oh, I still caught snippets of things that were happening in real life. The incessant sound of a heart monitor beeping. The incessant sound of daytime talk shows getting through. The incessant sound of Vanessa talking at my limp body. I don't think she cared that I couldn't respond at all. I do have to say, at least her voice was sonorous, and if I could be blabbered at every single night by her, I'd gladly take that offer up.

I don't think she even let the doctors and nurses get a word in edgewise, the handful of times they came in to check up on me. Just as well—I don't care for doctors or nurses, always sticking me with needles. "For your health," they always say, jabbing me with the business end of a junkie's wet dream. I've had enough experience with ice picks to know these so-called medical professionals must take some morbid pleasure in my discomfort. Those evil croakers. I was glad that my beautiful siren stayed and yakked them all away.

That all said, one thing that for sure got through my ear holes during my catatonic circumstance: the demonic racket of that soft rock torcher. "You're So Vain." In my subconscious, I had hoped to get a brief respite from that hellion Carly Simon. But apparently the powers that be enjoy adding insult to injury, and sure enough the song played faintly through the hospital room's TV speakers voluming into my mind, angering my core.

And then I awoke. Just like that. How else were you expecting?

I opened my eyes, lids heavy like an anvil dropping on some cartoon coyote. Vanessa was next to me, her blurry outline slumped over in a chair. As my vision became clearer, I realized she was sleeping. Though I heard whispers coming from her. Of course she's a sleep talker. Figures.

I let her lie there, staring at her dozing like a tractor. Her long, brown hair tangled down in front of her face. She wore a sheer tank-top, with a leather jacket over it, and I watched as her chest steadily rocked up and down with the rhythm of her breaths. Her tight jeans were crinkled like an empty potato chip bag. It looked like she hadn't changed or showered in a couple of days. She hadn't left my side. She was beautiful. I couldn't believe the first thoughts I was having was about how attractive she was. You're only human, Tracer.

A male nurse wandered into the room, making his rounds. "Oh, you're up!" he said, speaking much too loudly. His voice went right through me, making me shiver. Vanessa stirred next to me. "The doctor isn't in yet. He'll be here in an hour or so," he said, emulating a golf swing. I thought this was quite rude, validating an overblown stereotype like that. Plus, I could tell his form was terrible.

"Can you get him some food? He hasn't eaten solids in days now. I'm sure you must have some kind of sandwiches or chicken or beef stroganoff or mashed potatoes or cookies, chocolate chip would be good, but I'm sure Tracer will take anything at the moment. The kitchen might not be open yet, but you definitely have something lying around. Don't tell me you don't or I'm going to scream. That's just crazy if not. A hospital not even carrying leftovers for their patients. Don't tell me that," Vanessa said.

The nurse nodded, not wanting to interrupt.

As he turned to go, I called out. "Just no Jell-O. The way it jiggles creeps me out. Makes me dizzy. You wouldn't want me to get vertigo now, would you?"

Vanessa sat on my bed and leaned down toward me, caressing my broken face with her fingers.

"I can't believe you're finally awake. I was so worried about you. More worried and nervous than I can remember being. Except maybe that one time back in high school when Mrs. Leeds called me up to the chalkboard to finish that pre-calc problem. I could never quite grasp the concept of imaginary numbers. What even is that? Why would I care about something not real? Imaginary numbers. Just idiotic.

"So, I get on up there, just holding the chalk in my hand, staring at this dusty, dark green board with a bunch of letters and numbers written on it, and I'm supposed to solve for x, but come on, she barely taught us what a square root was, let alone how to solve for a letter. Who was she to chastise me in front of the whole class like that? You know, she called herself 'missus,' but I never saw no picture of a 'mister' on her desk. Frigid old crone. I bet she didn't even have a husband—

not that there's anything wrong with not marrying, just seems strange to lie to children that are supposed to look up to you—"

"Shhhh," I said, cutting her off. "Let silence have a turn at speaking, for once."

"I know. I'm sorry, I talk too much."

"Where do you even find the words? They just tumble out of your mouth like a ballerina on cocaine."

"It's…I had a lonely childhood. Never found it easy to make friends. Can't understand imaginary numbers, but imaginary friends…now that's something I get. So, I used to talk to them. And that turned into a habit of just talking to myself. I guess I never grew out of it. Maybe that's not a good excuse, but it's the truth."

This seemed like a good enough excuse for me, so I said that. "That's a good enough excuse for me." You're only human, Tracer.

Vanessa got a wild look in her eyes, like a dog who sees a wolf for the first time and wonders *what if?* Her breasts pressing against my body, she leaned over and kissed me.

She kissed like a sailboat: she took the wind out of my sails, her tongue rotated like a propeller, and there was a yacht of chemistry between us. You're only human, Tracer.

"Let me go see if that damn nurse found you any food yet," Vanessa said, smiling.

She left the room, this small ol' hospital room. This death trap. It was bisected down the middle by a green curtain. I was on the side closest to the door, hooked up to all these complicated machines meant to read my vitals: my heart beat, my blood sugar levels, my chakra count—whatever body things were inside me. The entire room was giving me a headache with how pristine and white the walls were, unless that headache was still from my knock-down drag-out.

I heard moaning coming from the other side of the room.

"Hey, pal, you alright over there?" I called and waited for a response, but none came other than a long whimper. "Alright, suit yourself. But I'm breaking out of this joint as soon as possible, and if you don't want in on the escape plan, you keep it to yourself."

I searched around for the bed remote, wanting to raise my upper body up. It must've been tangled in all these damn sheets, lost like an ancient minotaur in a labyrinth. I gave up. If I was going to be stuck in this booby-hatch, this loony bin, I might as well be uncomfortable to boot.

This gave me time to ruminate on how the Carly Simon case was going so far. Like any good private detective, most of my time working on a case was trying to comprehend what I've done after the fact.

Actually, I take that back. Most of my time on cases was spent unconscious. Either sleeping for the recommended eight hours per night or recovering from a horrific thrashing. One way or another.

My client, Marvin Hartley, had given me a terrible case. This was New York, the city that never sleeps. The city that never stops murdering. The city that never stops blackmailing. This was a city filled with drug dealers and embezzlers and thieves and jaywalkers and drivers who don't turn their blinkers on when changing lanes. I could've turned Marvin down and been presented with any number of other crimes to solve, but no, I had to choose this one. Something in me, maybe my inquisitive conscience or maybe my empty wallet, made this choice. I was tempted to grab a scalpel and remove the damn conscience from inside of me for all the good it's caused.

Sure, this assignment led me to Vanessa, much like a river leads salmon upstream to their reproductive mates. But it also led me to mysterious goons hired by some unknown entity, a flesh-eating enigma that couldn't digest bones, and then to a hospital. Much like a river leads salmon to the chemical run-offs of evil industrial businesses where the salmon grow two-heads, both of which are wanting to control which way to swim. And so the fish gets stuck in a circular path because neither head can gain full control of the body. It was exactly the same thing.

You're only human, Tracer.

In actual fact, you could say something was amiss with the assignment. You could say I was amid a mess of an assignment. You could say it was a mistake that I'd have to amend. You could say something was amiss with this mistake of an assignment that I was amid and maybe I could amend this mess. And if you could, you'd be a better man than me because that sentence is a helluva tongue twister.

One thing I couldn't figure out was what that goon Stuart had mentioned. He said his boss wanted something I had. Unless his boss wanted a second-hand trench coat, I had nothing worthwhile that anyone would want. I didn't even want the stuff I had, but that's the way of the world, ain't it?

I needed fresh air to clear my mind and think a little. I breathed deep but was only greeted by the chemical smell of the hospital: bleach, antiseptics, and baby wipes. I sighed. Never liked hospitals. Those scents were used to cover up the death that happens in hospitals on a daily basis. If I wanted death, I'd visit a back alley in the city. Or a farmers' market with all them trickster fruit vendors. Can't even decide if a tomato is a fruit or vegetable. Well, I ain't buying what you're selling, especially not any tomatoes.

At that moment, Marvin Hartley, speak of the devil, came into my room.

He blew in like a tornado in a china shop, a whirlwind of hot air carrying a twister. No, like he was actually carrying the party game Twister. I found out later it was a gift for his niece.

"You went to a bar? You went to a bar? You were supposed to be working my case!"

"Why don't you walk back out and try that entrance again, Marv, buddy? I think you meant to say something like, 'How are you holding up, Tracer? Can I get you anything, Tracer? Can I help you dig out of this hell-hole with a plastic spoon I got from the kitchen?' Maybe something along those lines would work."

"You. Were. Supposed to be. Working. My case," he repeated, punctuating every few words like a junior editor of *The Wall Street Journal.*

"I think I prefer the timid version of you from before," I said.

"And I prefer not hiring a drunk who wastes my time and money. The nurses told me you were in here. What'd you do—sit on the wrong end of your barstool? I can't believe you. I just can't believe you."

He seemed to really enjoy repetition when he was angry, like a broken record or a basic cable TV channel showing marathons of the same crime procedural show over and over again. I get it, USA Network, *Law and Order: SVU* is on again. Yeah yeah, people are disgusting perverts. Thanks for making that abundantly clear, Christopher Meloni. Their deviant fetishes require a carnal knowledge that I can't fathom. It's on so much I hear the "chung chung" noise in my head every time I even think about Ice-T now. Or even iced tea, the drink.

"How'd you even know I was holed up in here, Marv?"

"What? It's on your answering machine."

I must've looked confused, so he pulled out his phone and dialed my number. My cell rang, but I let it go to voicemail. Through his tinny speakers I heard my voice, "Heyyyyyyy, you've got Tracer Spence, PI extraordinaire! I can't come to the phone right now, as I'm probably in the hospit---hey! Hey! Mr. Ambulance Driver Man! Which hospital are you taking me to? St. Luke's? Oh yeah, that makes sense. Oh hey, can we stop for some cheeseburgers? I could go for a real greasy cheeseburger right now. A what? A concussion? No, you have a concussion! Come back and say that to my fa—am I bleeding? Why am I bleeding? What's my phone doing in my hand?" CLICK.

Marvin stared at me like I was a tax return filled out in crayon. "Sounds like you had a real fun night, Mr. Spence. A real fun night."

"Marvin, relax. I was there on your case. I had a lead."

"And I bet tomorrow morning you'll have a lead to a Bloody Mary."

"I wouldn't mind one, if I'm being honest." You're only human, Tracer.

He glowered at me again, so this time I explained what had happened.

"I knew it. I knew I should never have come to you or done anything with this. It's too dangerous! Maybe we should just quit before anything worse happens. Live with the song forever, you know? How bad could that really be?"

"That would be hell on Earth," I said. "And hey, I'm not giving up just yet. A few cracked ribs never kept Tracer Spence down." I looked around in my hospital room, bed-ridden and hooked up to an IV. "Well, at least not for more than a few days."

"I don't know, Mr. Spence. I think we should call it off. My therapist says I might just be obsessing about it. Maybe she's right."

I never believed in therapists. Not like I didn't think they could help. I just didn't believe in them like I didn't believe in ghosts. To my knowledge I never met someone who was a therapist, and I never met someone who was a ghost, either. You're only human, Tracer.

"Therapy schmerapy. Doctors don't know beans," I said, as a hospital doctor walked right by my door. "I MEAN TO SAY THEY DON'T KNOW ANYTHING ABOUT THE FOOD BEANS. BEST LEAVE THAT KIND OF STUFF TO THE BEAN FARMERS OF THE WORLD," I said, hoping the ill-timed sawbones wasn't eavesdropping.

I continued, "Look, Marv, I think it's a mistake to give up now. I don't know about you, but ol' Spence here ain't no quitter. Except that time in third grade when my dad coached my soccer team. Sport of the world, pshaw. Cleats tend to leave marks on your skin, let me tell you. I've still never seen another coach instruct the rest of the team to trample their teammate, but I never really understood team-building exercises anyway. Maybe that's why I work better by myself."

"I'm not foll—"

"What I'm trying to say is, we should keep going with this case."

"You were just beat up! Left for dead!"

"Yeah, and that means I'm on the right track! Someone out there knows we're on to them and their secret, and they're trying to get us to stop, damnit. Thrashing me to an inch of my life was blatant desperation on their part. They're getting sloppy."

I surprised myself with my own logic here. It seems Marvin Hartley agreed as he nodded slowly up and down.

"Alright, alright," he said. "What's...what's the next step then? What's your plan?"

9

The metal sign hanging above the door read "Tater Tatts," and it swung slowly in the wind, like a pendulum in a grandfather clock. I walked up the concrete stoop and pushed open the glass door. A bell rung above me. There was no way I could do this mission stealthily now. They knew I was here.

"Be right with you," someone called out. A gruff voice.

A desk was to my left. A cash register sat on top. Next to it was a black hardcover sketchbook, open to a page of photos showing horrible body mutilation. This was a sick place for sick sickos. My skin crawled just thinking about what went on here.

I looked past the desk to where the voice called out from. There were two people. A fellow with a shaved head sat in a wheelchair, shirtless. He was sweating. He was sweating more than any man I've ever seen. Why was he sweating so much? The second man was hunched over the sweating man, sticking some monstrous contraption, a mechanical needle, into the man's arm.

It looked like I was in the right place.

Earlier that morning, I found Harry Potter sitting at a counter in the arcade's food section. He was chowing down on a pizza slice the size of his head. Grease dripped from the folded crust backwards onto his paper plate. He had a string of muted pink tickets on the counter next to him.

One end of the tickets dangled off the edge of the counter. I picked it up, running the tickets through my fingers. "This must be a mile long, HP. Just imagine all the spider rings you can trade this in for."

"Tracer, what're you doing here?" Harry asked, snatching the tickets back. His hand smeared oil on a few tickets, dark splotches staining them.

"Easy there, easy there. I'm just looking for a little information."

"Look for it somewhere else. I'm busy."

"Yeah, I see that. That pizza's not just gonna jump down someone's throat by itself now, is it?"

He ignored me and grabbed a handful of thin napkins out of a chrome dispenser. He wiped his mouth, but the thin paper just smeared the grease along his stubble.

"Look, HP, what do you know about tattoos?"

"Tattoos? I know a bit," he said.

"Good. I saw an interesting one the other day. A star underneath this half circle."

"And?"

"And, what I need to know is," I said, pausing for dramatic effect, "where does one get a tattoo?"

"What? All you want to know is where to get a tattoo? That's it?"

I thought about his question for some time. Was that all I wanted to know? Was there something else that I was missing? Was Harry Potter trying to trick me? I looked in his eyes to get a sense of his mindset. I had to play this carefully. One wrong move and he would sense how desperate I was.

I nodded. Slowly.

"Look, people get tattoos at tattoo shops, Tracer. I can't believe I need to tell you that."

"Thanks," I said, slamming a quarter onto the counter. "This is for your next slice."

I turned to leave and felt a PING against the back of my head. Seems Harry Potter's greasy fingers dropped the quarter forcefully towards my cranium. Funny how often gravity seems to attract things to the back of my head when I leave rooms.

An hour later, I went back and found Harry Potter again. This time I had him show me how to use Google Maps to find the nearest tattoo place. I gave him another quarter, which somehow hit the back of my head again. I couldn't understand how someone could be so clumsy.

That's how I wound up at Tater Tatts.

"Alright, Tony, we're about done today, anyway," the second man said, powering down his torture-needle. "Sit tight, until you're feeling ready to leave." He wiped his brow with a towel and walked over. "Hey, pal, the name's Tater. What can I do you for?" he asked.

Both of his arms were covered in sleeves, which makes sense because he was wearing a red and black flannel shirt. He rolled up those same sleeves, and his arms were also covered in a multitude of tattoos. On one side, he had a menagerie of animals—wolves, deer, horses—all surrounding an old Native American chief. On his other arm, he had a full portrait of Gerard Butler in the Michael Crichton adaptation *Timeline*. Not even Gerard Butler in *300* or *The Phantom of the Opera*. I wasn't aware anyone even saw *Timeline,* let alone enjoyed it enough to have in permanently inked onto their body. Surely, this Tater fellow was a deranged mind.

"Well, Tater, if that is your real name—"

"It's not," he interrupted. "My real name's Robert Forest Moreau III. Tater is just a nickname from back in junior high."

"Well, Tater, you see, I'm looking for a tattoo…" I wasn't sure how to broach the subject. I didn't know if I could trust Tater.

"You've come to the right place then, since this is a tattoo shop. Have a look through this book if you want to see some of the art I've done before. Any custom ink jobs need to be booked in advance though." He pushed the black book forward on the desk, turning it around so I could see it better. "Hey, Tony," he called back to the sweating man. "You ready? I'll walk you out and make sure you're alright."

Tater pushed Tony's wheelchair out the front door. One of the wheels squeaked on every rotation.

What a break in my case! Sometimes the worst part about being a detective is having to talk to people. People tended to make me uncomfortable. Now I had time to search this tattoo shop for clues. I started in the last place a criminal hiding something would want me to look: at the pictures in the black book he pushed forward to me. If I were hiding the fact that I tattooed gang insignias, I would hide it right in plain sight.

I leafed through the book and yawned. Books are boring.

But I had to make sacrifices if I ever wanted to solve this case. A good detective needed to know what they were up against, and I was bound to come up against Stuart again, at some point. I think Jesus said it best when he said, "Know thy enemy." At least...I'm pretty sure it was Jesus. Who's to say? I never read the Bible, because again, books are boring.

Know thy enemy.

Stuart was thy enemy. Stuart had this tattoo near his neck, and I needed to find out what the tattoo meant.

RING RING.

My attention was cut off by the telephone. I had to play this cool. I could always pick up the phone, pretend to work at Tater Tatts, pump the unsuspecting caller for information, and use that info to blackmail Tater into giving me what I wanted, what I needed. It was a longshot, sure, but you know what they say—no risks, no rewards. I also think that was Jesus. Besides, what was I going to do? Sit and look through this book of pictures? No thanks.

By the time I was done thinking my plan through and went to pick up the phone, the caller had hung up already.

I got my chance a minute later when the phone rang again. I picked it up on the first ring, and then I cursed into the receiver because you never pick up the phone after the first ring; it just makes you look desperate.

"Excuse me?" the voice on the other line asked. It sounded familiar, but I couldn't place it.

I lowered my voice an octave, to disguise my tone. "Sorry, sorry, I didn't mean to say that. I just…I accidentally misspelled what this guy wanted on his chest. He said he wanted 'I Love Mom,' but I gave him 'Sic Semper Tyrannis.' Nothing that can't be fixed."

"Is this Tater? You don't sound like Tater."

"Oh, I'm not," I said, already forgetting my plan to impersonate the shop owner. "My name is…Tater. Yeah, I'm another Tater. But I'm new here. Tater…" I looked around the room. "Tater Couch…book…man. Yeah. Tater Couchbookman is my name."

"Hmmm…I didn't know the OG Tater was hiring anyone. Tell him I'm coming in later today for a touch-up. I'll get to meet you when I come in."

"I'll be here. Uh-huh. Because I definitely work here."

Holding the phone to my ear with one hand, I poked through some window blinds with the other hand. Tater was helping Tony load his wheelchair into the side of a black and tan minivan.

The voice on the line continued talking. "Yeah, I got in a brawl the other day. Scratched my tat up pretty good. I'll need Tater to do his magic."

Huh. Still couldn't recognize the voice.

"Sure, let me see if there are any openings…"

"Oh, there will be an opening. Whenever I come in is when Tater is going to see me. Or my name ain't Stuart."

This made it slightly easier to pinpoint how I knew his voice. I could cross off anyone I had ever met with the name Stuart. That left everyone else, which is like trying to find a needle in a stack of scrap papers with different names scribbled on them. Unless…unless the caller was lying, and his name was Stuart. If he was, could this be *my* Stuart? What were the odds that the pug I got in a dust-up with would use the tattoo shop—the only tattoo shop I had walked into—and call up at this exact moment? The coincidence was so contrived, it was hard to believe.

CA-CHUNK.

I peered out the window again. Tony had closed his car door and was speaking to Tater through the window. They were shaking hands. I didn't have much time. Tater would walk back any moment now. I had to turn the screws on this caller, be a little less subtle.

"Say, if you were to blackmail Tater into giving you some information on criminal activity, what way would you go about it?" I asked. "Just a hypothetical question," I added.

"Strange. But as long as it's a hypothetical question, I suppose I'll give you an answer. I would probably kidnap his girlfriend. Emotionally wreck him that way, and he'll probably tell you whatever you need to know, or do whatever you want. It's a tried-and-true method. I use it all the time in my line of work. Yep, I love kidnapping girlfriends. Hypothetically speaking, of course."

The door pushed open, and a gust of wind followed which lifted up the top pages of the tattoo book like they were wings of a bird getting ready to take off. Tater was back.

"Sorry, you've got the wrong number," I said into the receiver and then hung up. I turned to Tater. "Was just calling for some pizza." Perfect excuse. Everyone likes pizza.

"How was it a wrong number then if you were the one who called for pizza?"

I stood there, speechless, staring at him. Tater stared back at me, waiting for an answer. Neither of us moved, two obelisks staring at each other during an awkward moment.

This went on for some time.

"Ha ha, I know, right?" was the best I came up with after five minutes.

He waved me off. "So, you were looking for a tattoo. Did you find anything to your liking? Got a special right now. Half-priced apps. Like if you want a tat of some mozzarella sticks or sliders or hot wings. For some reason, those are all the rage these days."

"Actually, Tater, I saw someone with a tattoo the other day. Real unique. Maybe you could tell me the meaning of it?"

Tater picked up a legal pad laying on a chair and tore off a yellow page of paper. He handed it to me with a pen. "I'll tell you what. You draw it for me, and maybe that'll help."

I outlined Stuart's tattoo from memory. A five-pointed star underneath a downwards arc, sort of like a rainbow with only one crescent. I handed it back to him.

Tater studied it for some time. He was deep in thought. He turned the page this way and that, attacking it from all angles with his mind. Squinting, Tater held the drawing right up to his face, touching the tip of his bulbous nose. He must be a really great tattoo artist if he's this thoughtful for every piece.

"This is…completely inscrutable," he finally said. "Where did you learn to draw—garbage school?"

"I'm better at still lifes, drawing my gun," I said while pushing my jacket back to show the weapon on my hip. I realized this seemed intimidating and badass, but I simply meant that the only sketches I've ever done were of my third generation Colt Single Action .45. And those I did in crayon, in my spare time.

"Whoa, ease up there, buddy," Tater said, holding his hands up. "I still can't help you until you show me. Here's another paper."

This time I really went for it, getting all the details just right. It took me an hour and fifteen minutes and three tries before I felt ready to show Tater.

"Here's my masterpiece," I said, handing my artwork to Tater. "It's a regular, ummm…who's that artist? You know, that guy who invented the Campbell's Chicken Noodle Soup can and your dad spends the money that was intended for your college tuition on one of his prints? And then when he finally gets it, he hangs it up in what used to be your room, but no longer, because he says you don't deserve to breathe the same air as this painting, you little disappointment?"

"Andy Warhol?"

"Yeah, that's the guy. It's a regular Andy Warhol."

Tater looked at my picture. His face scrunched up, scared, just like he had swallowed a lemon rind. "I'm sorry, I can't help you. You better leave," he said, planting a large hand on my back and pushing me toward the door.

"Hey hey hey hey, what's the big idea, Tater?"

"I don't want no part in this, whatever it is your mixed up in. Now breeze off."

"I ain't planning on going nowhere. Except the barber shop, but my appointment's not until 4pm." I spun and slapped his hand down. "Now, you're going to help me, or I'll play you some chin music. You'll hate it because I can't sing, and you'll be left with a clef chin."

Silence descended upon the room like the curtains in a middle-school play: heavy and fast, because the weak arms of the prepubescent stage crew couldn't hold the crank in place.

"Look, I can't. I just can't tell you anything. If I squeal and it gets out that it came from me, I can lose everything," Tater said. "Unless…"

"Unless?"

"Unless you get a tattoo."

"Ha. I don't think so. Tattoos are for bikers and single moms, and I don't plan on riding no Harley."

"If you don't get a tattoo, I can't help you."

"You don't understand," I said. "My body is a temple." I believe that quote is actually from Chuck Norris.

"Look, it's the only way. We tattoo artists are bound by a strict code. The Hennacratic Oath." He pointed to a framed certificate on the wall behind the cash register. Sure enough, "The Hennacratic Oath" was spelled out in big, swirly letters. Looked official enough. "It's a sort of artist/patient confidentiality thing. You buy a tattoo from me, and you're my client. Meaning nothing we discuss today leaves my confidence. Got it?"

"Ugh. Fine. Got it."

I spent the next twenty minutes actually looking through his tattoo book, deciding on a tattoo to disfigure my body permanently.

While Tater stabbed me over and over and over and over again with a mechanical needle putting ink into my flesh, we discussed the star and arc tattoo.

"So, it's a gang sign, meant to show affiliation," he said.

"It is? I was right? I was right!"

"Stop squirming."

"Do you know how rare it is for me to be right about these sort of things? What gang?"

"They're called the Hidden Star Hill organization," Tater said. "I think they're from up north."

"Up north? What, like The Bronx?"

"I don't think so."

"Yonkers?"

He rinsed the needle off in a cup of water, dipped it into brown ink, and went back to work torturing me. "They're not from around here, but I'm not sure where exactly they're based out of. All I know is that they're some bad mothers. You don't want to mess around with them."

"That's too late, Tater," I said, through clenched teeth. My knuckles were pale as I grabbed the arm rests of the chair I was sitting in. "Hidden Star Hill. Hmmm…"

And that's how I wound up getting a tattoo of Secret Squirrel on the bottom of my foot.

10

"Tracer, why did you tell me to meet you in a parking garage?" Detective Hardholm asked. He was leaning against his '88 Dodge Daytona, sleek black with thin purple pinstripes down the middle. He had parked it diagonally, taking up two spots.

"Uhh…you know…Deep Throat?"

"No, really, why?"

"Deep Throat."

"And why specifically this spot?" he asked, taking a sip of coffee out of a paper cup. "We're standing next to a column whose stench is utterly unrecognizable, and I don't like it. And don't—don't you dare say 'Deep Throat' one more time. That's not an answer."

"But that's why I wanted you to meet me here. Deep Throat. This is what Deep Throats do."

"I swear to—do you even know what Deep Throat is?"

"Yeah, it's, you know, Deep Throat? Parking garage etiquette. Deep Throat. Like, *oh man, this is so Deep Throat, it's crazy.*"

He shook his head. "Will you get out of the shadows, man? I feel like I'm talking to a creepy lurker right now."

"Fine, but that ruins the whole atmosphere of such a clandestine meetup," I said, stepping out from behind the column I was half-hiding behind. Now that the blinding lights were surrounding me, me and Hardholm were face to face, and the mood was ruined. "You got what I asked for?" I said.

"Yeah, I got it." He opened up the passenger door of his car and picked a manila envelope off the seat. He tossed it to me, hitting me in the chest with it. "I still don't understand why you needed me here for this. Literally could've been a phone call. Or, you know, you could've looked up this information yourself."

"You forget I'm not a cop, Hardholm? I asked for arrest records." I started unraveling the envelope's string, figure-eighted around the two cardboard buttons to keep the top flap closed.

"Man, those are public record. You could've Googled that information."

"Oh."

"I don't know why I'm surprised you didn't know that, Spence. You're not even a licensed P.I. anyway. Luckily, you're harmless, and the rest of the New York Police Department doesn't have time to go after you for operating illegally."

"No, no, I did get my P.I. license actually," I said.

"You finally passed the test?"

"Well, no. It was a clerical error. But once the state sends it, it's hard to revoke it."

I pulled the papers out of the envelope. The first one said *New York Police Department – Arrest Records* across the top, with the NYPD's logo emblazoned in the top right corner. Underneath, the name of the culprit I was after was listed: *Sadie Marie Olivierri.*

"You sure this is the right person, Hardholm?" I asked. The mysterious caller on Ellie's answering machine never left her last name, so I was dubious about the detective just giving me information on a random Sadie Marie.

"Hell no, I'm not sure if that's the *right* person. I don't know what your case is about or how this broad relates to anything. I have no idea why you want information on 'em. But, that's the name that matched the phone number you gave me."

He took another sip of coffee. I hoped it was lukewarm.

I looked further down the arrest report. Which only took me a second. It was blank, white as the snow in Buffalo in Winter.

"This some kind of practical joke? I thought you said this was an arrest report. There's nothing here." I took a step closer to the detective and waved the papers in his face. I don't think he appreciated the gesture, because he pushed my chest to get out of his personal space.

"Of course," Hardholm said. "It's blank because there are no arrests."

"I don't understand."

"If there was no arrests to report, there won't be anything on the arrest report."

"Wait, let me get this straight…what?"

"Let me speak slowly and clearly, so a man of your…limited intellect will understand, Tracer. Lady good. No arresty."

"That can't be possible," I said, flipping the paper back and forth. "I heard the voicemail she left. She threatened Ellie Dayton, plain as Nebraska. This Sadie Marie Olivierri must be a criminal. Criminals get arrested and get on the arrest report. That's how this works."

"Well, let me put it to ya this way…if she is bent, then she's good at hiding it. She would be the first evil cupcake baker mastermind that I've ever come across."

I think the blank look on my face got across my confusion, because Detective Hardholm continued and said, "Flip to the next page." He twirled his right hand forward and waited for me.

The next page simply gave a Bridgeport, Connecticut address for some place called Take a Cakewalk on the Wild Side.

"And this is supposed to mean what exactly?"

"Jesus, you need everything spelled out to you, don't you? This Sadie Marie woman, that's her business. She owns a sweet shop. Again, if you just opened up the internet and typed in the phone number, this place would've been the first result. You wouldn't have needed to contact me and wasted my time, when I could do something more productive, like, literally anything else in the world."

"I suppose a thanks is in order," I said, folding up the information and stuffing it in my pocket.

"I guess you're welcome, Spence."

"Oh, right, you, sure. Thanks. I meant I should take a ride and thank this Sadie Marie for kidnapping my client's sister, because otherwise I wouldn't have this case."

"Look, just do me a favor, and next time you call the police, make sure it's because you're basically dead. That way, I can come and laugh at you while you're bleeding out in the gutter."

"Funny, that's the exact thing my dad said to me last time I saw him."

"Take care of yourself, Spence," Hardholm said. He took the lid off his paper coffee cup and dumped the rest of the bitter liquid on to pavement. It splattered at my feet and some coffee grounds dotted the asphalt, as the spill started moving downhill. Hardholm then got in his Daytona, shifted the car into gear, and took off.

Well, Sadie Marie was a baker who ran a sweet shop. I guess it was time for me to take a ride out to her store and see what exactly she had to do with my case. And maybe to scarf down a few of those cupcakes. Either way, I'd see to it that someone got their just desserts.

11

There is a subtle art to stakeouts that isn't spoken of much, at least the way I do 'em. People are more used to the way stakeouts are depicted in movies and TV shows. You know, the normal stuff. Detectives freezing their pants off in a sedan, junk food wrappers strewn about the backseat, a paper cup filled with hot cocoa in the detective's hands as they try to warm themselves up. Days of waiting just down the road from their target, surveilling them with binoculars looking through the smudgy car windows. The only activity to keep their mind off the ceaseless boredom is bickering with their partner about who snores louder in the passenger seat.

I suppose this is all true. I wouldn't know. I don't have a partner and was never on the police force. It's not how I do stakeouts anyway. Mine are more like tailgating parties, outside of a football stadium the morning before a game. They're more fun that way.

And, if I was going to learn anything about Sadie Marie Olivierri's criminal activities, it was time for me to throw one of my stakeouts/tailgates. I wondered if Connecticut allowed streets to be shut down for block parties.

There was only one issue. I don't own a car.

This was the curse I had to live with. Living in New York City meant that I never needed to own one. Taxis and the subway were my normal mode of transportation. Well…not *my* normal mode of transportation. *Most people's* normal mode. You know, people who could afford the luxuries of Metro cards.

It was my biggest regret in life that since I lived in the city and didn't own a car, I would never get into any sweet car chases. Like the one in *The French Connection*. I always considered myself just like Gene Hackman's portrayal of Popeye Doyle, only without the pork pie hat or the casual racism.

It was settled then. I would have to rent a car.

Which brought up yet another issue. I'm not exactly someone you could call "a responsible adult who has a good credit rating." Hell, I'm not even someone that you could call "a person who understands what a credit rating is." You know how people receive junk mail all the time from credit card companies with those fake cardboard credit cards glued to the pre-approval letters? My credit rating is so bad that I get those too, but the credit card companies send me pre-denial letters. The last one I got simply said, "Here's our phone number. Call us. We need a good laugh."

And that's how I wound up at Connecticut's very own local establishment called Shifty Ray's Rental "Car" Emporium and Empanada Shack.

I walked into the lobby, which had the overwhelming scent of new car smell and taco seasoning. Strange, because I didn't see any automobiles or any kitchens around.

A man got up from his chair, where he had been lounging with his feet kicked up on his desk and started walking over to me. His hair was slicked back, with so much product in it that if you could crack an egg on it and his hair wouldn't move an inch. He was wearing a suit without a tie, his shirt unbuttoned showing off his chest hair. The chest hair also looked like he slicked it with pomade to keep it in place.

Yep, he was a born salesman.

"You Shifty Ray?" I asked, as he got into hand-shaking range.

"That depends," he said, smoothly shaking my hand and placing his other arm around my shoulders, steering me into walking side-by-side with him. "Were you sent here by my wife? Ha! I kid, I kid." He thumped me on the back, with slightly too much force. I coughed. "Of course, I'm Shifty Ray. The shiftiest, the biffiest, as we always say here."

"I'm not sure what that means."

"Aren't we all."

"What?"

"So, what can I do for you, bucko?"

I had never been called *bucko* before. I kind of liked it. I wondered if it would catch on. The only nickname I ever had was *Four Eyes*. Which made no sense, because I never even wore glasses. But when your dad introduces you to your fourth grade class with that name, it's kind of hard to shake off.

"Well, Ray, I'm in the market for a rental car—"

"Oh, you mean a rental 'car,' right?" He used air quotes when he said the word. "You see, we're not legally allowed to call them cars per se."

"Why not?"

"Well, cars usually have things like seatbelts and airbags and engines," he said. We had reached his desk, where he picked up an air fragrance freshener and sprayed it. The aerosol can sprayed out a light mist which tickled my nose. I looked at the can. The scent said "New Car Smell and Taco Seasoning."

"Either way," I said, "I'm in the market for whatever 'car' type of thing that you're renting."

"See, now this is a true-blue businessman. I keep telling my wife this is why I love this business that I'm in. It's people like you. I say to her, I say, 'Wife, it's people like this guy why I'm in the automobile and empanada vocation.' She just doesn't get it. Women, am I right? Ha! I kid, I kid."

I shook off Shifty Ray's comment. I wasn't positive that he had a wife named Wife, but stranger things have happened.

"Now, listen Ray, I do have to warn you that my credit rating isn't…the best, let's say."

"Are you alive?"

"Y…yes?"

"Then your credit is good enough here. And we even throw in a free empanada with every rental transaction."

And, I was the proud rental owner of a *lightly used* 'car' after only twenty minutes or so of signing some papers. Papers with a lot of fine print. Fine print I had only skimmed. The only portion that I remembered was paragraph five of subsection 21a:3-3c, which pointed out, *consumption of any empanadas obtained from Shady Ray's Rental "Car" Emporium and Empanada Shack is strongly advised against.*

I parked my newfound rental across the street from Take a Cakewalk on the Wild Side, in front of a bail bonds place. It was located a couple blocks away from the water, in a very swanky part of town. Like, shutters on all the windows kind of swanky. Each building probably had running hot water whenever someone turned on the tap. Such snobbish decadence. Who needed that kind of hedonism?

I unpacked all my supplies from the trunk. I set my beach chair down on the street behind my car; you've got to set your stake for a good tailgate. The cooler full of beer and Mountain Dew was placed beside me, and next to that I put down my travel grill and small propane tank. I had all the quintessential food ready to go: burgers, hot wings, cocktail weenies. It's not a real tailgate party if you don't have cocktail weenies. Hell, I even got some of those plant-based burgers in case any vegans wanted to join. Tailgates are inclusive to everyone, and that's the way it should always be.

Next, I started handing out my flyers to all passers-by, inviting them in on the action. Nothing too fancy. The flyers simply said, "TRACER'S GOOD-TIMES STAKE-OUT!!! JOIN IN ON THE FUN! BRING YOUR OWN CHAIR!! From 8am to ???" The "???" part was key. I knew the stake out would probably last a few days as I gathered my intelligence on Sadie Marie, and if people wanted to party with me throughout the night, who was I to stop them?

I turned on a classic rock station—perfect tailgate music—on my battery-operated radio, cranked up the tunes, and sat in my beach chair, waiting for the good times to come to me.

Yes, of course, at some point "You're So Vain" was played on the radio station. There was no doubt that was going to happen. In fact, it happened all three days that I was camped out on my stake out/tailgating thing.

Between grilling up some food and pounding some brewskis with my new buds, I kept a watchful eye on Take a Cakewalk on the Wild Side. Spying through the large glass windows of the shop, I was like a hawk, eyeing my prey with my amazing vision. Also, I kept eating gummy worms out of a paper bag, which made me feel a lot like a bird of prey. I used my talons to scoop the unfortunate bugs out of the bag, flinging them up, and catching them in my beak. I'd whip my head back and forth, just like a hawk, those magnificent raptors, killing the gummy worms before guzzling them down my throat, making a hurking noise with my windpipe.

All the people hanging out with me saw me pretending to be a hawk and left immediately. I thought it was a good party trick. Oh well. Their loss.

The only other issue I was having was that the street meter only allowed for three-hour parking. This meant that every two and a half hours, I would have to pack up my lawn chair, my battery-operated radio, my portable grill, my gummy worms, and my cooler. I'd then throw all these items into the backseat and trunk of my rental car, and I'd switch between two parking spaces on the street. Then I'd fill up the meter with quarters and start the whole party all over again.

It wasn't until the third day that I realized I didn't even know what Sadie Marie Olivierri looked like. I kept watching random people enter and exit the bakery, with no recognition of who they might be. I didn't even see if there was a pattern with any of them.

It was time to change my tactics. And my Tic Tacs. I had run out of mints after eating so many of those veggie burgers.

I pushed open the door to the cupcake store. A digital bell chimed above me, three descending notes coming from one of those door sensor alarms positioned above the threshold. Damn technology. If there was one thing in this world that was the cause of evilness, it was technology like this. Automation stealing the jobs of hard-working, honest citizens. My first job was to stand quietly in the corner of a local coffee shop and ring a bell anytime a customer entered or exited. And now this? This was a mockery of everything decent and just.

I was overwhelmed with the scents of vanilla and ginger. The spices lingered in my nostrils, as if a cookie was literally placed up my nose. The place was brightly lit, made even more bright by the clean, white tiles that lined the walls. Stuck on the walls were pastel-colored decals of cupcakes. Cupcakes with faces. Happy, smiling, ecstatic cupcake faces adorned all over the clean, white tiles. What were they so happy about? What could anyone be that happy about? They made me want to puke.

Against the front windows were pink countertops and purple swivel stools—for eat-in customers, looking for a table to munch quickly on their desserts. Over on the left-hand side, there was a bathroom. One single bathroom. Co-ed. Like in college dorms. Those higher education schools that dealt in sexual depravity and open-minded debauchery. Sickening. A person should do their business in the privacy of their own restroom. Call me old-fashioned, but I was a strict believer in the belief that someone should only use one bathroom and one bathroom only, and that bathroom should be the one they own in their own house. That just goes to show what kind of disgusting, perverted monster must own Take a Cakewalk on the Wild Side.

Then there were the display cases. Glass cases in front of and to the right side of the door, the first thing customers would see when they walked in. Each with three levels of shelves, holding so many cupcakes. All different kinds, all beautifully decorated with loving care.

I'm no good at math, but if I had to estimate, there were at least four or six different types of cupcakes.

Directly behind the glass cases was a closed door, and to the right-hand side, there was a separate open room where I could just glance a large oven and fridge.

I was secure enough in my masculinity to know that all these bright, pastel colors, all these delicious pastries, all these smiling cupcake decals made me feel insecure in my masculinity. I wished there were something in this overly girly shop to butch it up. Maybe a pool table or a desk chair I could sit backwards in. Just something to offset all the feminine energy that freaked me out.

Because as it was, I was the only male in Take a Cakewalk on the Wild Side. Standing in front of the display cases was a woman, hair pulled up into a side pony. She was hunched over, looking at the different cupcakes, holding a little girl's hand. The little girl wore a puffy, currant-colored jacket and was dragging a stuffed bunny by the ears with her other hand. Lastly, behind the display cases, a brunette dame stood holding an opened box, mostly filled with cupcakes. She wore a brown apron, with a nametag that read "Sadie Marie."

There was no way to tell which of the three women was the Sadie Marie I was here to question.

"So honey," the side pony woman said, "last one. What kind would you like?"

"Ummm…" the little girl began, hugging her bunny rabbit to her chest. "Death by chocolate! Death by chocolate! Death by chocolate!" She chanted, like a Roman emperor deciding how to end a gladiator's life.

"Good choice," Sadie Marie said, reaching down with a tissue paper in her hand to grab the cupcake. "I'll just ring mommy up at the counter now, okay?"

While Sadie Marie fiddled with the cash register and the girl's mom ruffled through her over-sized pocketbook, the little girl walked up to me.

"This is Mr. Bun-Bun," she said, holding her stuffed rabbit up to me. Based on its name, I could rule out the stuffed animal from my investigation. Unless it was an alias that Sadie Marie used.

"He's very…charming," I said. I wasn't sure how to talk to children. Most of the time, they seemed to understand the world better than adults. That freaked me out. "My name's Tracer, what's yours?"

"Diedre. I'm four." She held up four fingers, showing me like I couldn't count up past three, the little brat.

I didn't think that a four-year-old would make up a fake name to throw a private eye off, but I couldn't rule out the possibility either. Diedre was still on my suspect list.

"Okay, Diedre, if that is your real name, have you ever been to New York City before?"

"My daddy took me and Mr. Bun-Bun once to see the Santa tree with all the lights. It was really, really pretty. Mr. Bun-Bun didn't like how crowded it was, but Daddy held our hands so we didn't get lost."

"That reminds me of when I was about your age. My dad took me to see a gas station though. We got out of the car, and he said to me, 'Son, this is where you live now,' and then he hopped back in the car and took off. He left me there for the weekend. Wasn't all that bad though—I did buy some Slim Jims. The only reason I found him again was that he forgot where he left me. He used to leave me a few different places, and just didn't remember which one it was this time around. Anyway, he showed up on Monday morning to get gas to go to work, and I hopped back in his car. That's also the gas station where he tried teaching me to smoke cigarettes—right next to the gas pumps."

Diedre said nothing. Instead she looked up at me with big brown eyes, scared. Maybe that wasn't the coming-of-age story I should've shared with the girl at this moment.

Stuck in a conversation that I had made awkward, I did what I always do in these situations. I blurted something out even more awkward.

"I'M HERE FOR A KIDNAPPING," I yelled to the entirety of Take a Cakewalk on the Wild Side.

Both Sadie Marie and Diedre's mother turned to look at me, and Diedre's mother rushed over. She grabbed Diedre's hand, and pulling the girl out of the store said, "Come on, darling, let's get away from the creepy man now."

Diedre waved to me as they exited the store.

"No! No! That's not what I meant!" I yelled after the two of them. No luck, the suspects were getting away as I stood there, helplessly not chasing after them. "That's not...that's not what I meant," I said to

Sadie Marie. "I'm a private eye, trying to find out who kidnapped a…friend of mine."

Sadie Marie looked relieved for a moment. Then she said, "Well, why are you here then?"

I had to play this just right. If this Sadie Marie who worked in this cupcake store was the same Sadie Marie who owned this cupcake store, I couldn't let her know I was trying to figure out if she had kidnapped Ellie Dayton.

"Did you kidnap anyone?" I asked.

"What? No. Between running this bakery and my marriage, I wouldn't have time to take care of a kid who's not mine."

"A kid, right," I said. "Mind if I ask you a few questions?"

"If you make it quick and stop running customers out of my store, sure. I've got a few things to do in the back."

"Where were you the day of November 22, 1963?"

"Well, I wasn't born yet. Wouldn't be for another twentyish years or so."

"Likely story," I said, mentally crossing Sadie Marie off the list of suspects who had shot John F. Kennedy. This was a cold case I had been working on for a couple years now. Some days it felt like I'd never get to the bottom of who shot the Magic Bullet.

"Alright, Ms. Sadie Marie, do you wear any jewelry?" I asked.

"Mrs. Sadie Marie," she corrected. "Just my wedding ring." She held up her hand, showing me the gold band on her finger. "Look, I don't mind answering questions if it'll help get a kid back, but I genuinely don't see how I would be connected to something like that. The thought gives me chills."

I was running out of questions for her. People didn't usually let me speak this long to them, and it's not like I had thought this through that well. In fact, I was still a little buzzed from my three-day stake-out.

Behind Sadie Marie, I saw a door marked "Private." Anything could be back there. There could be a tied-up woman behind there or the entrance to Narnia or an office with a desk and computer or a dozen monkeys dressed up like luchadores, all wrestling in a miniature boxing ring. In that moment, I made it my lifelong mission to discover what kind of sinister secrets were hiding behind that door.

"Well, you could help me out with this: is there a person bound and gagged behind that door back there? Is that where you're keeping them?"

"What? I already told you I didn't do anything. It's just an office," Sadie Marie said. "It's where I do my payroll, the ordering, the taxes, everything."

My lifelong mission now complete, I felt a hole in my psyche. That wasn't nearly as satisfying as I had thought it would be all those seconds ago.

Still though, the thought crossed my mind that maybe she was lying to me about the "Private" office. "Mind if I take a look in it? See if you're hiding anything? Maybe some cupcake trade secrets? Maybe a tied-up person? Maybe a diary of all your nefarious wrong-doings?"

Sadie Marie hesitated. A flash of anger appeared on her face. I had struck a nerve, it seemed. "Yes, in fact, I do mind. I don't know who you are from the next creep to come in here. Maybe you are some private eye and maybe you aren't. Maybe you're here to find out who took a kid, and if so, I still don't see what that has to do with me. Or maybe you're here for some other sick reason. Either way, if you're not going to buy anything, please get the hell out of my store."

"Okay, okay, lady. I get it. I only have one more question for you. How much for two cupcakes? I could definitely use something to sober me up right now."

After I bought two cupcakes, I left my card on the counter and pushed it her way. "Look, if you think of anything, give me a call, okay?"

She picked it up. "This is the four of hearts from an actual deck of cards."

"Yeah, and? I wrote my phone number on it."

I was heading out the store. That's when Sadie Marie said, "If you're really trying to find out who kidnapped your friend, I hope it works out."

I turned back to her. "Ah ha! So, it *was* you! I never mentioned anything about kidnapping!"

"You did though. It was literally one of the first things you said."

"Oh. Right," I said, recalling how my awkward conversation with the girl ended only five minutes beforehand. So, I said my goodbyes and shoved a whole cupcake into my mouth hole.

12

By the time I got back to my office in New York, evening had settled in like a bad houseguest. I was exhausted from my three-day trip to Connecticut. I was frazzled after thinking so hard about my cases. And, I was sticky from eating the two cupcakes. Frosting had been piled high on them, like a tower made entirely of sugar. And now that tower had adhered to the corners of my lips, and I planned on showering the sugar tower off as soon as I possibly could.

But I had notes and equipment that I needed to drop off in the office before heading to my apartment. I made it a habit not to bring work home. Which wasn't too difficult as my apartment was about the size of a janitor's closet. It was about that size because it was, in fact, a janitor's closet. It was *still* a janitor's closet. I had to share it with Pete, the janitor. Nice guy. We had come up with the system of taping a ribbon down the middle to split the room, but secretly I would leave my clothes on his side when he wasn't there. You normally wouldn't think that a Murphy bed could fit in a room that size, and you'd be correct. Whoever had installed it had done a trash job of it, and when pulled out of the wall, the bed only fully extended to a 45-degree angle. The good news was that with all the cannisters of ammonia products Pete kept on his side of the room, I still had an easy time of falling asleep.

Which is why I headed to my office first. Trouble was, I wasn't the only one with that idea.

I was rummaging in my coat pocket for my keys, walking up to my office door in the darkened hallway. You know how spies like James Bond and Jason Bourne usually keep a hair lodged in between their door and the door frame, just so? That way, when they're returning to their rooms, if the hair has fallen to the ground, they know that someone's been inside? Well, I do the same thing, only with a large cardboard sign that says, "TRACER'S OFFICE. KEEP OUT. I'LL KNOW YOU'VE BEEN IN HERE IF THIS SIGN IS ON THE FLOOR."

That sign was, indeed, on the floor.

Nonetheless, I entered my office. This was a mistake.

I was greeted by a right hook to my temple. Unlike most greetings, the fist didn't say, "Welcome back, Tracer. I'm so happy to see you." Instead, it said THWACK. I fell to the floor and to pieces.

The fist was connected to one of three thugs in my office. The fist guy had been standing next to the door, another mook was going through my files, and the third was Stuart. He was sitting in my chair, feet up on my desk.

The place was a mess, even more so than usual. Papers littered the floor, thrown around with abandon. Stuffing from my seat cushion was strewn on to my desk; they had cut open my chair. And candy wrappers were tossed in every direction.

"You know," I said, rubbing the side of my head, "I don't mind you guys coming by for a late-night party, but I hope you plan on cleaning up before you go. The maid service here is great, but even they might balk at this mess."

"Tracer, you know why we're here, right?" Stuart asked.

"I almost never know why anyone is anywhere. That's what makes me so great as a detective. No biases."

"You've got something our employer needs."

"An adorable personality?"

"Why don't you just tell us where it is, and we'll be on our way?" Stuart cracked his knuckles. One by one, they made gross, arthritic popping noises.

"It's something that was given to you but doesn't belong to you. Let's leave it at that, so as to not implicate ourselves in something bigger than you'd want to be a part of."

"You mentioned something like that last time. Whatever I have, you see in this room."

"Boss," one of the other guys said. "All he has is a bunch of candy hidden around. Every hiding place we've found so far, it's just different candy bars. I think there's been like seven different hiding spots."

I thought to myself, *The false desk leg, the fake electric outlet, above the fiberglass ceiling tile, underneath the desk lamp, on top of the ceiling fan blade, the licorice string inside the pen instead of an ink cartridge, and the hollowed-out book that's supposed to be my finances.*

Yep, they'd found all seven of my candy stashes.

"I hope you guys left me some. When my blood sugar gets low, I get cranky because I haven't eaten any candy."

"We're evil henchmen," Stuart said. "Of course we didn't leave you any candy. Whatever we didn't eat, we tossed out the window just so you couldn't have any. The pigeons will feast tonight."

"You bastards."

"Now don't make things get ugly," he said. "We know you have the thing. Maybe it's just in a secure spot around here. A safe maybe? Do you happen to have any safes lying around?"

My eyes darted right to my *Little Giants* poster, betraying me like the sixty senators who stabbed Julius Caesar in the back. *Et tu, pupils?*

"The poster," Stuart said, pointing at it. "Tear it down."

"No, no, no, wait, I spent five dollars on that on eBay plus three bucks for shipping and handling! It's a collector's item!"

That didn't stop Fist Guy from ripping the *Little Giants* poster right in half. Now, it really was like Rick Moranis would never reconcile with Ed O'Neill, whose face was on the other half of the torn banner. At least, not without some masking tape.

"Here it is, boss," Fist Guy said, finding my hidden safe. "I guess you were right. It was a real safe poking through the poster. I didn't think anyone would be that dumb."

"Now, here's where it's gonna get interesting, Tracer. You're gonna tell us the combination for that safe, so we can take the thing out of there, and then we'll be on our merry way. Got it? You ain't gonna make this any harder than it needs to be right?"

Unfortunately for all involved, I was going to make this harder than it needed to be. I didn't remember the combination. I told him that. He didn't believe me.

"I guess we're gonna have some fun then," Stuart said. "Hey, Enzo, cover the snail up."

The guy who was throwing papers around, Enzo, took his jacket and covered Moby's terrarium.

"Moby!" I called out. "Moby! You're going to be alright, buddy! Don't worry. I'll get you out of there." To Stuart, I asked, "Why'd you do that? What are you covering him up for?"

"We may be evil, but we don't hurt animals. Not even with mental scarring. And trust me, if Moby saw what was about to happen to you, he'd need years of therapy to work his way through it."

The two other henchmen grabbed the tops of my arms, lifting me up off the floor. They heaved me onto my chair. Enzo held me down, his arms wrapped around me from behind, while Fist Guy put some plastic zip ties around my wrists and ankles, tying me to the chair.

I was trapped. Just like one of those dead butterflies. Except instead of being in a glass case with my wings tacked back, I was stuck in my own office. And I didn't have any wings. If I did have wings, I'd either be an angel or a half-human half-bat hybrid of some kind. Either way, I probably wouldn't be a detective that wound up in this dire situation. If I were an angel, I probably wouldn't even have to worry about money anymore, living up in Heaven and all that. Or if I were the half-human half-bat hybrid, I bet I could make a decent enough living in a traveling circus as part of the freak show.

"What are you talking about?" Stuart asked.

"Huh?"

"You were just mumbling something about being a half-human half-bat hybrid."

"I said that out loud?"

"For a good three minutes, yeah," he said. "And it doesn't even make sense. If you were a half-human half-bat hybrid, you'd be hunted by the government, and your lifeless corpse would be on display in a museum."

"I don't know," Enzo said. "I think the populace is much more accepting of people's unique biological conditions these days. It's not like when we were kids when we'd get bullied for having cryptotia."

"Cryptotia?" Stuart asked.

"Yeah. It's the medical term for when part of the cartilage of your ear is buried beneath the skin on the side of your head." Enzo showed Stuart and me his right ear, which was just like he explained. "It makes it difficult to wear glasses. Thankfully, I have twenty-twenty vision. But my point is that I think half-human half-bat hybrids would be much more welcome in today's society."

"I think you guys are getting a wee bit off topic," I said.

"Right," Stuart said. "Back to the torture."

I regretted changing the focus of our discussion back to the subject of my imminent pain.

"Torture? We can do this a different way, instead. My doctor says I should stay away from torture and all torture-related activities," I said. "You know what? You could strap me to one of them lie detector tests. Not only would I tell you what you want to know, but I'd be able to give you tonight's lotto numbers. Not being able to lie and all."

"That's not how those work," Stuart said. "You can't tell the future with 'em."

"Really? That's two hundred bucks I'll never get back from that police auction."

"Hey Enzo, bring in the *implement*," Stuart said. He turned to me. I could see the wrinkles of his face change as his smile curled upward. He had enchanting dimples. "We're gonna make your worst nightmares come true, Tracer."

"Don't you even joke about quicksand."

Enzo walked back with the implement in his hand, held as far away from his body as he could get it, as if it were a plutonium rod. It was just a toothbrush—a nice one, at that, with different angled bristles and an ergonomic handle—with some toothpaste already on it. I didn't understand what was supposed to terrify me.

Fist Guy came up behind me and pushed the back of my chair into a reclined position. I was stuck looking up towards the ceiling, like at the dentist's office.

"Open wide," Enzo said.

Let me tell you, the act of someone else brushing your teeth for you—it was a strange, yet not unpleasant experience. And Enzo was good at it. You could tell he took pride in his work.

"You know, I'm studying to become a dental assistant," he said. "This henchman thing, it's just to make ends meet."

I could feel the bristles on my teeth, a satisfying pressure being applied. The back-and-forth motion scraping the day's food away from my enamel also helped apply the toothpaste throughout my mouth. The mint flavor stung but felt fresh and clean. Enzo made sure to focus on every section of my teeth: the fronts, the backs, the tops of the molars. He even scraped my tongue with the rough patch on the back of the toothpaste.

"Have you been flossing every day?" he asked, while the toothbrush was still dancing its way across my teeth.

"I twy bud thumdimes I forgedd, if I'm beweeing honethed," I said.

Enzo looked at me with disappointment. "It's the best way to fight off plaque and dental disease. You should really be more vigilant about it. Just five minutes a day and you'll be thanking yourself for the rest of your life. Now spit in the cup, please," he said, and held a small paper cup in front of my face.

I did as he said. "I'll try to be better about it in the future."

"You ain't going to have no future," Stuart said. "Not unless you tell us the combo to your safe."

"I told you already. I don't remember it. I had it written on a piece of paper a while back, but I stuck a wad of gum in it and tossed it out."

"Okay, then. We'll play it your way, Tracer. Enzo, time to bring the pain."

"The brushing wasn't the torture?" I asked.

"What kind of torture would that be? No, that was just the prep," Stuart said.

Enzo walked back over to me, holding a thermos. It looked heavy. If he bashed me in the skull with it, I think it could've done some brain damage. Or at least give me a bruised welt that would've popped out of my forehead like a unicorn. In retrospect, I wish that's what would've happened, because what came next was cruel and unusual.

"I'm so, so sorry," Enzo said, pouring the thermos' liquid into my mouth.

The bitter taste hit my tongue and the back of my throat. I could tell that there was supposed to be some sweetness in there, but with the lingering minty toothpaste flavor, my mouth was just consumed by the taste of rancid shampoo. Bile rose up my esophagus, an elevator of disgust. I coughed, most of the drink sputtering on to my chin and shirt.

"Orange juice? You sick fiends. Orange juice!" I spit some more, right on to the floors of my office.

"The combination, Mr. Spence. What's the combination?" Stuart asked.

"I don't know! Try one!"

"One?"

"Yeah, try zero zero one!"

Stuart nodded to Fist Guy, now standing by the safe. He spun the dial with the code I gave. A red light blinked from the safe and loud buzzer emanated from it. A digital display read "INCORRECT CODE. PLEASE TRY AGAIN."

"Enzo, hit him again," Stuart said.

The revolting orange juice and toothpaste mix hit my palette like the liquified form of dirty socks. I was shaking, rattling against my binds, but the zip ties wouldn't budge. I swallowed the drink this time. It was even worse hitting the back of my tongue.

"Try zero zero two. Just don't give me any more of that stuff. Please. Zero zero two."

Fist Guy took the code I gave and spun it around the combination lock. Same thing. A loud buzz and a red flash. The digital readout said, "INCORRECT PASSWORD. ONE MORE ATTEMPT BEFORE TOTAL LOCK-DOWN."

"Boss," Fist Guy said, "we may have a problem. It says we only have one more try."

"Tracer, you sure sprung for a high-end safe, didn't you?" Stuart asked.

"If I'm going to protect what's most important to me, I figured I might as well."

"Enzo, go ahead."

This time, the drink felt like someone had puréed undercooked salmon and poured it down my gullet. Tears swelled to my eyes. If my tongue had its own consciousness, it would've torn itself out of my mouth and issued me a restraining order.

"We're waiting," Stuart said. "If you're wrong this time...well, I hear the Hudson has a very comfortable river bed at the bottom."

"I don't...I don't know. I'm not sure," I said. I really wasn't. Numbers were never my strong suit, and remembering three in a row, especially in these dire circumstances, was difficult to do. "Try...try zero zero three."

Fist Guy slowly maneuvered the combination lock around. Zero-zero-three. The safe shot a green light from its display and a rising arpeggio chimed. With a final read-out of, "WELCOME BACK TRACER, OUR DEAR AND GLORIOUS OVERLORD," which I had programmed the safe to say, the locking mechanism clicked.

"Zero zero three?" Stuart asked me.

"Yeah. I remember now. I never wanted to get locked out if I forgot the combo. Three made sense, since the safe only allows that many attempts."

"Boss, it's...the arm bracelet's not in here!" Fist Guy called out.

Oh, the arm bracelet, I thought.

"What do you mean? It's got to be," Stuart said.

"It's not. It's just more damn candy." Fist Guy turned around, holding a jar of jellybeans.

Stuart grabbed my shirt collar and pulled, my face an inch away from his. The zip ties cut into the skin around my wrists. I felt a drop of blood run down the palm of my right hand and onto my ring finger.

The door to my office opened. We all looked. It was the maid, pushing her cart with cleaning supplies on it.

"You're lucky today, Tracer," Stuart said, putting me back down in the chair. "But we're going to be back and we're going to find the bracelet."

The three henchmen all walked out the door, squeezing past the maid. I heard Stuart say to her, "Sorry, we were just playing *doctor.*"

As the maid was untying me from the chair, I thought of how lucky it was to not keep the arm bracelet that Serena gave me for safe keeping in my safe. I mean, I did think to do that at first but couldn't remember the combination. Instead, I put it in the most secure place I could think of: the United States Postal system. I picked out an erroneous address in Alaska, and I mailed it in a box, knowing that it would be return to sender in the near future. Probably right when I was ready to wrap this case up, I bet.

I rubbed my sore wrists and licked the blood away.

"Mr. Spence," the maid said, tapping me on my shoulder, "I'm not going to clean this mess up. I told you last time. It's incredibly rude of you."

"That's okay. I got it. Just leave the cart for now."

13

The Rolling Stones. Keith Richards. Ronnie Wood. And of course, Mick Jagger. Classic. Legendary. Who else espouses the credos of Rock and Roll more than these septuagenarians?

More importantly for me though, who else would know the facts behind "You're So Vain" than the uncredited backup singer? Yes, Mick Jagger would be my focus tonight, thanks to the very expensive clue from Harry Potter. I was banking on the hunch that Jagger's time with Carly Simon resulted in him having some insider knowledge about the song. And if I was lucky, maybe he knew who it was written about. That was the secretive gossip that I had heard or made up in my imagination. Who could tell the difference between the two anymore?

The risk on my end was that these guys are one of the biggest bands in the world, and they'd have the home field advantage. Super popular. Rich as Croesus. More famous than the President of the United States— seriously, who can even name the President? There's been like forty, fifty of those guys? Who can keep up? Give it a rest already, willya? But still, much like the President has his secret service, the Stones have their roadies. Remember Altamont? The Hells Angels? Roadies don't mess around as security. It was going to be tough and dangerous to get to Jagger. But if anyone's up for the task, it's a private eye by the name of Tracer Spence.

That's right, me. My name is Tracer Spence, in case you had forgotten.

I had one thing going for me, the one rule of war that works in the opposition's favor. The element of surprise. I *knew* where they were going to be, and the Stones had no idea I was even coming for them. Hell, I doubt they even knew who I was. Suckers. It was going to be like taking candy from a baby. But not Tootsie Rolls. Because, ew, gross. They get all stuck in your teeth and taste like chocolate-coated plastic. You can keep your disgusting Tootsie Roll, you dumb baby. Because I'm going for the big prize. Which in this metaphor would be a Reese's Peanut Butter Cup, I guess.

Vanessa was shocked when I asked her to accompany me. I guess she couldn't believe a smokin' hot ten out of ten would ask her out on a date.

"You got tickets to the Stones as Madison Square Garden? How is that even possible? They were sold out months ago! I couldn't even get through in the pre-order! The website was so slow because so many people were logging in, and then I heard its servers crashed. I tried for an hour and twenty minutes, minus those five minutes when my tea kettle went off, but I was waiting for the page to load anyway while making my tea. Chamomile, because it was evening, and I didn't want the caffeine to ruin my sleep. Tracer, do you have any idea how much this means to me, to see them live?"

"Keep it in your pants, Vanessa." Yeah, she was so in lust with me.

Every good private investigator goes into their case with a plan of action. It's in the rule book. Or it's in my rule book. I'm not sure there's an official rule book anywhere, but I've been writing one in my spare time. Right now, it's scattered across some loose leaf paper and sticky notes, but I do plan on collecting it all together and editing it down. Maybe I can sell it on eBay or Etsy. I'm not sure I'd want to go the publishing route and be labeled a sell-out. Man of the people, that's what I am. In fact, that's rule #52: *Always be a man of the people.* Right before rule #53: *Rubber duckies make good bath time toys, but they'll make you lose concentration, and next thing you know, you'll have been in the bath for two hours and all pruny, just like a raisin.*

My plan of action was to sneak backstage while the band was playing their set. Get the drop on 'em. Then I could question Mr. Jagger and slip away unnoticed. In my experience, rock bands normally played at dark clubs and tiny hole in the walls. This would be easy-peasy. How much bigger could Madison Square Garden be?

I met Vanessa just outside of Penn Station, and she caught me shoving a couple dirty water hot dogs down my gullet. There's nothing better than one—or seven—of them with some lukewarm, greasy onions scattered on top. I don't care that it is mystery meat that's been sitting there all day. Hot dogs are a staple of a successful detective's diet, what with stakeouts or holding a gun in one hand and a bun in the other. And for a dollar a dog, it's perfect for budgetary reasons. Still, I was embarrassed to be caught in the act by my date.

And then Vanessa ordered two for herself and shoveled them into her mouth. I was in love. I still couldn't believe how beautiful she was. I wanted to airbrush her likeness on the side of a van and drive around town blasting some Molly Hatchet.

She smiled at me, licking a spot of ketchup off her lips. Walking through the crowd on the sidewalk, she tossed her napkin into a garbage can.

"Ready?" she asked, smoothing out her black T-shirt with a psychedelic picture that sported the band Journey's logo across her chest. Over top, she had on her leather jacket, and she wore some distressed blue jeans.

"Sure thing. What back alley are we going down to find this place?"

She pointed to the giant, circular building that was right next to us with a big purple sign that said "MADISON SQUARE GARDEN" near the entrance. Oh. This may be more trouble than I originally thought. This place looked like it could hold at least 100 people.

We walked inside, and I saw another flaw in my plan—the stadium-like seating wrapped all the way around the stage. How could I sneak backstage if backstage was just more seating?

As we made our way to our seats, Vanessa went on and on. "I can't believe I'm here right now. You know, it's been my dream for ages to get to perform here, to get to be in the middle of everything. It's not about the fame or money, though, come on, that would be great too. But to have people listen and love your creativity? I know it'll never happen since we're just a cover band, but hey, maybe in the long run. I've got some songs worked out. Got one called 'Blue Jean Dragon.' Not sure if the classic rock crowd would like that though…but hey, they did give Ted Nugent a voice. But man, Madison Square Garden. Maybe someday." She was like a typewriter ribbon, and I was expecting a ding after every sentence.

"I think you'll get there, Ness. You're that good. And I'm in the same boat. I'd love to be memorialized in the Private Detective Hall of Fame someday."

"There's a Hall of Fame for that?"

"Sure. I mean, the eligibility rules are real strict. You either have to be a fictional detective or killed in the line of duty. But a man can dream can't he?"

Vanessa just laughed and touched my shoulder.

By this point, we had found our seats. Looks like Harry Potter did me a solid, as we were toward the front. But I wondered if he got rid of the tickets because he knew how uncomfortable the seats were. Why anyone would want to sit willingly on hard plastic is beyond me. You're just asking for a lifetime of back problems. Why do people even make chairs or seats out of plastic anyway? Seems like bad business to me. Just more corporations out to get the little man. Probably Big Chair in cahoots with Big Chiropractacy.

The stadium was huge. Like, imagine a seedy bar, and multiply that by at least eight, maybe eight and a half. That's how big Madison Square Garden is. The stage was set up in the very center, with all the seating looking down on it, like the audience was some snooty socialite. And the TVs, oh those giant TVs. Hanging down from the ceiling right over the stage, four screens were faced so all the audience could see them. My local pub is lucky enough to have an antennae television propped up on a rickety chair. But that's what gives my local pub character—that and the threat of violence breaking out at any moment. The problem with these high-tech arenas is no character. At least that's the judgement call I made after being in MSG for the very first time for a total of five minutes.

As people were milling in, Vanessa and I sat quietly, listening to the pre-concert music they were playing over the venue's loudspeakers. She knew what was coming. I knew what was coming. I'm positive you know what was coming. "You're So Vain." Can't even have a nice date-slash-work function without it ruining my night.

As soon as the song started, Vanessa reached out and held my hand, squeezing it three times. We were in this together, she seemed to say. It had been a while since I've gotten to hold hands with someone of the opposite sex—Trina Williams in the 7th grade, and when my father found out, he bribed her away with the promise of ice cream on a weekly basis if she would never speak to me again. I think they still meet for Fro-yo every week, actually. Strange how some friendships are forged—so nervousness instantly overcame me. My palms became sweaty, as wet as the inside of a porpoise's blowhole.

Vanessa didn't seem to mind and kept her hand in my lap, wrapped around my fingers.

Ten minutes had passed when the music stopped, and the lights dimmed. The first notes of "Satisfaction" dropped as loud as a bomb, amplified through the entire building. The Rolling Stones came out, rushing the stage as Keith Richards hit his riff over and over again. These elder statesmen of rock and roll, with a career spanning fifty-something years were still somehow doing this, jumping and running around like lunatics. When I reach their age, I could only hope to be in half as great shape as them. Then again, being spoon-fed pudding while watching daytime TV shows and lying in bed also sounds like a viable option.

I focused in on Mick Jagger himself. The reason I was even here tonight. The man was spry. He was athletic. He was a monster, dancing around the stage, hands on his hips like he was thirty years younger. You could say he had moves like Adam Levine.

Other than clapping between songs, Vanessa's hand never left mine. Her fingernails were freshly painted, pink with black stripes, rubbing against the callouses of my knuckles.

It was during "Sympathy for the Devil," the Stones' ode to the Dark Princess (I envisioned an early '70s, long-haired Carly Simon, with her flowy, ruffled shirts) that a break in my case came.

Pyrotechnics shot off during the last chorus, lighting up the room like a charcoal grill that someone poured too much lighter fluid on, and the burst of flames burns off half your eyebrows. Even with smoke rising from your face, you could still see your Dad holding six canisters of lighter fluid and cackling. You walk around high school the next two months looking like ET. Where was I now?

During that half-second with the arena lit up, on the jumbotron screens I saw a familiar face seated behind the band. Stuart. That mook. He tried to kill me twice, and now he was at the same concert as me? It couldn't be a coincidence. Unless it was…

If he was here for a sinister purpose, I didn't understand. Would he have followed me to Madison Square Garden just to get an arm bracelet that I didn't have? It made no sense to me. Not that most things do right away, anyway.

However, he wasn't looking in my direction. If he had followed me, maybe he had lost me in the crowd. But, I had to make sure it was him. Like any good detective, I came prepared with some of my detective's toolkit.

Out of my jacket pocket, I pulled out my magnifying glass.

I had to get a better look across the chasm that was this arena. And what better way than my trusty magnifying glass. If it was good enough for Sherlock Holmes, it was good enough for me. I think. I never actually read any of Arthur Conan Doyle's stories, but I was sure based on the pictures I'd seen that Holmes used a magnifying glass, like, all the time.

Like a good billiards player, this was all about getting the angles right. If I held the lens just right, I might be able to see across to Stuart's section. If only I could identify him for sure. I bent my arm this way and that way, hoping something would work. While doing so, I wondered how big my eye looked from the opposite direction. That made me giggle.

If only the sun was behind me, I'd be able to melt Stuart's head like a plastic army man.

All of this was for naught, though. I couldn't make him out. He was going to get away, and it was all because I wasn't as good a detective as Sherlock Holmes. Maybe I should've sprung for the industrial sized magnifying glass. "Drats," I said.

"Did you just say 'drats?'" Vanessa whispered in my ear.

I explained to her my predicament.

"What?" she asked, directly afterwards. "It's too loud in here. I couldn't hear you."

I explained to her my predicament again, two more times. She got the gist of it.

"Here," she said, shoving binoculars into my hands. "I brought these because I wasn't sure how far away we were going to be. Use 'em. Maybe they can help you, and you can get the drop on him later."

If Vanessa ever joined the detectiving business, I might be out of a job. Still though, how perfect could one woman be?

The binoculars were heavy and bulky, an expensive pair. I was nervous holding them, worried that for sure I would drop them. But, through shaky lenses, I could see that it was in fact Stuart on the other end of the cavernous room. Confirming it was him, I then turned the binoculars backward and looked in the wrong side. He looked so small and puny like this!

Nonetheless, I'd have to keep an eye on him throughout the concert. Make sure he didn't leave and sneak up behind me, with a chloroform rag or a car jack or a car jack dipped in chloroform.

I completely failed in this goal, being caught up in The Rolling Stones' concert. Damn them and their menacing talent. They must be working with Stuart and his boss, plotting to distract me. This had to be a conspiracy of epic proportions.

The main concert finished up, with the Stones playing "Gimme Shelter." Perfect closing song, right? Total professionals. They thanked New York City and left the stage through one of the tunnels on the ground floor. The audience continued clapping, knowing that an encore had to come next. I looked back into the binoculars and realized that Stuart was no longer in his seat.

He was probably making his move to attack me already. I had to get to Mick Jagger before Stuart got to me.

"I have to go!" I threw Vanessa's binoculars into her lap, no time to waste. I then bent down and laced up my sneakers.

"What, now?" She asked. "Let me come with. I can help."

"Sorry. I work alone. Like a lone wolf. I stalk my prey alone. I attack alone. I even howl at the moon alone."

"Okay. Fine. Just don't forget about me after your job is done. I'll meet you by the merch table. I'd like to get one of their hoodies, with the lips on the front. Always wanted one, and it might be chilly by the time we get outside. I can get one for you too, and we can match!"

I nodded my head, and then I took off, bolting like a medium-talent high school sprinter. Good thing I tied my shoes, otherwise I definitely would've tripped down the stairs. Pushing past other concert-goers, I somehow made it backstage, slipping by both security and the band's roadies. Sometimes it's best to look like you couldn't intimidate a duckling, so you could just appear invisible to the security guards.

The lanyard around my neck with the laminated backstage pass began to itch. I hated wearing jewelry.

Couldn't harp on that now, though. I had to get to Mick Jagger before anything happened. Stuart had gotten a head-start on me. But maybe he also stopped for a paper bag of popcorn, like I did. It was my only hope. The smell of the buttery snack wafted into my nostrils as I ran through a room with extra amplifiers and guitars. Rounding a corner, I crunched on a handful of popcorn, spilling some down the front of my shirt. I found the dressing rooms. My father used to say I couldn't walk and chew at the same time, but the joke was on him now that I learned after twenty-something years.

There it was. A black-painted door with a star and temporary label which read "Mick Jagger." I kicked it, the sole of my sneakers connecting near the handle. It didn't budge, and pain radiated through my leg. I don't know why I ever try kicking in doors; it never works. I tried the handle. A-ha! It was unlocked.

I was too late. A corpse laid dead in the center of the room. Laid? Lied? One of the two. Either way, the artist formerly known as Mick Jagger was now crumpled up, bleeding out of a knife hole in his chest. I had just seen him two minutes ago, jumping around on stage, singing his heart out. And now, here he was, heart literally cut out, never to jump around again.

On the bright side, this was a pretty major clue. As clues go, you couldn't get cluier than this.

I didn't understand why Jagger was dead though. Maybe Stuart wasn't after me. Maybe he didn't even know I was here. But if that was the case, why did he kill Mick Jagger? The Rolling Stones wouldn't have the arm bracelet, unless they tampered with the United States Post Office parcel I put it in. I wouldn't put it past them, but even that was too big a leap in logic for me. Was Stuart somehow connected to the "You're So Vain Case" as well as the kidnapping case? How? Why?

"Damnit, man, this is the second time this year," a voice came from behind me. I spun around. It was Keith Richards, Fender Telecaster still slung around his body.

"What? What do you mean?" I asked. "Oh, and this isn't what it looks like," I added. Perfect way to set up an alibi.

"This is another 'You're So Vain' thing, right?" Keith Richards asked, his accent all British-like.

"Y—yes? How'd you know?"

"Damn song's been the death of him for years, now."

I didn't follow him. I was confused. I told him that.

"I don't follow you. I'm confused."

"Look, man," Richards entered the room and poked the body with the head of his guitar. Blood stuck to the wood and a drip ran down towards the fretboard. "This ain't the real Mick. Hasn't been for near on thirty or so years. He's a fake. A dummy. We've got lookalikes on retainer."

"You mean a clone?"

"No, no, no. Nothing like that. This isn't some sci-fi hullaballoo. He was a Mick Jagger impersonator. And when the last one died, we hired him, got him the best plastic surgery out there, and brought him into the band. It was harder back in the day, of course, but we find them on YouTube now. We've all got 'em. Except for me. Ronnie's on his third iteration. And Mick, we lose an average about one of them a year it seems. You'd be surprised how many people want to murder the Rolling Stones. Nine times out of ten, it's that Carly Simon song with Mick though."

"But, wait, you said not you?"

"Yeah, yeah. I'm the real me. The original Keith Richards."

"How?"

"Easy. I don't go to bed without checking for booby traps. Don't eat anything without a taste-tester. Always wear a bullet-proof vest. Once you know what you're looking for, it's simple to stay alive."

"So, this was a fake Mick Jagger, then? He didn't know anything about 'You're So Vain?'"

"No, this guy wouldn't know who the song was about, if that's what you're asking. I think his name was actually Frank Benigno from Jersey City. Decent enough chap. Used to make us boys some real good spaghetti and meat balls. Poor guy."

I started putting two and two together, because of this conversation where Richards spelled everything out for me. It was a real talent of mine, to puzzle things out while someone was clearly explaining to me what was going on.

"Why would anyone kill him, if he knew nothing? Maybe they knew I was coming to question him, and they killed him to silence him and stop the secret from getting out. But if they've murdered countless Mick Jaggers before, they would realize he was a fake."

"Look, kid," Richards said while grabbing a handful of M&Ms out of a ceramic bowl on a dirty counter. "If you thought you murdered someone and then found out he was still alive singing for the greatest rock band ever—"

"Greatest? How humble of you. Maybe top ten."

"Like I was saying," he rolled his eyes. "If you found out he was still alive, your mind wouldn't jump to the fact that he's a replacement. You'd just think that your last flunky failed to actually murder him."

"I gotcha. Thanks, Mr. Richards. Looks like I've gotta figure out where to go next with my case."

"You want my advice? Follow the money, kid. Now get the hell out of here, I've got an encore to do."

14

I made my way back to my office after the concert. Confused. Alone. I spent the walk kicking rocks down the street so I could kick them again. Or until they fell into a grate. I did this until I kicked a rock too big and bruised my big toe. Now I was confused, alone, and limping.

Confused, because of Stuart's presence at the Rolling Stones concert. How was he connected to both cases?

Alone, because I forgot to look for Vanessa after the whole debacle with a dead Mick Jagger doppelganger and my conversation with Keith Richards. By the time I remembered to look for Vanessa, I had already walked ten blocks out. When I turned to go back, she was already gone.

Limping, because I had kicked a big rock and bruised my toe, which I just said. Pay attention, dummy.

Just like the night before, my office door was ajar, creeped open just an inch. Who would've thought that two nights in a row I'd have intruders waiting for me? Actually, the odds weren't that bad—every year the local Girl Scout Troop ambushed me night after night, attacking me and bullying me until I bought their leftover cookies. It was an annual tradition for them now. They even had a badge made up, the Cato Fong badge, named after the *Pink Panther* character. It was nice making a difference for the community, even against my will.

Since it wasn't cookie season, I had to be ready for anything. Anyone could be in my office, and I didn't want a repeat of last night's events. I reached for my revolver. It was so rare that I used the weapon that I barely remembered I had it on my person. Actually, I had reached for a pack of Skittles in my pocket but brushed against my revolver. Luck was on my side. I was packing heat, and my heat was packing a wallop.

I kicked open the door, cursing under my breath because I used the foot with the bruised toe. In the middle of the room, I saw a figure sitting in a chair. They were illuminated from only the light outside the window, so I could only see their silhouetted outline.

It was time for the trespasser to meet the welcoming committee, which consisted of me, my gun, and whatever friendly dummies were in the gun's chamber just waiting to say their hellos.

I opened fire.

Thwip. Thwip thwip thwip. Thwip.

Huh. I looked into the barrel. Clean as a whistle, including the spit that I used to polish my gun. I swung out the cylinder. I must've forgot to load any bullets into the gun. In fact, I couldn't even remember the last time I loaded the damn thing.

The mystery figure didn't even move. I flipped the light switch on.

I blinked a few times, adjusting to the light. Once the blurriness retreated from my vision, I saw her body, duct taped to the chair.

I had only ever seen Ellie in the pictures from her house, until now. Even in her death, the pictures didn't do her justice. Although her black, straight hair was now unkempt and tangled, years of taking care of it still stood out. There was no makeup on her face, which held a deep purple bruise on her upper cheek, but she was still smiling—a slight one, with her right side upturned, as if she had passed while keeping a secret. Just a faint dimple underneath her bruise.

Her throat was also bruised, black and purplish. I wouldn't be surprised if the cause of death was strangulation. But the rest of her skin hadn't yellowed yet. It couldn't have been but a few hours since she was killed.

I tossed my gun on my desk. I failed her. I couldn't find her before this had happened. I failed Ellie. I failed Serena, her sister. I failed.

Now that I was on the other side of the room, I saw the message left for me. On the wall next to the door, "YOU ARE NEXT TRACER,

TRUST ME" was written on a tilt. At first, I thought it was written in blood, its scarlet color glinting off the light in the room. However, after a thorough examination (taste test), it was simply ketchup. Which raised further questions. Questions like:

Who carries this much ketchup around with them, especially when they're planting a dead body in someone's room?

What kind of monster wastes ketchup?

And, *is it spelled "ketchup" or "catsup?" Is there a difference between the two products? And what happened to all that gross, green ketchup marketed in the early 2000s? Did anyone really eat that?*

So, now I had a threatening message and a dead body in my office. It didn't look good. I panicked. And, I did the first thing I normally do when I panic…I called the police.

"What the—what the hell, Tracer? It's, like, three in the morning right now? Why the hell are you calling me?" Detective Hardholm said, answering his cell. "I swear, if this is another pocket dial, I'm going to arrest you for harassing a cop."

"Body. Dead body," I said.

"What?"

"There's a dead body in my office. And some ketchup on the wall. But I think the dead body's probably more important."

"Fine. Just…okay, I'll be right there. Give me fifteen minutes," he said. "You know there are other numbers for the police that you can call in these situations, right? Like 9-1-1? I don't see why I'm your first call."

"That's what friends do, I thought. You're number two on my speed dial."

"I'm not your—okay, whatever, Tracer. Just hang on, and don't do nothing stupid, okay?" He hung up.

Doing something stupid would've been not trying to figure out who had done this. So, I did the opposite. I did something smart. Which was getting down to the business of determining who had left this message and Ellie's corpse for me.

I opened my desk drawer, pulling out the detective's tool that I normally went to first in these kinds of situations. My Magic 8-Ball.

"Who did this?" I asked, shaking the mystical toy.

REPLY HAZY, ASK AGAIN, it said. So, I did.

VERY DOUBTFUL, was the reply this time. That's when I remembered I needed to ask it yes or no questions.

"Do you know who murdered Ellie Dayton and snuck her body into my office?" I asked.

YES—DEFINITELY.

"Was it somebody that I know?"

SIGNS POINT TO YES.

"If I guess the right name, will you let me know?"

BETTER NOT TELL YOU NOW.

I cursed the spiritual item and tossed it back in my drawer. The little occult weasel, hiding its secrets from me.

Sometimes it was better to be direct when finding things out. I grabbed my Rolodex and slid it closer to me. Using the metal wheels on the side to flip through the cards, I got to the letter I was looking for— M—for "murderers."

These were the killers connected to all my previous cases, that I had helped put away. Or that I had been around while the police put them away. Either way.

I dialed the first number.

"Hello?" the voice on the other line said.

"Hi. Is this Alan A. Anders?"

"Speaking."

"Hi, buddy. This is Tracer Spence, private eye extraordinaire. I'm not sure if you remember me, but I was the private detective who was working on the case where you had killed your wife in a hot-blooded rage a few years ago."

"Oh, I remember you alright. Why are you calling so late?"

"Well, there seems to have been another murder, and well…let's just come down to it. Did you do it?"

"Are you…are you kidding me? Listen, pal, I did my time, and I got the help that I needed. Prison was the best thing that ever happened to me, and I'm rehabilitated now. And here you are, accusing me of another murder? I can't believe you."

"Well, not accusing per se…just, you know, well you did commit one murder before…"

"I'm gonna come down their and rip your…no. No. Remember what the doctors said, Alan. Breathe. Count to ten when you're feeling stressed. Breathe. In and out…Listen, Mr. Spence. I'm not your guy. And I'd appreciate you not calling here again." He hung up.

Most of the other calls I made either went straight to voicemail, probably because it was so early in the morning, or had cell phones that were turned off, probably because the owners were still in prison. This wasn't getting me anywhere.

I stared at the message on my wall for a couple minutes. Luckily, I was a master sleuth, and something came to me. I realized that the letters in "YOU ARE NEXT, TRACER. TRUST ME" could be rearranged to spell "A EXTREME TRUE CRONY, STUART." That bastard. Only that lunatic would waste so much ketchup by leaving me a cryptic message. And, you know, killing someone. That was bad too.

If only I hadn't walked home so slowly from the Rolling Stones concert. I could've got here soon enough to save Ellie, instead of giving Stuart two kills on the night. *If I have to see one more dead body tonight*…I thought to myself. But I didn't want to finish the thought since I didn't want to tempt any cosmic fate out there.

Six sharp raps on my door interrupted the uncomfortable silence, like a polite Tommy gun.

"Door's open," I said.

Detective Hardholm walked in, carrying two paper cups of coffee. He looked over at Ellie and made his way toward me, hugging the sides of the room. Still looking at Ellie, he placed one of the cups down on my desk. He finally turned to me, pushing the cup my way, and said, "I think you need this, Tracer."

I nodded silently, taking a sip. My way of saying thank you.

The coffee was black and bitter. Just like how tonight turned out. I thought this was a cool thing to say in the moment, so I did.

"Black and bitter. Good. Just like how tonight turned out."

"What the hell are you talking about?"

"Nothing. Nevermind."

"The morgue guys will be here soon, with some other cops coming to take pictures and look around," Hardholm said. "So, who is she?"

"Remember that librarian-looking woman you sent to me the other day? The one looking for her sister?"

"Gotcha. Looks like you found her."

"Wish it was a little sooner though."

"I'm not going to lie, Tracer. You're off this case. Us actual cops— now that it's a murder, we'll be taking over. High priority. The way you bungled this mess? You should be happy that's all that's happening, us taking it from you." He paused. "But, if I find out you're still working on it, make no mistake—I will have you thrown in the joint for obstruction of law and interference."

This was it. There was no way in hell I was going to stop working this case, but now I had to steer clear of Hardholm and the cops? I had little time left to solve Serena's case, or what was left of it. Sure, Ellie had turned up, but who had done this? Why? What was the reason behind the kidnapping in the first place, let alone her murder? With all their resources and manpower, the police were in a better position to move quickly. Maybe that was for the best, to be honest. But this was personal now, and I was more determined than ever to follow through.

"You know anyone who has it out for you, Tracer? Any ideas at all?"

Sure, I knew there was Stuart and whatever the Hidden Star Hill gang was. But if I was going to keep this case, I wasn't giving Hardholm any leads. Maybe that was a bad idea brought about by it being past 3 in the morning, but when had I let a bad idea stop me before?

"How long ya got?" I replied.

"That many, huh?"

"Let's just say you don't get in this line of work to make friends."

"Yeah, but you don't get in it to make enemies either."

"Just a perk of the job, I guess."

We both took sips of our coffee, letting the silence wash over the room. Distant sirens in the night got louder, the altering of their pitch dizzying.

"Why *did* you get into this job?" Hardholm asked. "Is this what you wanted? To be a private eye?"

"Actually, I always wanted to open a laundromat. I'd call it 'Spence Cycle.' You know? 'Cause my last name is Spence? And it's like spin cycle, like what a washing machine does? 'Spence Cycle?'"

"Yeah, I get it. Why didn't you?"

"I have an irrational fear of getting stuck in a dryer and shrinking down like a wool sweater."

"You're an idiot sometimes, you know that?"

"I said it was irrational."

Over the next handful of minutes, I explained to Detective Hardholm some of my case—leaving out certain aspects. I didn't mention Stuart nor did I mention Sadie Marie; I still didn't know the connection between the two of them, and I was pretty embarrassed by the whole toothpaste/orange juice torture scene. Even just being in my office 24 hours later was giving me flashbacks.

But, as it turned out, leaving most of the specifics out of the story was problematic.

"You mean to tell me," Hardholm started, "that you've been on this case for the better part of two weeks now, and all you've done is break into Ellie's house to look for clues? And then you got a tattoo? That's it? And then, cut to a few days later, and her body is placed here because someone has it out for you? Whoever it is behind this, do they know how little you've actually done on the case?"

"I don't have to answer that. You're not my lawyer."

The door swung open again, with more cops spilling into the room. The next hour was a blur. Police snapping pictures, guys from the coroner's office inspecting the body, detectives searching my office. Eventually, Ellie's body was moved out on a gurney, one of its wheels creaking with every rotation. I was so exhausted that the incessant squeak gave me a headache right behind my left eye.

"Tracer, I asked if you got that," Hardholm said. Apparently, he had been talking to me while I was pushing on my eyelid, trying to dull the pain.

"Sorry, one more time."

"I said that I'm going to call this Serena Dayton tomorrow morning. Have her come in to the station, tell her about her sister, identify the body. I suggest you call her as well. Tell her everything that's happened. Maybe give her money back."

"Uh-huh."

"And leave the crime scene tape up. We'll swing by tomorrow morning to take it all down and make sure we haven't missed anything."

"Yeah. Gotcha. Thanks."

He knocked twice on my desk as a goodbye. Then he crossed the room, and ducking under the crime scene tape, left my office. The door had barely closed before I had conked out, feet up on my desk, reclining in my chair.

15

Serena Dayton tried lifting up the crime scene tape to enter my office, forcing the tape to give a little more than its fastened ends would allow. Her small, white satchel kept slipping off her shoulder when she bent sideways to step through, and by instinct, she kept shrugging the purse back up before it touched the floor. Her stiff movements looked like a gazelle trying to maneuver around some crime scene tape while carrying a satchel on its shoulder. You know, like gazelles do.

When she entered my office, she clung to the walls as she made her way around, not wanting to step into the middle of the floor. I guess she was unsure of where Ellie's body was found last night and didn't want to desecrate the place where her sister was found. That or she was put off by the big puddle of orange juice I had spilled five minutes ago and still hadn't cleaned up.

Though she was still smartly dressed, just like our last meeting, this time around, she seemed a little worse for wear. Her hair was pulled back in a bun, but frizzled flyaways stuck out, escaping the grasps of her bobby pins. Her makeup betrayed how she had spent the morning. Pale tear tracks ran down her cheeks like paths made by a bicycle on a sandy beach.

I knew she had just come from the coroner's office to identify the body of her sister.

She sat down and looked me over.

"You look like hell," she said.

It was true. As out of it as she looked, I was much worse having never went home from the night before. I had glimpsed myself in the bathroom mirror earlier, and woof. My eyes were bloodshot. I had a cowlick that Alfalfa from *The Little Rascals* would bully me for. I hadn't shaved in a couple of days, so I sported a patchy five o'clock shadow. And my clothes were so wrinkled they looked like they had been trampled by bulls with cleats on.

"Nothing that a bitter cup of black coffee won't fix," I said, raising up my mug. I was proud of the mug. It was emblazoned with *#1 Pirate Eye* on it—a typo that was all my fault when I ordered it from some website late at night without proof-reading what I had entered in the personalization field.

I opened one of my desk drawers and pulled out a bottle of Irish Whiskey. Pouring it into my coffee, I added, "And whatever the coffee don't fix, this might do the trick."

Serena rapped on my desk and with two fingers, motioned for me to pass the fifth of whiskey over to her. I did. She took the bottle, wiped the mouth of it off with the sleeve of her emerald green knit sweater, took a couple of hefty guzzles, wiped it off again, and set it back on my desk.

"I hate whiskey," she said.

"That's okay. Drinking whiskey isn't about liking it. It's about hating yourself as much as you hate it."

Serena moved her mouth as if to reply but stopped short. I wish she had just stopped altogether, because when she spoke again, it was a simple, "You're fired."

"Probably the right move," I said, offering her the bottle again. She took it, took another sip, and then got up to take her leave.

"Before I go, though," she said, looking around the room, "where did you find Ellie? Her body, I mean."

"Just about right where you were sitting," I said. This seemed to freak Serena out, so I quickly added, "Don't worry. It was in a different chair. And a couple inches over to the left."

Serena turned to go, but stopped, turned around. "You were supposed to find her. My sister. You were supposed to find her, and everything…everything was supposed to be alright. How could you fail like this?"

"Technically, I did find her. You know, in a different chair, and a couple inches over to the left," I said, pointing again. "Sorry," I added, after I noticed Serena's expression that could've dried concrete.

"This isn't what I wanted," she said. "This isn't what I meant to happen."

"Meant to happen?"

"Huh?" she asked.

"This isn't what you meant to happen, you said."

"I—I meant—I meant I wanted you to find her alive. I wanted to have my sister back. From before. From before she became obsessed with that—" Serena cut herself off. "From like when we were kids. She looked up to me, Mr. Spence. Our mother passed when I was eleven and Ellie was eight. She didn't remember much of our mother, but I did. The way she used to look at Ellie, the way she brushed her hair before bed every night, the way she left little words of encouragement on sticky notes in Ellie's lunch bag every morning. All the little things that she used to do with me when I was that young. And then she passed on—our mom was out riding her bike and hit by a car. Not even a drunk driver or anything. Just a dumb accident.

So, I sort of took over for our mother. I started doing those things for Ellie. Our father was working two jobs, making sure we were taken care of, but he wasn't exactly around most of the time because of it. Which meant that I had to take care of Ellie. I had to grow up. I never really made many friends in my teenage years; I was always taking care of Ellie when she got home from school. I made sure she did her homework. I made sure she knew to cross her legs when sitting down. I taught her how to apply makeup. I taught her that when boys teased her, it meant that they liked her. But I never had much time for myself. Never had boys—or anyone—tease me.

And then we grew up, Mr. Spence. We were always close, but we grew up and apart. Or grew differently. She stopped looking up to me, like I was her mother, and we were more like friends. She was so smart, so talented, so wild. She went off and did things on any whim that crossed her mind. That was her. Which may explain the mess she got herself in, goddamn her. And I found my partner. I was able to live for myself finally.

Ellie was doing great. I was so proud of her. And more than that…she was proud of me. But then, maybe twelve, thirteen years ago, she became obsessed with something, and everything changed. Gradually. Slowly. But things still changed, Mr. Spence. And now, because of that, I think, she's dead. She's dead, nothing makes sense, and you're fired."

She palmed the whiskey bottle, tossed it to her other hand, and downed the rest of the liquor. It was, and I'm not exaggerating, one of the top five sexiest things I've ever witnessed. Right behind Vanessa singing the other night and right before witnessing a koala giving birth in a zoo for my fifteenth birthday party. Well, not exactly *for* my fifteenth birthday. More just *on* my birthday, when my father threw a candy bar down into the koala enclave and convinced me I should climb down to get it. Despite what most people may think, it was a deeply erotic experience.

"What was Ellie so obsessed about?"

"What? Oh, nothing," Serena waved her hand, dismissively. "That doesn't matter."

"It might."

"Not if you're not on the case anymore. The police said they're taking over now. I don't need you. Not that you had helped anyway."

"And you trust the cops? They're the same people that suggested me to you."

"That's a fair point."

"I don't know how it is in your world, Ms. Dayton, but in mine, I don't give nobody the chance to do my job for me. Trust isn't easy. If you're going to trust anyone, it might as well be yourself. Even then, I only trust myself every other day."

"Is that…is that how you're trying to stay on the case? By telling me I should do it myself?"

"No! I was telling you to continue to trust me! What didn't you get about that? I was being pretty clear."

"You were not being cl—you know what? This is pointless anyway. There's no reason for you to be on the case anymore, if the cops are going to do it and you haven't solved anything yet."

"Not true. There's one reason to keep me on. It's personal."

"Of course, it's personal. She was my sister."

"No, I meant—for me. It's personal for me," I clarified. "Like, yes, it's obviously personal for you as well, with it being about your sister and all. But I meant that the case is personal also to me."

Serena stared at me, nothing but silence emanating from her. Her blue irises accusing me.

"Serena, they killed Ellie and left her here. In my office. They left a threatening message for me. Whoever did this to your sister, they want me off the case."

"That makes at least two of us then."

"Give me another chance."

"That's just the point, Mr. Spence. You shouldn't need another chance. Your failure got my sister killed."

"That's what we in the industry call an 'oopsie whoopsie.' Look, the police may try to find who murdered Ellie, but they're going to be stopped by red tape—"

"As opposed to you, who just gets in his own way." She breathed out a sigh. "I'd like my payment back. The arm bracelet."

"That…well, that might be a problem," I said. I explained to her my safekeeping process of mailing it to a fake address so it would be returned to me and the intricacies of the United States Postal Service. "You can certainly have it back, if you insist on firing me, which I strongly, strongly, strongly suggest against. But you'll have to wait until it comes back from Alaska."

"You know, I regret the moment I ever laid eyes on you, Mr. Spence."

"Funny. That's word for word what my father said to me, every Thanksgiving dinner. We'd all go around stating what we were thankful for, but he'd only say that. Every year."

"I can understand where he was coming from."

"Listen, Ms. Dayton, wouldn't it be better having one more set of eyes? One more guy following his own leads? In a different way than what Hardholm is gonna do?"

Again, Serena opened her mouth to say something, and then stopped herself. She sat back down and leaned forward, her elbows resting on the opposite side of my desk. "What are you saying? You're saying you have a lead?"

"A few leads," I said, lying.

"And the cops don't know about them?"

"They didn't come up, no. Let me guess though…you want me to share my ideas with Detective Hardholm and leave it alone?"

Serena leaned back, and her right heel started tapping against the floor like a jackhammer in high heels. She chewed on her bottom lip, contorting her face, like she was thinking things over. "No…no—I don't know. I'm not sure…" she trailed off.

"You're not sure?"

"Yes…no…I'm not sure. Hypothetically speaking…where would you start with one of your leads?"

"Well, I have an idea of who may have wanted Ellie out of the picture. I found some incriminating evidence in Ellie's apartment, and then I spoke to the suspect, but they were elusive. So, my next move would be to sneak into their office and try to find a motive."

"You think…you think you can find a motive at this person's office? Really?" Serena rubbed her left shoulder, her right arm pressed tightly across her chest.

"Listen, don't get hysterical, Ms. Dayton. I'm not positive what exactly I'll find. Leads are just about connecting the dots. That's all being a detective is. Connecting the dots, like one of those kids' picture thingies. There's no way to know just how you're supposed to connect the dots, so sometimes you just wind up with a bunch of random squiggles on a sheet of paper."

"What? There are numbers on the dots. You connect them in order. It's supposed to make a picture at the end."

"Only if you play by the rules," I said, hoping this smooth line would cover up the fact that I didn't realize that's what the numbers were for.

"And…hypothetically speaking, how dangerous would this…what would you call it? Reconnaissance mission? How dangerous would this reconnaissance mission be?"

I liked the sound of that. *Reconnaissance mission.* I let it play off my tongue to feel how good it felt coming out of my mouth.

"Reconnaissance mission. Yes. That's EXACTLY what we call it. And, to answer your question, it would be very dangerous. I don't exactly know what I'd be getting into, and that's the way I like it."

"If, and this is a big hypothetical if, I keep you on, and you go on this reconnaissance mission, and you get caught, how likely would it be that they would find out that I was behind your little visit?"

"I think I get what you're getting at," I said, tapping the side of my nose with my pointer finger, which is somehow a known social code implying understanding, though I have no idea why. "Let's just say, if anything—anything at all—goes wrong, I have this…" I lowered my voice to a whisper; it felt like the right thing do, like she and I were co-conspirators. "…This cyanide pill."

I pulled the pill out of my jeans pocket, wiped some lint off of it, and held it proudly to Serena in between my thumb and pointer finger.

She took a good, long look at it. She got up close, really studying the miniature capsule, my guess is because she had never seen one before.

"That's a B-12 vitamin. It says right on it. It's supposed to help with your metabolism system."

"…Like superpowers?"

"No, not like superpowers. Like, with digestion or something, I guess. It's good for you."

"How many would I have to take to kill myself? Like, in terms of being apprehended during clandestine operations?"

"I don't know. A hundred? A thousand?"

"Ah. That's probably expensive, right?"

"Probably."

I thought about the implications of hiding a thousand pills somewhere on my body and ruled it out as improbable. I could probably stuff like twenty in each ear, but that still left 960 to be hidden elsewhere. And those forty would taste like ear wax. Gross. If I was going to die, the last thing I wanted to taste was scotch and steak, not my own bodily secretions.

"In that case, I'll have you know that I've been classically trained in the art of resisting torture. Well, maybe not *classically trained,*" I back-pedaled, "but I'm well-practiced in the form."

"How so?"

"I once tried to infiltrate and stop what I thought was an illegal cock-fighting ring. Only, I found out, it was actually people betting on Roombas with knives and balloons strapped to them. Whichever Roomba popped the other's balloon first was the winner. It turned out to be pretty popular on the internet honestly. Anyway, when the people running the event found out I wasn't there to participate in the betting, they tortured me by making me participate in the competition. It's a lot harder than you'd think to go up against one of those robots with a balloon strapped to your butt. I swear they smell fear. But, I never gave up my benefactor."

Serena rubbed the lower knuckle of her ring finger while thinking. She bit her lower lip, the other side plumping up.

"You're sure it's going to be dangerous?" she asked.

"If my last few days have been any inclination, they've only been a precursor to what's to come danger-wise."

"Good. Good. Or, I mean, bad, I guess." Serena said. "Sorry, I'm grieving, you know. Speaking without thinking."

"It's okay. I say stuff all the time without thinking first. It's kind of my modus operandi."

"Okay. Mr. Spence, against my better judgement, you can stay on the case. But on one condition. You report back to me with anything, and I mean literally anything, you find. The second you find it."

"Well, I guess I've got some work to do then," I said, letting the conversation end naturally.

Though, I felt real stupid about saying that and nothing else, as Serena had to run the gamut of standing up, walking around the spilled orange juice, and ducking underneath the crime scene tape, which all took a good five silent minutes. When would the police come to take the crime scene tape down? And when would the janitorial service come and clean up the juice spilled in the middle of my floor? Only time would tell. Only time would tell.

16

I was back in Connecticut, standing in the alley outside of Take a Cakewalk on the Wild Side. If I was to figure out why Ellie was murdered, I had to get in the back room that Sadie Marie was so intent on keeping secret from me. And that meant sneaking into the bakery.

The big question was: how?

It was a one-story brick building. In front, there was the glass door and windows like I had seen last time I was here. Around back in the alley, a metal security door opened up from where the kitchen would be. This was of course locked. Above the door and to the right was a vent, the slanted cover discolored but free from rust or dirt.

My first thought was to gain access from the roof. Maybe there was a giant skylight up there that I could silently cut through and slip into the building quietly from. I didn't remember seeing any giant skylights the last time I was standing in Take a Cakewalk on the Wild Side, but I could've been misremembering. Or Sadie Marie could've had one installed within the last two days. Barring the skylight, maybe there was just, like, a door. Or a fireman's pole that I could slide down heroically into the kitchen. Or a Star Trek-esque beaming transporter that could dematerialize my organic material and reconvert it into the bakery.

The point was I had literally no way of knowing what was on the roof, but I was determined to find out.

I looked around for anything that I could climb on. The only thing I saw was a dirty, green dumpster, lined up with the opening of the alley against the building across the lane from Take a Cakewalk on the Wild

Side. I scooted behind it. It appeared more filth and garbage was smeared on the outside of the dumpster than was ever thrown into it. Nonetheless, I steeled myself; this may be my best shot at getting access to the roof.

I pushed with all my strength.

"Ew ew ew ew ew ew ewwwww ew," I muttered, my hands pressed against some unknown substance not quite squishy and not quite dried. No luck. I couldn't even budge the damn thing. I guess that was why garbage trucks had those mechanical levers to pick them up.

I sucked in my gut and scooted back from behind the dumpster. I did my best to wipe my hands off on my shirt, which was now also smeared with whatever mystery substance that was encrusted on the dumpster. The first thing I would do when I got into the bakery was wash my hands off. And unless Sadie Marie had a medium-sized men's shirt just laying around, mine would have to do for now.

I circumnavigated the building again, being careful not to be seen through the front windows. No ladders, no staircases, no piles of boxes that I could stack on top of each other. No nothing.

Back in the alley, I stared at the air vent. It was a bucket list item of mine to crawl through a vent on a spy mission. Maybe this was my chance. Standing on my tippy-toes, I could just reach the bottom of the cover with the tips of my fingers. If I could jam my fingernails into the screws holding the vent cover in place, I might loosen them up, maybe.

Righty-tighty, lefty-loosey…

I couldn't tell which way was left or right though. Does left and right even match up with clockwise and counter-clockwise? I cursed, giving up, wishing my dad had taught me basics of tools instead of just throwing socket wrenches at my head whenever I entered the garage.

My time to crawl through a vent would have to wait.

Instead, I focused more on the brick wall that the air vent was built into. I grabbed hold of one of the recesses between bricks at eye level. Sure, the concavity was tight, but with the right climbing grip, it was possible for someone to scale the side of the building.

I jumped, reaching above me for another nook to sink my fingers into. I jumped again. And again. Again. Again. Again.

Out of breath, hands on my knees, feeling the urge to vomit, I conceded it may be possible for someone to scale the side of the building, but that someone was someone else—not me.

I also came to the realization that I should probably start going to a gym because being winded after six jumps did not bode well for my health or longevity.

Take a Cakewalk on the Wild Side was no Fort Knox, but I had to admit, it was proving to be more secure to infiltrate than I thought. I knew I should have invested in a grappling hook when I had the chance. From now on, when a strange man offered to sell me military grade equipment in a back alley for dirt-cheap, I was going to take him up on his offer, damnit.

Unfortunately, my failures only meant one thing: I would have to sneak in through the front door.

I hung off to the side of the front window furthest away from the store's entrance, hoping that Sadie Marie wouldn't catch me peeking in every so often. I bided my time, waiting for an opportune moment.

That opportune moment was interrupted.

"What'cha doing here, boy?"

I turned around and was confronted by a luxurious, bushy mustache. Attached to the mustache was a police officer, his uniform and badge glinting in the sun.

"Just testing the tensile strength of this sidewalk, officer," I said. I stomped my foot twice, hoping this would prove my smart-ass claim.

"What's this sign say?" he asked, ignoring me. He pointed to a street sign a couple feet away.

"No loitering."

"Good. So, it seems you can read, boy. You can read, but not follow directions. Because it sure seems like you're doing an awful lot of loitering in these parts."

"You don't have a group of skateboarders you can bust right now? No tickets to write for parking a minute after the meter's expired? I'm the most important criminal happening right now?" I asked.

I regretted mouthing off as soon as the sentences left my mouth. Mainly because Officer Lip Foliage was quick with his truncheon. It was out of its holster and whacking against my knee within a second. Pain radiated through my body like a gamma ray. I dropped to ground.

"Now, are you going to move, boy, or do I have to strike the opposite side as well?"

Through heavy breaths, I said, "I thought night sticks weren't used any longer. How the hell do you still have one?"

The officer stood up straight, proud. "I petitioned the city council to keep mine. Said it was more effective in combatting the riffraff."

"Lots of riffraff loitering around here, yeah?"

"When you really set your mind to it, doesn't everyone look like they're loitering?" he replied. "Now, amscray, boy. Captain told me to clear the area of any suspicious undesirables. Apparently, some big city cop is coming, working a murder case. And I've never seen you before, but you certainly look like a suspicious undesirable, so get." He lifted his baton, threatening to swing it at me, making me flinch.

"Look," I said, pushing myself to me feet, "let me…just…get to my…feet…and I'll be…out of your hair." On the last word, I yanked at his mustache, grappling it and throwing him off balance. I took off sprinting past the open windows of Take a Cakewalk on the Wild Side, hoping Sadie Marie would only see a blur as I ran. I turned the corner, into that old familiar alley, not even looking over my shoulder. Never look over your shoulder while running from someone. The movement only creates wind drag and slows you down. It's basic aerodynamics.

Now that I was back in the alley again, I wasn't sure what to do. I looked around for a hiding spot. The only one I spied was the dumpster. I could hope that my thesis was right and that the inside of it was cleaner than the outside was.

I heard footsteps rounding the corner. I had to decide.

I sprinted towards the dumpster. Instead of lifting the lid and jumping in, I swung the lid high and took off running again, around the other corner, back to where me and Officer Caterpillar Face started our mad dash. With any luck, he would hear or see the lid close and think I had hidden in the dumpster. This would buy me, oh, five or six seconds before he opened the lid and realized I wasn't in there. But every moment counted in a life-or-death chase. And if we did this loop twenty times, those five or six seconds would add up, and he'd never know where I was.

That was the plan anyway, until I was running past the bakery a second time and noticed Sadie Marie wasn't in the main room anymore. Now was my chance. I opened the front door.

I had a single moment of victory for successfully infiltrating the store. In that moment, I was home-free—just had to sneak around quietly to not gain Sadie Marie's attention.

Then I heard the three descending notes of the automatic door chime above me.

I cursed.

"Be there in a minute," I heard Sadie Marie call out from the kitchen. Her sing-song voice would've made any Disney princess envious.

I couldn't let her see me. I couldn't let the cop outside find me either. I needed to get in that back office, but there was no way I could sneak around the glass bakery cases before Sadie Marie came back out front. The smiling cupcake decals on the wall mocked me and my predicament.

Ducking into the co-ed bathroom, I held my breath, opening and closing the door as quietly as possible. The click of the latch bolt catching in the strike plate was the loudest noise I'd ever heard, with my ragged breathing currently in a close second. But I hoped that both were noiseless enough in real life that Sadie Marie would think her customer had left as soon as they walked in.

The automatic light clicked on, sensing movement. The bathroom was spacious. Both the toilet and urinal were clean, with an extra roll of toilet paper in a wicker cozy laying on top of the tank. A matching wicker cabinet was across the room from the sink, no doubt holding extra paper and napkins. However, there was also a closet in here, the door to it right next to the cabinet. On the walls were, of course, more of those sinister smiling stickers, the pastel baked goods creeping me out.

"Hello?" I heard Sadie Marie ask, her voice muffled because of the closed bathroom door.

Her footsteps got closer and closer; I heard them rounding the corner of her countertops and walking across the main floor. The fluorescent lights in the bathroom made me feel naked—they were so bright, and I was way too in the open. I felt my heartbeat pounding in my temples.

I shuffled towards the bathroom's closet. Opening it, I saw there was just enough room for me to crouch between the shelves holding cleaning products and the door. If Sadie Marie checked the bathroom for her disappeared customer, my only hope was that she wouldn't check the closet as well. I felt good about my hiding spot. I had experience with hiding. My expertise stemmed from that summer when my dad volunteered me for summer camp on a private island, which turned out to be a *Most Dangerous Game*-type situation.

Knock knock knock.

"Hello?" Her voice echoed in the cold bathroom.

"Hello?" she asked again. "Is anyone in there?" She waited a beat and then said, "I'm coming in."

I heard the bathroom doorknob turn, and the door opened.

"Huh, that's weird," she said. I realized she was talking about the automatic light which had never shut off. If no one was in the bathroom, the light should've clicked on when she walked in.

Her steps got closer.

I covered my mouth with my hand, trying to stifle my breaths.

The lever handle to the closet door turned down.

The door slowly opened, a sliver of light creeping across my right eye.

DING DING DING.

The store's front chimes went off, followed by a familiar voice saying, "Hello? Ms. Olivierri?" It was the mustachioed cop from outside.

Sadie Marie turned, closing the door. I heard her say, "Yes, I'm here," and then she left the bathroom.

"Ms. Olivierri, this is Detective…I'm sorry, sir, what did you say your name was? I'm terrible at remembering," the cop said.

"Hardholm. Detective Hardholm."

Damnit.

"Right, Detective Hardholm. He's from New York. Investigating a mur—"

"It's nice to meet you, Ms. Olivierri," Hardholm said, cutting off the officer.

Of course it was Detective Hardholm, the big city detective that the cop was talking about.

I opened the closet door, scooting like a dog itching himself on carpet out into the larger bathroom area. I sat on the cold tile floor, trapped like a grizzly caught in a bear trap, only with slightly less hair on my chest. I matter-of-factly cursed things. Plenty of things. I cursed the timing of cops. I cursed pretty women who owned bakeries. I cursed those damn smiling cupcake decals. But most of all I cursed fate itself and its cruel sense of humor.

"Did he say you were investigating a murder?" Sadie Marie asked.

"I'm sorry, Ms. Olivierri, Officer…what was your name? I couldn't remember either," Hardholm said. I could hear the sarcasm in his voice.

"It's Officer Dre—"

"Doesn't matter," Hardholm interrupted. "He spoke out of turn. Yes, I'm investigating a murder, Ms., but I'd appreciate it if we discussed further down at the station."

"Right now? I'd have to close up shop then."

"Right now, yes. I apologize, but it'll only take half an hour."

Sadie Marie agreed, went to her office to get her purse, and then I heard the electric chime of the front door interrupt itself a few times, as the three of them left. I was in the clear.

I walked out of the bathroom and over to the office. I opened the door and stood in the doorjamb. Finally, I saw what was inside of the private office. It was nothing more than a boring, old office. A desk with a computer monitor, picture frame, telephone, and large water bottle on top of it. Filing cabinets. Leather chair. Wall-to-wall cheap carpeting. A safe in the back corner of the room.

Yawn.

However, I did notice that hanging up from the ceiling to the right of the desk was a closed-circuit television displaying footage from security cameras around the store. The videos cycled through current images of the store: one looking towards the customer side of the register, one looking towards the other side of the register, one in the kitchen pointed towards the back door, and one pointed towards the safe in this office.

That last one meant the camera had to be right above the door's entrance.

In case these surveillance videos were being recorded, I didn't want to be caught on the security footage. I deduced the angle of the camera and figured that I wouldn't be caught if I army crawled into the room.

Dropping to my hands and knees, I inched my way forward. My face and chest scratched across the utility carpet. Goose bumps ran down my body, and I shivered from the feeling of the carpet bristles rubbing along the fibers of my shirt. I giggled from the ticklish feeling.

James Bond-like, I pushed and vaulted with my feet, tumbling into a somersault. Being out of shape, the roll was sloppy and took a full minute. Also, I misjudged how far away I was from the desk, so my lower back crashed into the steel front plate. The collision knocked the water bottle over, the contents spilling over the side of the desk, directly onto my pant leg. My left calf was as wet as the inside of a waterbed.

I rolled over to the side, out of the camera's line-of-sight. Standing up, I used the metal filing cabinet next to me to balance myself. A stack of red plastic cups was on top of the cabinet. I pulled one cup off the top, figuring I could use this to cover the camera.

Standing on my tippy-toes, I reached up, balancing myself with my right hand, the cup in my left. Water trickled down my leg, like a trail of ants down a tree trunk. I slid the plastic cup over the camera, trying to balance it, so it wouldn't slide off. I nudged the cup a couple of times, trying to catch it on one of the camera's ridges.

That's when I lost my balance, grabbed the entire contraption, and ripped the camera off of the wall, exposed wires ripping out of the electrical box. The camera hit the floor, and my forehead hit the camera.

In pain, I rolled over, glancing at the television. The office footage was only static now. Mission accomplished.

I stood up and searched the room for something to fix the mess. This was only made more difficult by seeing double with a blinding headache. Luckily, I had my fair share of practice with this condition walking from my local hole-in-the-wall bar to my hole-in-the-wall apartment. I spied a roll of Scotch tape in one of those plastic holder thingamajiggers on the filing cabinet.

A few minutes later, the camera was secured, amateurishly, back on the wall, with, I'd estimate, a solid pound of tape holding it up.

My mess cleaned up, I walked over to Sadie Marie's desk.

Sitting in her chair, the first thing I did was open up all the drawers of her desk. Mostly, I just found rubber bands, staples, push pins, reams of paper. Boring office supplies. But, in the bottom drawer, hidden underneath a manilla folder, I found something I had seen once before. Ellie's secret journal. The notebook had somehow made its way from Ellie's apartment to Serena Marie's bakery within the last couple of days. And I doubt it had sprouted legs and walked from New York to Connecticut on its own. Though that would be cool. Like an alien in disguise or something. Maybe I could sell a screenplay with that as the big twist. Either way, Sadie Marie had somehow gotten her hands on this diary and concealed it. I didn't know why. I didn't know what was so important about the journal. And I didn't know the number to any

Hollywood big-shots that would be interested in a Sci-Fi detective movie. But none of that was going to stop me from solving this case.

I took the journal, shoving it into my jacket pocket.

Sitting in her chair, I turned her computer monitor on. The black screen flashed, and a spreadsheet popped up. The store's finances. I combed through the entries, hoping to crack some kind of code that would stand for "paid for hitman to murder Ellie Dayton." But I got real bored real quick and started zoning out. Numbers do that to me. That's why I never kept my own financial logs—I preferred to be surprised when my checking account was in the red. Though, it was more of a surprise when I wasn't in debt.

I minimized the file. Below it was the internet browser, with about 30 tabs opened up. Most of these were recipes for cupcakes, research on different types of flours, or links to purchase baking items. However, one specific tab caught me eye. It was a YouTube video, "How to Gavotte," showing a couple young women—one playing the violin, the other doing some sort of Baroque tap dance. Every so often, the women would explain in slow detail the basic dance steps.

I know I had seen something like this before, but I couldn't place it. While I was thinking, trying to remember, I noticed a picture on Sadie Marie's desk from the corner of my eye. I snatched the frame and brought it closer. Sadie Marie was smiling, leaning her head on the shoulder of an equally happy Serena Dayton.

I had so many questions. Serena? With Sadie Marie? How did they know each other? What was going on? Would I ever understand the last season of *Lost*? How'd Serena get her teeth so white, and could she possibly give me the number to her dentist?

I had no time to process this, however. I heard the chimes from the front door again, and Sadie Marie called out, "I'm so sorry! I'll be real quick. My wallet is right on my desk."

Sure enough, a thin leather wallet sat right next to where I had picked up the picture.

I panicked. I was sitting in her office chair, her computer screen was on, a security camera was ripped from her wall and taped back up, and a puddle of water soaked into her office carpet. Things didn't look good. I only had a few moments to come up with a plan.

I crawled under her desk. The anxiety-ridden panic made my armpits sweat. But I had to hold it together. Earlier, I had noticed a phone hanging on the wall in her kitchen. If I could call the store's number, hopefully I could distract her long enough to sneak out of the office and back into the bathroom.

I dialed the phone number.

Just like I had thought, the kitchen phone started ringing. Unlike what I had thought, so did the phone sitting on the desk right above me.

Making things even worse—her phone's ringtone was a MIDI melody of "You're So Vain." I heard the digital synthesizer notes blare out the chorus of Carly Simon's ditty, without feeling.

I hung up. Also, with the best idea I had in maybe my entire life, I turned my cell phone on silent, in case she called the number that appeared on the missed call display.

I heard her walk into the office. She picked up the phone and said, "Huh," and then placed it back onto the desk. She grabbed something else off the desk—I assumed it was her wallet—and then left the room. A couple moments later, I heard those damn chimes go off again and the front door open and close.

She hadn't even noticed the puddle of water or her monitor being on or the camera or the full-grown man breathing heavily and sweating under her desk. She had just been told that she was somehow connected to a murder case, so she was probably dazed.

Not all of us can handle pressure like that, I thought, using the torso part of my shirt to absorb my underarm sweat.

I crouch-walked out of the office, behind the glass displays and counter, and through the kitchen. I used that back door to leave, just in case Sadie Marie and the cops were out front.

In and out, without a trace. That was my style.

17

It was evening, and I was standing outside of Serena Dayton's house in Connecticut. A few hours had passed since I snuck out of Take a Cakewalk on the Wild Side. During the interval, I had bought a change of clothes since mine had been wet from garbage juice, liquid from a water bottle, and sweat—in that order. Now though, I was pacing back and forth in Serena's walkway, rehearsing in my head the confrontation I was about to have with my client.

How did she know Sadie Marie? Why was she so…familiar with this evil, kidnapping baker in a photograph on Ms. Olivierri's desk? Did she get a good deal on all these solar lights that were next to the entrance path in her front yard?

The dim blue lights emanating from them were tasteful, illuminating the landscaping in front of her split-level house. The shrubs were well-trimmed, neatly planted in speckled white stones behind a brick barrier. I supposed this was what realtors meant by *curb-appeal.*

That said, I never understood why anyone would live in a house in the suburbs. Why would you when you could give all your money to a landlord who, instead of fixing the leaking ceiling above your bed, spent his time making his own wine in a bucket down in the basement of your apartment? That was the big city hustle-bustle that you just couldn't get in the suburbs. *That* was atmosphere.

I rang the doorbell.

"Coming," someone shouted from inside. A moment later, Serena opened the door. "Tra—Mr. Spence? What are you doing here?"

I was glad it was her. This was the third house I rang the doorbell at, and the first homeowner was quite irate about being interrupted during their dinner. I tried explaining that it wasn't my fault that all the houses on this street looked the same. They shot back that I should pay attention to the address numbers on the houses and mailboxes. The second time was simply because I got distracted by all the fireflies and was wondering where I could get a mason jar to catch them.

I was about to reply to Serena when she said, "No, it doesn't matter. I've had a long day, including seeing you this morning. I need you to leave. Whatever it is that you want can wait."

From behind her, a voice called out, "Honey? Who is it?"

And then Sadie Marie appeared in the doorway.

She and I said, at the same time, "What are you doing here?"

"Jinx. You owe me a Coke," I said.

"Mr. Spence, why are you here? And why have you been stalking my wife all day?"

"Your wife?" That would explain the picture I found in Take a Cakewalk on the Wild Side. It also put Sadie Marie's voicemail to Ellie in a new context: *taking her out* may not have been a sinister threat, but a friendly invitation instead.

Still, the hushed whisper of the voicemail played in my head. Why would a friend call and leave such a quiet voicemail? Especially one that seemed so angry in the beginning. Something didn't sit right. I needed to listen to that voicemail again. Soon.

"Yes. Sade is my wife," Serena said, hugging the baker with one arm, while never taking her eyes off of me. "Now, answer my question. Why did you break into her bakery today?"

"How did you know I snuck in?" I asked.

"We watched the security footage," Sadie Marie said. "After I was taken down to the police station and found out Ellie...her sister was...was..." She trailed off. I hadn't noticed before, but Sadie Marie's eyes were pink and puffy, like she had just been crying. "Well," she started again, regaining her composure, "we decided it was best to look through the tapes to make sure we were safe."

"You're terrible at sneaking around, Mr. Spence," Serena said. "Despite all your crawling around on the floor, it was like you didn't even try to get out of sight of the cameras. So again…why were you investigating Sade?"

I was still convinced Sadie Marie was the culprit in Ellie Dayton's murder, though I wasn't sure how. And since I still didn't have any proof, I didn't want either Sadie Marie or Serena to know that.

"I…I had…well, it's for the same reason you were just watching your security footage. I had intel that whoever murdered Ellie was also interested in Sadie Marie. Or in something she has, some kind of info, something that they think belongs to them. That they've been staking out the bakery. I needed to sneak in to find what they were looking for before they could find it."

As lies go, that one wasn't half bad for me.

"And, did you?" Serena asked.

"Did I what?"

Serena glared at me with a look that would've had the moon questioning why it orbited the Earth. She said, "Find what they were looking for."

"Y…yes," I said, stalling. I patted my torso, pretending I was looking for something on my person that I had misplaced. When I tapped around my chest area, I felt the hard cover of Ellie Dayton's notebook in my pocket. I took it out. "This. I found this."

"Is that…where did you find that?" Sadie Marie asked. She snatched it out of my hands. She looked pale, like she had just seen a ghost—a ghost that had found a secret journal stolen from the dead sister of her wife.

"In your office," I said. "Duh. I just said that. Keep up, lollipop."

"What is it?" Serena asked.

Both me and Sadie Marie stayed quiet, waiting for the other to speak first. It was a game of chicken, like two cars driving towards each other, waiting for the other to swerve out of the way first. Which one of us would break first? Which one of us would spill? Who was the strongest of the—

"It's your sister's secret diary," I said.

"And what was it doing in your office?" Serena turned to Sadie Marie, who was still clutching it to her chest.

"She asked me to keep it safe," Sadie Marie said. She was so good at lying, I almost believed her.

I held out my hand to Sadie Marie and fake coughed. Worried that I was too subtle, I said, "I need that back, actually."

While Sadie Marie reluctantly gave it back, Serena asked, "Why? What's in it? It's just a diary, right? Why wouldn't she come to me for safe keeping?"

That was a good question. I wish it had popped into my mind to ask, but at least I was lucky that someone here was thinking through things logically.

"I don't know, honey," Sadie Marie said. "I just assumed she asked you first. It's just…Ellie said it was just a record of all the times she heard that song. Apparently she kept a log of the times and places, every day."

"What?" I asked.

"Oh, that's it?" Serena said.

"What song?" I felt my palms sweat.

"Yeah, honey, that's it. If she didn't ask you, I guess it's just because it's such a silly journal."

"No seriously, guys. What song?"

"Okay. I guess that makes sense. Why would anyone be after that though?"

"Am I a ghost? Do you two see me?" I waved my hands at them. "This is important. I need to know what song."

"I don't know. I guess we should be glad your private eye took it out of my office though, if someone's after it."

"IF YOU TWO DON'T TELL ME WHAT SONG YOU'RE TALKING ABOUT, I'M GOING TO FILL ALL OF MY POCKETS

WITH BRICKS AND WALK INTO THE OCEAN, SO HELP ME GOD."

In retrospect, even I could admit that was too dramatic.

"That '70s song, 'You're So Vain,' from uh, what's her name, Carly Simon," Sadie Marie said. "Ellie was obsessed. She used to say it was stalking her. That she heard it every single day."

At that moment, all the lights in the neighborhood dimmed for two seconds. The solar lights lining Serena's walkway, the streetlights, the outside lantern hanging next to the front door—everything went dark at the same time.

"What the hell was that?" Serena asked, looking around.

"Probably a power surge," I said. "Either that or a cannibalistic tribe of creatures that control shadows and light."

I turned back to the matter at hand, and I flipped through the pages of the notebook, turning towards the end. "The last entry says it's day 4752. That means that she heard the song for at least—"

"Just about thirteen years," Serena said.

"Nearly thirteen years," I repeated. Thirteen years. I had only heard the song once a day for just slightly over a year, and I was already feeling crazy. Ellie had been—*stalked* was the word Sadie Marie said, and that fit—stalked by Carly Simon for almost thirteen years. Was this what I had to look forward to? What would someone who heard that song once a day for thirteen years do?

Serena broke the spell. "I don't understand though…why would her killer want this diary? What is this for?"

"I don't understand either. Not yet, anyway," I said. "But I'll figure it out, don't you worry, Mrs. Dayton." Considering I had lied about the bad guys wanting this journal, I hoped I could come up with another good lie in a couple days to explain this whole thing.

"Are you…are you sure you need to take that with you, Mr. Spence?" Sadie Marie asked.

"Yes." I still didn't know how she was involved. Why did she have this notebook that I last saw at Ellie's apartment? She didn't seem like the murderer now, but what was she hiding? Why had she lied about

Ellie asking her to keep the journal safe? Did "You're So Vain" have anything to do with Ellie's murder? Was I ever going to get that Coca-Cola from Sadie Marie that she owed me?

We said our goodbyes, Sadie Marie and Serena going back into their nice, suburban house. I walked down their driveway, pulling out my phone. I forgot it had been on silent since early in the day at the bakery. I had three missed calls, all from Vanessa. I also had a text from her. A simple *we need to talk.*

That was a good idea. I needed someone to talk to after the day I just had. Someone to bounce some ideas off of. I dialed Vanessa's number as I got to the end of the driveway.

18

If there's one thing that could be said about me, it was that I was a man of patterns. I looked for 'em in my job, and I followed 'em in my day-to-day life. And that's how I found myself at my favorite hole in the wall—named The Hole in the Wall—the next night.

It was the pattern I fell into all the time: blowing it with the ladies and then drinking myself stiff.

Vanessa and I had gotten into an argument. Or she had gotten into an argument, and I had gotten into a being-yelled-at-ment. She had answered my phone call, fuming like a lit cigar stuck in the tailpipe of a pickup. Point of it is, Vanessa didn't like that I never came to find her after the death of the false Mick Jagger. She was upset. And good ol' Spence, he did the same thing he does every time a girl gets upset with him—made it worse.

"I thought the date was over," I said into the phone. "You know, with the situation and all."

"Look, I didn't mind you running off to work on your case. You should know that. I know how important it is to you, but you should've come back to find me. It was like leaving a little kid at a water park during a family vacation on accident. I just waited there, planting myself by the wall next to the merch table, thinking you'd come back."

"You know, that same thing happened to me. Only, I guess it was less of a water park and more of an abandoned rock quarry that my dad took me too. He told me it was a scavenger hunt and to go look for any leftover TNT lying around. He even gave me a book of matches to light up any caverns that I'd look in. But he must've forgot we were playing a game, because his car was gone within an hour. I never did find any explosives, but there was an unopened bag of beef jerky in the driver's seat of an old excavator. That was the highlight of the trip, I'd say."

"How dare you change the subject."

"You don't like beef jerky?"

"I bought you a sweatshirt at the concert. I just hung on to it. It was pathetic. Some security guard even came up to me asking if I had been stood up. I told him you were coming right back. An hour later, he asked me the same thing. I've never been more embarrassed in my life."

I had found the sweatshirt on my office desk later that night. Vanessa had folded it, the sleeves overlaid each other. I thought it was a nice gesture, even with the trespassing on private property. I told her that, hoping that would smooth things over.

"Tracer, I need some time alone."

She hung up the phone, I hung up my hat, and we were both hung up on my issues.

That evening, I threw the sweatshirt on and went to The Hole in the Wall. It was one of those places where no one cares about your name. The lighting was dim as were the patrons. I sat at the bar which was sticky with spilled drinks. The bartender, Joe, apparently hadn't wiped it down yet. That was okay. I'm used to dealing with adverse situations.

"Ah, Tracer. What'll it be today?" Joe asked me. He had a deep voice, grunting as if he was in the middle of working out. Which made sense—you could snap a baseball bat in half on his forearm. His V-neck t-shirt was too tight, and the dark skin of his muscular biceps glistened in the poor lighting of the bar.

I had built up a repertoire with Joe over the years, and he was the best friend money could buy.

"I'll start with a beer, please. Yuengling. I've always said that the world looks clearer through the bottom of an empty glass."

"Didn't get the keg shipment in yet," he said, putting down an aluminum can in front of me. "This is all we have for now."

"Erm…I've always said the world looks clearer reflected from the bottom of an empty beer can."

It had been a few hours, and I had moved on to harder stuff. Liquor that you could build a foundation on. Cheap whiskey was the way of escape, and there was plenty I wanted my mind to escape from. Vanessa. Mick Jagger's dead "clone." Finding Ellie in my office. Man-eating shadows. My cases in general. And with tomorrow's hangover, I'd want my mind to escape from my own cranium.

I had plenty of beer cans, shot glasses, and whiskey glasses lined up in front of me, a line of dead soldiers. I tipped the next drink into my mouth hole, and placed the glass, rim-side down, in rank with the others. Joe came by to clean them all up, a rag draped over his shoulder.

"You're being uncharacteristically quiet for a change, Tracer. Anything wrong?" Joe asked.

I nodded. As a private eye, there's one thing I'd learned, and that's that you can trust no one. As it happens, Joe was that no one. He was a world traveler turned bartender, a man of the people, so to speak. He had an easy way about him, as all good bartenders should. Private detectives had their own codes of conduct to follow, and so did bartenders. They had to be like therapists and archeologists, only with the ability to make margaritas. Joe was all of the above, and with a name like Joe, how could he be anything else?

"So, what is it, son? Girl problems?"

"Ew. Like ovulations and cycles? Joe, you know I don't want to talk about that."

"No, that's not what I—never mind, Tracer, never mind." He started to walk away.

"Joe, wait a minute," I called out. "This thing's been bugging me all day. I've always thought that dreams could be prophetic, and I think I had one last night. Maybe it means something."

"No, no thank you. I don't want to hear it. Listening to other people's dreams is as boring as watching paint dry."

"No, no, really Joe. I need this. Please."

"Okay, but if you start being a drip, I'm moving on."

"Last night, I dreamt…I dreamt of a barren wasteland. An apocalyptic hellscape. Of a warrior on the road, a burnt-out shell of man. Maybe he's demonic, maybe it's just his nature. A traveler like yourself. Searching the desert wilderness for meaning and for fuel. But he happens upon this settlement out in the middle of nowhere, isolated like everything in this calamitous future. And there he finds meaning, as this settlement is attacked day in and day out by a roving gang of marauders. In trying to save this group, this replacement family, he befriends this kid, feral, wild. And suddenly he's not alone anymore. Joe, what do you…what do you think it all means?"

Joe paused, clearly thinking about this dynamic Delphian vision of the future and the latent psychic powers I must have.

"I think it means you fell asleep watching one too many Mel Gibson flicks. That's the plot to *The Road Warrior*. The first one's better if ya ask me."

"Huh." I shifted on my wooden stool. It was uneven and kept rocking back and forth.

"Is that all that's on your mind, kid? There's got to be more you want to talk about."

My mind, clouded with alcohol, thought of the horrors I'd seen the other day, after meeting Vanessa. The shadow figures. Bones stripped clean, like bodies dumped into a muddy pig sty.

"Yeah, I got something else. You're a smart man. You know a lot about a lot. You know anything about shadows that eat people?"

"Ah, you're in to some supernatural thoughts? Interested in the paranormal?" Joe replied, like I had asked a totally normal question. But Joe was used to the lunatic ravings of alcoholic rumpots in these parts.

"You could say it's been a slow business for me lately," I said, not wanting to tell Joe the truth. "My mind's been on other things."

"I mean, yeah, I've heard a bit about shadow figures. The *black mass*. Dark mist. Beings that light kind of just evades. There's a few things in folklore about them. Cherokee legend believes it's the spirit of dead Native Americans come back to prey upon the living. Unfinished business and what have you. Sort of like their version of Purgatory. Maybe it's that they have to redeem themselves before moving on. Maybe it's that these Cherokee refuse to move on to the next plane of existence."

"Where'd you learn all this? Spent some time with the Cherokee in your younger days?"

"No," he said. "Wikipedia."

"Ah. And you believe this folklore?"

"Can't say for sure. Never saw these dark mist figures myself. But you know the old saying: there are more things in Heaven and Earth than are dreamt of in your philosophy."

Joe poured two shots of whiskey. He plopped one in front of me and held the other. We clinked and downed them, toasting silently.

"That said," he continued after a moment of coughing, "some say it's just a psychological condition. Sleep paralysis. Something that affects 5% of people regularly, but anyone can experience it. A dysfunction of the REM cycle. Right on the edge of waking life and sleeping. People tend to hallucinate and can see things that ain't necessarily there. These figures approaching them while the victims are laying in bed. Maybe sitting at the edge of the bed frame. Maybe crouching over the person hallucinating. Sitting on their chest. Any of that kind of creepy atmospheric stuff."

"And you think these…these things are cannibalistic?"

"Cannibalistic? Only if you consider them human, right?" His voice was barely above a whisper now, almost conspiratorial—like we were talking about the JFK assassination or Stanley Kubrick filming a fake moon landing or the Flat-Earth theory or, well, shadow creatures that eat people. He continued, "But kid, I don't know. I just don't know. Beings that exist on the edge of your peripheral vision and that consume humans? Stranger things have been known to happen. Like you finally paying your tab." He tapped his fingers on the bar in front of me.

"Maybe when you get any quality alcohol in here," I said. "Or when you send some mafia enforcer after me to break my legs."

He laughed. I smelled the alcohol on his breath. Or was that my breath?

"Want me to call you a cab, Tracer?"

"No, that's alright. I'll walk home. The air'll do me good. Or do me in." I threw down some cash on the bar and walked out.

The temperature difference between the air-conditioned bar and the balmy New York night made me pause. It was muggier than a mug. I began perspiring, my sweat clinging to me like the condensation on the drinks I just had. The acrid smell from my pores betrayed me—my sweat was more liquor than water at this point. I shook my head, chastising myself for drinking so much. I needed to take myself down a peg and a shower.

I rolled up the sleeves on the hoodie, hoping that would alleviate some of my body heat. The curving lips of the Rolling Stones logo seemed to mock me. The tongue stuck out, giving me a silent raspberry. I stuck my hands in the front pockets and cursed.

I turned down an alley, a shortcut between The Hole in the Wall and my apartment. I had the drunken stride of a pirate power walker— you know, because their wooden peg leg would be all uneven, especially when walking briskly? I wonder if that's why they always have a parrot on their shoulders, to balance themselves out.

In the lonely street, with only the dull bricks of the buildings as my friends, I was hit with a thought. That thought was "ow," because I was also hit with the butt of a gun. I fell forward, spilling onto the pavement.

"Sorry," a voice from behind me said. "That was supposed to knock you unconscious."

"Well, it didn't." I turned around, rubbing the back of my skull, still lying on the concrete. Two men had snuck up on me. The taller one had a pistol in his hand, having just used it to give me a concussion. "If you ruined my hoodie, you're going to pay for it. I just got it a couple hours ago, damnit."

"I said I was sorry."

"I don't accept. I mean what kind of man does that?"

"We're bad guys. Hired henchmen." His voice was reedy and nervous.

"Henchmen? No thank you. I've had my fair share of your kind lately." I thought for a second about who would hire some punks to hurt me. "Wait, did Joe actually hire you to shake me down? That was just a joke."

"Who's Joe?" the main guy asked the silent one behind him.

The quiet goon just shrugged, his tight red jeans rustling with the movement.

"Oh wait," the same guy said, "We should make sure this is who we're sent here for. What's your name, pal?" he asked me.

"The name's Tracer Spence. My friends call me Tracer Spence," I said. "Never was one for nicknames, really."

"Yep. You're who we're here for. Well, whatever, I guess. Just come on, we're supposed to kidnap you. Follow us," the taller one said, waving his gun haphazardly, indicating I was supposed to follow him. He had a lumberjack's beard and a lumberjack's plaid button-down shirt. However, this was the city which was a dead giveaway that he wasn't a lumberjack.

I should say that I went with them because it was a good lead and that I was just playing the hand I was dealt. I should say that. But in reality, I followed because I was still pretty drunk and didn't want to be lonely in my apartment.

"Oh, I almost forgot," my captor said, "close your eyes. Please and thank you."

"Close my eyes?"

"Yeah, you're supposed to be blindfolded as we bring you to our secret hideout. But we didn't have the blindfold ready. So, you'll just have to make due."

"How am I supposed to follow you with my eyes closed?"

That stopped the two of them in their tracks.

"Huh. Well…fine, then. Keep 'em open. But if anyone asks you, be sure to tell 'em we blindfolded you."

19

The talkative captor looked around the hallway, checking to see if we were followed, before rapping on an apartment door.

KNOCK. KNOCK-KNOCK KNOCK. KNOCK.

"Secret code," he said to me. "So our roomma—I mean, business partner—knows it's us on the other end. Real professional of us. Got to have a secret code."

"What's the password?" A woman's voice said muffled from the other side of the door.

"The glass key," the guy said in reply. He turned back to me, elbowed my side, and said, "See? Even have a two-step form of identification validation. We did our homework."

It was a real swanky place they led me too. Swanky by my standards anyway. It was an apartment with an actual lock on the door! Not just propped closed by a wooden chair balanced under the door knob. The living room was carpeted wall to wall, and there was even a recessed area in the middle where a love seat and an L-shaped sectional were placed. And there was central air conditioning! I didn't even think New York City apartments came with AC. Hell, I couldn't remember the last time I cooled off my own place without pouring ice cubes into a plastic kiddie pool.

"Nice place you guys got here," I said. "Any rooms available in the building? I've been in the market for another place for, oh, seven years now."

The woman answered me. "Ah, this whole place is rent-controlled. I could ask the landlord though? Put in a good word? My name's Ruth." She was an attractive twenty-something, with her bright red hair pulled back into a tight bun. She shook my hand, her soft skin giving off a faint vanilla scent.

"Ruth! We said no names!"

"Oh, right, sorry. Sorry. Never mind. My name's not Ruth. It's something else. Uh… Linda. Always wanted to be a Linda." She walked down to the love seat, picking up some needles and thread that were left on the cream-colored cushions. "Do you guys still need the blindfold? I'm almost done making it."

"Well, keep at it, Ruthie…err, Linda. We don't need it now, but maybe in the future."

Ruth/Linda nodded and said, "I may have went too big with it now. But I suppose you could use it as a scarf as well if I keep going." She sat on the love seat and kept working on her crocheted blindfold.

Behind Ruth/Linda were three large windows, with flowing curtains hanging down to the floor. Any time a good detective enters a room, he needs to be aware of all entrances and exits, in the case he needs to make a quick getaway. One of these windows could be said getaway for me. If things got bad, maybe my three captors would huddle up, discussing their game plan, and they'd leave me unguarded. We were on the eighth floor, so leaving through the window would be tricky. But I could make a rope out of sheets in, like, eleven minutes if I rushed.

But for now, I'd wait to see how things played out.

"So, Mr. Tracer, please sit," the main kidnapper said to me. He tugged at the end of his beard. "Would you like a drink?" he asked, opening up the fridge. He pulled out a white carton of orange juice.

After the other night, I had had enough of orange juice to last me a lifetime, and fearing it to be poisoned, I said, "No. I like my OJ like I like my fiction—pulpy." This wasn't true, but in my business you had to know when to lie. These hoodlums would never find out that I despised pulp, that I thought it should be annihilated from the face of the Earth, because seriously, who drinks any liquid with slimy chunks of debris floating around in it? And they would never find out that the last time I read for fun was the back of a cereal box. Those riddles that Kellogg's publishes are tough.

Still though, I kind of wished I had taken up his offer of a drink. All of that alcohol earlier had dried me out.

Walking to the sofa, I plopped down. Everything seemed to be going alright so far, at least to my still inebriated self. But much like the *Titanic,* I had a sinking feeling—and only part of that was how the cushion warped around my body.

"So, who do you all work for? You kidnapped me. Now tell me why."

Everyone stayed silent. Even the silent captor who hadn't said a word yet all night.

"Um. No one? No one at all." Ruth/Linda said. She continued weaving her garment and her lies.

"No one, huh? Well, in that case I'll be off." I started to stand.

"Now, hold on, friend-o," the main guy said to me, pushing me back down to the couch. "We don't know their name. They only identified themselves as W.B."

I searched my brain vault for anything that "W.B." could possibly stand for. Like every great detective, I store all information in what I call a brain vault. You might call it "memories," but the difference is mine sounds way cooler.

I felt like I had ran across the initials at some point, recently.

"W.B.? Like Warner Brothers?" This made sense to me. Carly Simon had signed with Warner Bros. Records in the '80s. Maybe this nefarious record label was trying to keep a secret a secret. "So, that would make you Yakko, Wakko, and Dot."

The three of them stared at me with blank expressions on their faces.

"*The Animaniacs?* The cartoon from the '90s? *Hellllloooooo, nurse?* Nothing?"

"Oh, is that the cartoon about the rabbits? I think that's a little before our time," Ruth/Linda/Dot said, shrugging her shoulders as if she were sorry I was so ancient compared to them.

"Look, Mr. Spence," Yakko (the tall, talkative one) said, "We have to move on. We've got a job to do. Supposed to question you and see what you know. And if you're—what's the word he used? Reluctant? Resistant? Whatever—and if you're resistant, my associates and I are supposed to get it out of you any way we can." He indicated the quiet Wakko and Ruth/Linda/Dot. "That means torture, if you hadn't inferred it."

"I got it, thanks," I said. "So, what, Wakko over there…he's supposed to be a silent enforcer or something? He hasn't said anything all night."

"He's taken a vow of silence actually. As a form of protest. Against Burger King and their evil corporate practices."

"Why? What did they do?"

"He thinks they're implementing anti-democratic ideals, trying to stir up support for monarchist tendencies. Why's it got to be the Burger King and not the Burger President? Who put him into power? And all that stuff. He's very politically motivated with his personal life, and Ruth…err, Linda and I do our best to support him with that."

"How very virtuous of all of you. How long's his vow of silence gone on?"

"Nearly five hours now," Ruth/Linda/Dot said. "We're very proud of him. You've got to have principles to stand on, I always say."

"Sure, sure. What else is there to stand on, otherwise?" I leaned back into the couch, letting it caress me like a masseuse with corduroy hands. "You three don't seem like the type to be mixed up in something like this. What're you—all college students?"

"Yeah!" Yakko said. "Actually, we were told this could be considered an internship in lieu of college credits. And you know how it is out there right now—you need some sort of experience even for an entry level position. But let's get down to brass tacks. What do you know, Mr. Spence?"

"I think you're going to need to be a bit more specific."

"Playing hardball, huh? This isn't going to end well for you."

"No, I'm not. I know a lot of stuff. I could recite the theme song to *Boy Meets World*, if you want. I could list all fifty states, if you give me hints along the way. I just don't know what you're asking me about, specifically."

"Actually, could I change my name to Lena? I like the way that one rolls of the tongue more," Ruth/Linda/Dot/Lena said.

"Mr. Spence, help us help you. You're working on a case, and our employer needs to know what you know. That's all there is to it."

Wakko cracked his knuckles behind my ear.

"Keep doing that, and you'll end up with arthritis, you know?" I turned back to Yakko, and said, "I'm a busy guy. Working a lot of cases for a lot of people. What say we just call it a night now? I leave, and you go back to your employer saying I didn't tell you nothin'? Actually…that would help spread the word around that I can withstand intense questioning. I could see a big increase in jobs. People like their private detectives to be good under pressure like that. Not some wimp that breaks down and cries anytime an authority figure looks at them with a stern face."

I paused, looking around at the three kidnappers.

"Not that I do that. Just a hypothetical."

"Hypothetical?" the girl asked. "Oh, wait, I remember that from Intro to Geometry. That's the longest side of a right-angled triangle." She bobbed her head, seemingly pleased with herself.

Yakko ran his fingers through his dark beard and ignored her.

"Mr. Spence, I'm afraid if you don't tell us anything about this Carly Simon case, we're gonna have to get rough with you. I've got some torture ideas that I'm just itching to try out."

"You do?" Ruth/Linda/Dot/Lena asked.

"Yeah…I didn't want to go into this job without any know-how," he turned and said to her. "Like just yesterday, I was practicing waterboarding on my full-body Anime pillow."

I sniggered like Muttley, Dick Dastardly's dog sidekick.

"Don't laugh!" Yakko said to me. "How dare you yuck my yum! They're called dakimakuras, and they're very socially acceptable now!"

"I'm sure they are. But torturing a human is different than something stuffed with feathers."

"Actually, she's stuffed with 100% polyester. Shows how much you know, Mr. P.I."

"I'm not sure I want to waterboard him," Ruth/Linda/Dot/Lena said. She twirled her red hair between two delicate fingers, a maneuver that would have plenty of hot-blooded men frothing at the mouth. I wondered if that was something women like her learned or it was intrinsic. "Isn't that kind of barbaric? I don't want to violate the Godiva convention or anything."

"Geneva," I said.

"No, I'm pretty sure Geneva is from King Arthur times."

"Ruth…errr, Linda…Lena, I don't think we'd be breaking international laws or anything with waterboarding. I still think the U.S. is undecided on if it counts as torture or not," Yakko said.

The girl pouted. This was the practiced coquettish gaze of someone used to getting others to write term papers with no fight.

"But, if it means that much to you, I suppose we can try something different," Yakko relented.

"So, that settles that then," I said. "No torture for me."

"Relax, Mr. Spence. We'll figure it out. This is a safe space, and all ideas are welcome."

"I like my idea of no torture. But I respect the creative process. There are no wrong answers in a brainstorming session."

"What about having him drawn and quartered?" Ruth/Linda/Dot/Lena suggested. "That gives us the benefit of petting some horses too."

"I'm not sure, Ruthie. Where are we supposed to find horses?"

"They've got them over in Central Park, right? Those carriage thingies?"

"The hansom cab rides?" Yakko said. "Where do you picture this drawing and quartering taking place?"

"Well…" She looked up to the ceiling and absentmindedly stuck her tongue out. "I think it would have to be in here. We can't risk anyone else see us. So, we just tie up each of his limbs. We can use my yarn! It's stronger than you'd think. I've got a big stockpile of it in the other room I can go get. And then, each section of Mr. Spence gets tied to a horse. So, we'd have four horses. After it's done, and we learn what we need to from him, we can hang out with the horses and return them in a few days."

"This apartment wouldn't be big enough for one horse, let alone four."

"You never like my ideas!" The girl pounded her fists on the arms of the love seat.

"I just want to make sure we do everything right. We need to be by-the-book on this."

"Who even put you in charge? It's just like that time during Spring Break when you made the itinerary for everyone and we wound up in Idaho, on a historical tour of steamboat traffic over at lake Coeur d'Alene! We all said we wanted to go to Santa Catalina! But noooooooo, Mr. Big Shot had to book us for the most boring trip ever."

"You…you…you Judas! You said you loved that trip!"

"No one loved that trip. Worst vacation I've ever been on."

"I think you three are doing a bang-up job," I said, trying to build their confidence back up. I hated seeing confrontation among friends, tearing them apart. "Really. Just top-drawer. I'd be proud of you guys if I were your employer."

"Thank you," Yakko and Ruth/Linda/Dot/Lena/Judas said at the same time.

"Now, the two of you need to apologize and make up. Let me give you some advice: your job should never get in the way of your personal friendships."

Sheepishly, they both apologized.

After a few minutes of awkward silence, Wakko began waving his arms wildly around. He was either imitating a pigeon, trying to swat a pesky mosquito, or trying to get the attention of the others. He looked like an epileptic octopus, except he only had two limbs instead of eight and I doubted he could breathe underwater. There was no way to be sure of that last one though.

"What is it?" Yakko asks. "You have an idea? A good one? Yeah? Alright, let's hear it."

Wakko nodded.

What happened next was the worst game of charades I'd ever witnessed or been a part of. And that's including the game of charades that ended with my father stabbing my thigh with a 12-inch BBQ fork. But it was my fault for not being able to guess *Close Encounters of the Third Kind*. My father has always stated that turned into his favorite family get-together in the years since.

Wakko stomped around the apartment like a dinosaur with steel-toed boots on. He moved his arms in definitive motions, sometimes shaking them violently and sometimes pulling something invisible towards his torso. His head rocked back and forth, and I was worried he'd give himself whiplash with the way his neck was snapping. For someone who had taken a vow of silence, I was surprised by just how terrible he was at communicating through movement.

Not that the other two were any better at guessing.

Yakko didn't even understand that holding up two fingers meant "two words." Or that pulling on your earlobe meant "sounds like." Ruth/Linda/Dot/Lena/Judas repeatedly called out "Melissa McCarthy's character in *Gilmore Girls!*" As if guessing that over and over again would somehow change what Wakko was trying to say. And she wasn't even guessing the character's name. I just wanted to yell at her *Sookie St. James!* But I wouldn't tip my hand that I watched the *Gilmore Girls*. A man's got to have some dignity, and I wanted these youths to think I was cool.

I also refrained from pointing out to the group that Wakko could easily write down what he wanted to say on a piece of paper or on the magnetic white board hanging up on their fridge.

It was a solid twenty minutes of this, and I was developing a migraine. Wakko was visibly sweating, his perspiration blotting on his forehead, near his widow's peak. I felt bad for the kid, even if he wasn't helping himself. At a certain point he was going to break down crying, moving his hands through the air in a zig-zag motion.

I couldn't help myself.

"It's 'electric shock.' He's trying to say to electrocute me, damnit. How are you two not understanding? He's moving his hands like a lightning bolt and then pretending to be in an electric chair! It's so simple!"

Realization dawned on Yakko, and his face lit up like a hand-drawn picture of the sun, only without the cartoon sunglasses.

"Ohhhhh," Yakko said. "So, when he was opening his fingers upside down, that was indicating a fork in an outlet. I get it, now."

"I still think it was the *Gilmore Girls* thing, if I'm being honest."

"You know what? Electrocution is as good an idea as any we've had. Go for it, broski. I'll let you do the honors," Yakko said to Wakko.

How were they going to do this, I wondered. Did they have an actual, working electric chair? Were they going to just rip some wires out of a wall? Hook me up to some electrodes—whatever they were— and turn up a menacing-looking dial? How much would I be able to withstand?

My mind raced with these questions, just like the old Adam West *Batman* series. The narrator would close out the episode, just as Batman and/or Robin were being lowered into some vat of green acid, and the audience would be left on a cliff hanger, worrying about their intrepid super heroes. Until next week: Same Bat Time, Same Bat Channel.

20

Wakko took off his shoes. This was unexpected. This was unprecedented. This was unseemly. I mean, it's one thing to take off your shoes in the privacy of your own house, but with guests? What a terrible host this kidnapper was.

He wore argyle socks, checkered in bright colors of yellow, baby blue, forest green. His right big toe stuck out of a large hole. It was bulbous and hairy, like Fred Flintsone mixed with a hobbit. And the bottoms of his socks were filthy. Darkened with dirt, they were in desperate need of a wash or a full-on Exorcism. I know I shouldn't judge people based off of what socks they wore, but I knew in that moment I could never be friends with this monster.

He hopped down into the recessed section of the living room and placed his hands on my shoulders. He held eye contact with me, as he held me captive. His irises exuded pure evil, if evil was some Bushwick hipster with horn-rimmed eyeglasses.

"Do your worst," I said to him, hoping it sounded cool.

"Gladly," he said, and the other two audibly gasped.

I had to admit it—he out-cooled me. Staying silent all day then dropping that bombshell? How could I even compete? I shouldn't even try to, is the answer. Of course, I realized that in retrospect because I did try to one-up him, and I totally failed.

I said, "I double dog dare you," and immediately regretted it.

Wakko started shuffling around me and the sofa, never lifting his feet off the carpet. I could feel his eyes burrow into the back of my skull like some kind of animal that burrows into the ground. Like, uhhh, a squirrel that digs, only slightly fatter though. Like a walrus. Or a hog. A fat squirrel hog that tunnels itself into the ground. Only the ground being my skull and the animal being his eyes.

I could hear the carpet rasp against his socks. The fibers of both *scratch scratch scratching* against each other. It was making me itch just thinking about it. If this was the torture he was going for, it was working.

He circled me four times over. A buzzard flying over some carrion, waiting for roadkill to expire. Lucky for me, the only thing about to expire was my parking meter. I had found a great spot in front of my apartment back in 2010, and I wasn't about to let real estate like that go to waste. But I did need to feed the meter within the next twenty minutes. I hoped this whole torture thing didn't take too long. I'd hate to have my 2001 Kia Optima towed. I didn't trust New York City tow trucks not to scrape the light baby blue paint job. Who knows if that would buff out?

"It's time," Wakko whispered.

He stuck out his index finger. It stuck out like a sore thumb. He inched closer and closer to my body, never once lifting his socks off of the carpet.

SCRATCH SCRATCH SCRATCH.

He touched my chest.

ZAP.

Static electricity ran through me like the Energizer Bunny. Even with the lights on, the charge was big enough to see a flash as the connection was made. It hurt. The pain was searing—I was his London broil, and his finger was a charcoal grill set to high. The electrocution was so powerful, even my sweatshirt began to smoke.

I didn't think I could withstand another shock like that.

"You've…you've got a real talent there," I said through gasping breaths. I rubbed my chest. He may have given me a third-degree burn while giving me the third degree. "Ever think about becoming a psychiatrist? Your shock therapy could cure wonders."

"Funny guy." He rubbed his hands together. "Tell us what you know, or there's more coming to ya."

"Try me again. You might just jolt something out of me next time."

He called my bluff. Big time. This go-around, Wakko shuffled along the carpet around the sofa for five minutes straight. I know five minutes doesn't seem like a long time, but you try sitting still while everyone's quiet and a psychopath tracks an oval path around you. Five minutes seems like an eternity in that case.

There was nothing I could do, except sit there and wait. Sure, they hadn't tied me up or anything. But I didn't want to be impolite. I was their guest.

Wakko stopped in front of me. His voice was a rasp. "You sure you want to do this?"

I simply nodded.

"I can't look!" Ruth/Linda/Dot/Lena/Judas buried her face in her arms. I was proud of the courage that she showed until this point.

Wakko extended his finger again. I could see up close that he had a crick in his knuckle, but his fingernails were very well-manicured. I'd have to ask where he got them done. My motto was: *you've got to treat yourself every so often.* I also had another motto: *leave no stone unturned, except for pebbles because they were too small to hide clues.* And actually, my main motto was: *a motto for every situation.*

It's a damn shame I didn't have one for the circumstance I found myself in now. I'd have to create one. Maybe something like: *never follow two kidnappers into their apartment and allow them to torture you, but if you do, make sure you definitely get the orange juice that they offer you, otherwise you're going to be parched while they're electrocuting you.*

I licked my lips. They were cracked and dry. His finger kept inching closer, accusatorily.

"Didn't your mama ever tell you it's rude to point?"

ZAP.

He nailed me in the same exact spot as before. I cried out in pain. I smelled burnt toast.

My vision flickered. Either the torture was too much and it was affecting my ocular system, or the lights in their apartment had gotten dim. Was his static electricity affecting the wiring in their apartment? I'm no science doctor, so I couldn't refute my theory.

"Talk. Now. Tell us everything."

"Everything?" I could barely lift my head up, and it felt like two anvils were tied to my eyelids.

"Everything."

"Okay. Okay," I said. "I believe in ghosts, but only because they keep rewinding my VHS tapes after I fall asleep. I put my shoes on before my pants. I think chipmunks are a type of lizard. I'm aware people say they're related to squirrels, but I don't buy it."

"Why are you telling us this stu—wait, before your pants, you said? Why? That's heinous."

"I like the challenge. It's almost like a puzzle, you know?"

"Okay. Fine. What's this got to do with anything though?"

"You're the one who said to tell you everything." I was being obstinate.

"That's not what I meant."

The torture and the exhaustion of binge-drinking all night were getting to me. My sight was growing darker. Shadows extended along the walls. Outlines of tendrils, of creeping limbs reached out onto the carpeted floor. I looked to find what lamp or chair or whatever would've been creating these silhouettes and found nothing. That's when I realized it wasn't my eyes imagining these illusions.

It was my shade warrior stalkers. They found me again. They were here.

I looked behind me. Yakko and the dame hadn't said anything in a while. They were gone. Vanished. Darkness had fallen behind the sofa. Wakko and I had been so engaged in each other, we hadn't even noticed they were disappeared. There hadn't been a scream. There hadn't been a yelp. There hadn't been a nothing.

I shivered. I knew their fate. They didn't deserve it. They may have kidnapped me, hit me with the butt of a gun, and threatened to torture me, but they didn't deserve it.

Wakko followed my eyes and realized his friends weren't there. "Guys? Guys?" Wakko called out. He wandered around the floor, looking for them. He bumped into an arched brass floor lamp, which shook in its spot. The vibration of it played even more tricks of the light, as shadows danced around every corner. Wakko was just like a lost puppy, searching for its owner who just left to go grab a carton of milk from the grocery store. He was confused, and why shouldn't he be? Who would expect an unseen cosmic entity to have eaten his friends?

After a few moments of his eyes darting around the edges of the apartment, he stopped in front of me. He had no words, but not for the same reasons as earlier. His face was contorted in alarm. Panic. He looked at me. All the animosity between us melted away. He wanted— needed—help, just someone to explain what had happened to his friends. What was happening to him. What was going on.

"I—" was all he got out before he, too, was taken.

Slithering tentacles of darkness had wrapped around Wakko's limbs. They bent in ways not even yoga instructors could manage, all right angles perpendicular to his spinal cord. The tentacles pulled him back, lifting him off the ground, ripping him like he was a lawn mower cord and they were starting the engine.

Again, no screams. No shrieks. Just silence.

And then, just like that, the darkness lifted. It receded into the corners of the room, a balding hair line sped up. All that was left of my kidnappers were three piles of viscera and bones. A mess of heaping body parts, oozing and sliming the stained carpet.

I needed coffee. Enough coffee to keep me awake for hopefully the rest of my life so I'd never have nightmares about tonight. Enough coffee to make a woodpecker's heart explode. Normally, I'd drink my coffee black. Today—this morning—I was going to put enough cream in it to make it as light as possible. Enough cream so that when I stirred it, there'd be clouds in my coffee.

21

Follow the money.

The next day, my mind kept returning to what Keith Richards had said to me.

Follow the money. I sat in my office ruminating on these words. My office, my home base. Police tape finally taken down. Moby the Mollusk by my side as always. Bare brick walls surrounding me. Window behind me, light shining in, making my shadow grow long across my desk and segmented onto the floor. *Follow the money,* he said. Keith Richards, one of the richest men out there, told me to follow the money. As I sat quietly, thinking my plan through, I came to one conclusion.

I had no idea what "follow the money" meant.

It was a sweet nothing, something to whisper in your sex partner's ear after making tender love above them. It was a lie they would quietly speak, tickling the bristles of your ear hole, making you giggle until you realize you never actually heard what they said. Then you have to ask them to repeat it. Which makes the moment fade as they say, slightly louder this time, "Can you move over? You're crushing my hand."

Follow the money.

I'm used to following suspects. You know, *actual* people with arms and limbs and legs and movements. Well, okay, not *actual* actual people. Digital actual people from video games. Those missions where you have to stay close behind perps as they lead you to the bigger bad—but not too close! Otherwise they may spot you! And not too far away either, otherwise you'll lose them. Video games are a great detective's tool. Taught me everything I know about tailing someone. Not even real life experience is that good of an instructor. Real life doesn't have the text boxes that pop up to explain the controls. And if the IRS ever comes calling, that's the justification I'll give why *Murder Spree 7: Detective KillPunch's Revenge* is the perfect tax write-off.

Follow the money. Follow the money.

Now, I know what you're thinking. You're thinking *Tracer, follow the money means to look into bank accounts and transfers and to literally see where money has been paid and spent.* I know you're thinking this because you're an artificial construct of my mind, and I'm making you think this. You're also thinking *You're so damn good-looking, Tracer. Just downright sexy. And adorable to boot! You're like a kitten with six-pack abs.* Thank you. I appreciate that. You're too kind.

But back to the money thing…I'm no idiot. I've seen movies and TV shows. I know about wire transfers and off-shore accounts and Swiss banks and tax shelters. I know I've *heard* of those things. But guess what, guys—I don't have any experience with that stuff. I'm not a hacker, typing away super-fast at five keyboards, tracing this stuff to local coordinates. The heavy typewriter sitting on my desk is a testament to my computer literacy. And if you think I trust banks enough to even have a checking account, you're crazier than I thought. Banks are nothing but government-sanctioned sleazy motels for your money to stay at while the cheap prostitutes out front babysit you because your father can't be bothered to drop you off at a friend's house. I'd rather throw my money away than let those repulsive bankers get their grubby little hands all over it, sliming it up with whatever inhuman mucous membrane is covering their fingers.

Which gave me an idea…

I opened the window behind my desk, the frame sliding up with a CLUNK. I also slid the brown, moldy screen up as well and scared away the birds that held their meetings on the ledge there. Pulling out my wallet, I grabbed a hundred-dollar bill. I was going to go with a one, but there are probably thousands of Washingtons just littering the streets of New York. How could I tell which one was mine? I thought of the two-dollar bill I had as well, but that was my lucky money that I refused to spend.

I tossed the hundred out the window.

Don't give me that look. What better way to follow the money than to literally follow the money? It made perfect sense. And it's not like I just crumpled up the hundred and chucked it. No, I made preparations.

I turned it into a paper airplane.

There's a real artistry to crafting a paper airplane. Your folds must be crisp and neat. The nose must come to a perfect point, not just a flat, crooked thing like a witch pre-plastic surgery. And the wings need to have the correct ratio in accordance with the body proportions. Most important is the paper…you'd be surprised how many people overlook the paper part of a paper airplane. But, duh. Come on. That's obvious. Most amateurs will use regular copy paper, but I prefer a lighter weight paper. A4, maybe A3 if I'm feeling saucy. You should also let the paper sit for an hour beforehand, so it becomes accustomed to the moisture level of the room. But that's all basic 101 stuff.

My hundred-dollar bill paper airplane obviously didn't meet my standards. The cotton/linen composure doesn't make for the most suitable of flying conditions. But under the situation, I was pretty dang proud of it. I named it *Bold Boy.*

And man did *Bold Boy* soar.

I envisioned myself as the pilot, a World War I flying ace. Green helmet snugged tightly around my head, big aviator goggles keeping the dust out of my eyes. A machine gun was welded onto *Bold Boy.* Trusty weapon that it was, it saw me through so many dogfights. Those damn Krauts always on my tail. But this mission…this mission was different. I'd be going up against my nemesis, The Red Baron. Never taken down by any in the allied forces, The Red Baron represented the best of the best of the German air force. I'd been lucky so far, being forced out of a few fights with him, retreating while licking my wounds, but never anything too serious. This time though, I had my flying partner with me. Woodstock, a small, yellow bird…

Damnit. I realized I had been getting my life confused with Snoopy's again.

I came out of my reverie, just in time to watch *Bold Boy* soar across the back alley that my view looks out on. Just when it was about to hit the opposite brick wall, a gust of wind took it toward the main street.

I booked it out of my office, which is to say I tripped over a pile of library books I kept under the front right leg of my desk. It's wobbly. And putting a matchbook underneath won't do much help. I'd probably need like 5 million matchbooks. The leg to the desk is so much shorter than the others that most of the leg is made up of library books, to be completely honest. I'm not sure how that came to be. I blame the Swedish instruction booklet that got me all turned-around when I was putting the desk together. So yes, I use library books to prop it up. I'm not going to use my *own* books. Every week, I return a few and check a few more out, so I don't incur the wrath of those petty librarians and their 15 cent fines. Don't worry, it looks very professional as I only use titles related to detecting. *Sherlock Holmes, The Maltese Falcon, Eat Pray Love.*

Crashing onto my wooden floor, I tucked and rolled James Bond-style. It was super cool and badass. I wish someone was there to see it. Not even Moby was watching. Stupid slug.

I took the steps two at a time, which wasn't difficult considering my office was on the first floor and there were only six steps.

Turning towards the street, I glanced at *Bold Boy* floating leisurely across the lanes of traffic, like a 13-year-old boy in bright yellow swim trunks going 'round the local water park's lazy river for the twentieth time. All because their father drove off without the boy, "forgetting" they came together. Even though it was only the two of them that went together.

Nonetheless, I darted between angry cabbies and bicycle messengers and out-of-towners stuck on this aggressive New York City street. I leapt between them, emulating one of my childhood heroes: Frogger. That green frog was the closest thing I had to a role model. He was fearless. He was driven. He was cold-blooded. He was everything I ever wanted to be. As the driver of a black limousine yelled obscenities my way, I could only think about how proud I must've been making Frogger. I hoped he looked down on me from his place up in Digital Amphibian Heaven and smiled.

Can frogs smile? I made a mental note to look that up later.

Either way, I made it to the other side of the street, relatively unscathed. *Bold Boy* had arrived safely on its landing strip: a New York City sidewalk in front of a hot dog vendor. I stood for a few minutes watching as throngs of people walked around the hundred-dollar bill. Makes sense. This is the city. If you stop for even a second—to pick up some loose change, to tie your shoe, to hail a taxi—the savage pedestrians around you will trample right over you, swallowing you up like some tasty pizza slice from Tony's on Knickerbocker over in Bushwick. The city is unforgiving. I had personal experience. In fact, at that moment as I was stopped watching my money, I was bumped into by no less than, like, conservatively 2000 people. I was being pushed further and further away from *Bold Boy.*

I watched in horror as dozens of people stepped on my paper airplane, crumpling it into a misshapen mess. There was nothing I could do to even stop it, being jostled by the city's unfeeling pedestrians. Much like that music video from the '90s about that Sinead O'Connor lady who was upset about walking around creepy statues in parks, a single tear ran down my cheeks. RIP *Bold Boy.* You lived a fruitful life.

Luckily, before I lost sight of the money, a passerby bent down and pocketed my hundred-dollar bill. He was wearing a red, puffy vest and a black baseball hat with no words or logo on it. This was going to be easy to follow him; baseball caps with no words on them were so rare. Where does one even find something like that? This was going to be a walk in the park. Literally, since he led me through all four acres of Bryant Park. I tailed him for an hour and a half in the park, 43 minutes of which was watching him play a single chess game with an acquaintance.

And then the bastard lost the game. He handed my crumpled up money to his opponent. Who plays high stakes chess games in a city park? Only a monster, that's who. I was glad to no longer be following this degenerate gambler.

Instead, I now followed his acquaintance around. An older gentleman, gray hair but still thick—good for him! At his age? If only we could all have his genetics. He wore a dusty, brown trench coat. That was a dead giveaway. He was certainly a member of the New York City underground Mafioso. Only two types of people wore trench coats: Italian mafia types and private detectives like myself. Only, I'd never be caught dead in one so dusty. I considered myself a fashionista.

Therefore, by process of elimination, the man had to be an underground criminal. Or a stripper, pre-act of stripping. I suppose they were known for wearing trench coats too. And those weird Goth kids I always saw hanging outside of the mall, listening to The Cure on their cell phones. They sometimes dressed in trench coats. And how could I forget Harpo Marx! Possibly the most famous trench coat-wearer in all of history. Oh, flashers too—but maybe they were already covered under the "stripper" category. Were they technically considered strippers? I wonder where the line was drawn between strippers and flashers? Is it intent? Surroundings? Do strippers have certifications or licenses?

So really, sixish types of people wore trench coats.

It was my job to follow him, no matter which one he was. I was really hoping he was Harpo though. I wondered if the man had any comedy props stuffed in his oversized pockets, like a candle burning at both ends or a lit blowtorch. But my money, literally, was on mafioso.

To be fair, he didn't make it easy to follow him. He stayed in Bryant Park for another two and a half hours playing chess against random people. Man, was I bored. I never even understood the rules of chess, so it's not like I could even follow along with the games.

I put the hood up on my Rolling Stones sweatshirt, now peppered in dirt and blood from the night before. And peppered in pepper from my eggs benedict this morning. I couldn't risk my tail making me. I didn't want any other looky-loos that may be lurking around sniffing me out, and the hood would give me appropriate cover. I still felt guilty over how things ended with me and Vanessa, and wearing the sweatshirt was my way of grieving, I suppose. Plus, now with the bonus of espionage concealment, it was a tactical garment as well.

The older gentleman didn't lose a single game. Flush with cash, he exited the park and wandered down to the Port Authority bus station. I, of course, followed. For the first few blocks, I became paranoid with the sound of my sneakers slapping against the sidewalk pavement. It was so loud. So, I changed to walking on my tippy toes.

If you've ever been in the Port Authority, you know it's basically the definition of the word "drab." Light brown tile floors. Fluorescent lights beaming off of smudged metal railings. If a man wanted to disappear into his surroundings, here was the place to do it. But I was going to make sure that didn't happen; I'd be on him like a fly on rice.

At the bus station, my tail met up with one of his friends. They shook hands, and I was immediately wary of this new feller. Anyone who was friendly with this older gentleman I was following must've been up to no good. They got in line to buy tickets and afterwards sat down in the waiting area.

I knew I had to keep following. So I also got in line. When I reached the counter, a cashier in her twenties with frazzled hair greeted me. Her voice was so monotone that you'd get confused between her and the voicemail lady, even standing in front of the cashier, watching her mouth move. Before I could even say hello back, she asked where I wanted to go. I stammered. I stuttered. I stumbled.

Problem is, not wanting to stand too close to my tail and tip him off, I hadn't heard where he bought tickets to. I did the only logical thing I could think of. I bought tickets to every city listed on the digital board, above her bullet-proof window. Although she processed my transaction, the cashier displayed a scowl that would make a grizzly bear hibernate during the summer.

I took my seat a row away from my target and his accomplice, straining to hear their conversation.

"I'm ready for a big score," the old guy in the trench coat said, pulling out his cell phone. "I need it. I'm trying to buy a house in the suburbs, finally move out of the city, and it would really help me."

"Yeah? How high do you think it's gonna be?"

"I'm thinking around 750. I guess we won't really know until we get to the bank."

How brazen of these two criminals to be discussing their heist in the open like this! I had them. I wondered which family they were working for. The Gambinos? The Lucchese family? The Gottis? Were the Gottis even still around? More importantly than that, how was all of this connected to Carly Simon? That rancorous doxie, she had her hands in every pie, didn't she?

I was so lost in my mind that I almost missed the next part of the conversation.

"What kind of mortgage do you think you can get with a credit score that high?"

Oh.

Still, the pair never once said that they *didn't* work for a crime family. My evidence could still be admissible in the court of law. Not to mention the court of public opinion. Or even a royal court. Or even a basketball court. LeBron could reside over any of the above, considering he was King James.

A tinny voice came over the Port Authority loudspeaker: "Nwheegh deparghhieng. Botth Fweefwelph to Eggphlantegg Schifty." Turns out, it actually said "Now departing. Bus Three-twelve to Atlantic City." I've never been able to comprehend the Port Authority loud speakers. Must be a talent that people are just born with.

My pair of guys got up from their seats and stepped up into the metallic bus, handing their tickets to the driver. I sifted through all of my tickets, found the right one, and did the same. I sat one row ahead of them to not arouse suspicion. How could someone be following someone else if they were in front of them, huh? That's right, I was always one step ahead.

By this point, the afternoon had grown long. I had been out in the sun since early morning following the money. Just like a Segway, I was too tired. And just like a segue, my mind transitioned from one thought to the next. The sun was already setting, and since we were stuck on this bus for nearly three more hours, I took a nap.

In my sleep state, I heard whispers in the back of my mind. "He's following the money." "He'll find out for us for sure." "But he's sleeping." "Needs a guardian." Tiny voices. Nearly incomprehensible. The sounds of your eyelashes scratching your pillow case while you're asleep.

I woke up, startled by them. The bus was just entering Atlantic City. Looking around, I saw no one that could have been whispering in my ears. It was dark outside of the rattling window, darker than I had been expecting. But that was okay—a good detective thrives in the shadows, much like an ocean thrives on the gravitational pull of the moon.

Ah, Atlantic City. The Las Vegas of New Jersey, only with more heroin, corruption, and New Jerseyites. Truly one of the worst cities the East Coast has to offer. Its boardwalk infested with rot. Its government infested with rot. Its infestations infested with rot. Of course this was where my criminals were heading to. Probably some bigwig meeting between these representatives of the New York City mafiosos and some unscrupulous Jersey hotshot.

The bus took us directly to the Tropicana. Politely, I let the pair of thieves I was trailing get off before me. This held up everyone else on the bus, who started hurtling insults my way. Really mean things. Phrases I could never repeat in mixed company. In retrospect, I should've gotten off first.

We walked along the boardwalk, more cardboard than wood, and into the casino slash hotel, me a couple steps behind them.

I heard the older gentleman say quietly to his companion, "Careful. The weirdo behind us has been following me literally all day. I don't know what his deal is, but he's making me super nervous."

This shocked me. I looked around, checking my environment, checking the faces of the surrounding crowd to see if I recognized anyone from earlier in the day. Who else could've been following my guy?

I didn't see anyone, so they must've been even better at hiding in plain sight than I was. Were they wearing a hoodie making them practically invisible too? If they were, I wondered how their break-up went with the woman of their dreams and if they were in as much anguish as me.

With the blinking lights from all the slot machines and the loud noises of change clanging in metallic catching tins, I found it hard to focus on my prey. It was a detective's worst nightmare. Well, second worst. First place belongs to that recurring dream I have where I'm standing at a subway stop, but it's somehow pouring rain. I look down and realize I'm missing my feet. When I look back up, I see a guy juggling them in the middle of the track, bones sticking up through the torn off ankles. He's laughing as he tumbles my limbs over his head, catching them with ease without even looking. Every time he tosses them up in the air, they circle his head in a perfect arc, a rainbow of juggling talent.

It's not so much the missing feet that frightens me. It's the juggler. They're creepy. Anyone with that much time on his hands to learn such a useless skill curdles my blood like lumpy milk.

Nonetheless, I managed to follow them through the meandering casino. They walked with purpose, like a dolphin. Finally, they reached their destination: the Tropicana Showroom's box office.

The older gentleman bought two tickets to whatever show or concert was playing that night. He slid the money—my money—to the cashier, and he and his companion walked through the event center's doors.

"Excuse me," I said, sliding up the cashier, some young kid in a black and red suit uniform two sizes too large. "Who's behind this?"

"What?" they said back to me.

"Don't play dumb, punk. I'll slap your dirt stache right off that face of yours. This nefarious scheme going on. Who's behind it? Where's the money going to?" It's better to get straight to the point with these grunts.

"I don't know, man. Probably him," the cashier kid pointed at a poster that was hung up next to the doors of the event center. It was a nicely framed picture of an elderly guy holding an acoustic guitar. James Taylor. Of course! Carly Simon's first husband. I knew my follow-the-money plan would work out!

"How do I get to him?" I asked.

"With…a…ticket?" The kid talked to me like I was younger than him.

"Ah, I see, a bribe, huh? All you young punks are the same. How much for one of these quote-unquote tickets?"

"It comes out to $86.75."

"Okay, well, that guy you just took that money from? That was my money. So, just take it out of there, and we'll be all squared up."

"What the hell are you talking about, man?"

"That money, the hundred-dollar bill, that was mine. I lent it to that older guy that was just here. Sort of. So, just use that money and give me my ticket."

"Sorry for my friend here," a mystery voice from behind me said, and I felt an arm wrap around my shoulders. I turned to face the newcomer. It was Marvin Hartley. He continued, "He's just teasing you. I put him up to it as a joke. No worries, we'll be on our way." Marvin turned me away from the cashier.

"What're you doing?" I hissed to Marvin. "I had him right where I wanted him."

"You're thinking too small, Spence. You're gonna what? Go into the concert and somehow make your way backstage to confront James Taylor?"

"You'd be surprised. It's worked before."

"Look, come with me," Marvin said, steering me like cattle towards the elevators. "You don't go to James Taylor. Let him come to you."

This was another side of Marvin I hadn't seen yet. He had showed me his meek as a lamb side in our first meeting. He had shown me his angry side in the hospital. Now he was showing me his devious, scheming side…his underside, if you will.

I thought nothing of his obvious out-of-character traits, as a man has many layers in real life. Just like a college girl in Autumn, with their undershirts and sweaters and jackets and bras and whatever other layers they might be hiding from twenty-something boys aching to find out. Well, I was one of those horned-up twenty-somethings finding out how many layers Marvin Hartley had to him.

We entered an elevator, and Marvin pressed the top floor button, flashing a key card over an RFID security checkpoint.

"Why are you here, Marv?"

"Same reason you are."

"*Bold Boy?*"

"What the hell is *Bold Boy?* I have no clue what that means."

"It's my paper airplane."

"I'm going to pretend like we're having a normal, different conversation, Tracer. No, I'm here to get answers. And James Taylor is going to give them to me. To us."

Yes, this was definitely a different Marvin: more confident, more slimy, more cocksure. Maybe he was putting on an act originally, and now his desperation was showing his true self. I shook my head. It's not like I really knew Mr. Hartley. I was being overly suspicious.

I was looking for paranoia in all the wrong places.

DING.

The elevator doors slid open, and Marvin handed me the key card.

"Here. Use this to get into that room."

"These are the executive suites, Marv."

"Yeah, and that's James Taylor's room."

"How'd you get this?"

"I told you when we first met, money wasn't an issue. Now use the card to break in, will you?"

I knelt, ear to the wooden door. I slid the plastic card through the side of the door, trying to catch the lock. I used to do this with old credit cards that I maxed out and didn't feel like paying the exorbitant interest rates. Whenever I needed to break into a suspect's house, or more regularly, my own apartment after drinking all night and forgetting my keys, this was my go-to. I was a master at it. Ol' Locksmith Hands, I called myself.

"What the hell are you doing?"

"Shhhh, you'll break my concentration, Marv. I've almost got the latch. Give me fifteen more minutes."

"What? Just use the card slot on the front of the door."

I looked. Yeah, there was an RFID slot, just above the handle. I slid the card into the exposed pocket mechanism. The four lights turned from red to green. DING. Just like Ol' Locksmith Hands, able to sneak into any room he pleased. We were free to enter James Taylor's private suite. But the question was: should we?

22

The answer was no, no we shouldn't enter James Taylor's hotel room. But we still did.

The suite itself was stupid expensive. The kind of expensive that only a rockstar like him could afford. Or maybe the President, but I doubt even he could book this kind of room. There was a whole wall made out of a fish tank. With actual, real life fish swimming in it, just like at the aquarium. There was an entire room for the toilet, complete with a phone and a television in it. I'm not saying there was simply a bathroom; no, I'm saying there was a bathroom with an extra room in it, like a Russian nesting doll of bathrooms. Tell me, who's on the John that also needs to make a call while watching the latest episode of *Black Mirror*? Do rockstars really do that?

There were no actual walls on the outsides of the suite; the entire length was just windows. Sure, it gave you a great view of the sewage-rotten ocean in AC, but anyone flying by in a helicopter could just see in! Or maybe…that's what these rich cretins wanted. Those disgusting voyeurs. It's not enough that their entire lives need to be filmed by the paparazzi. No, they also need their private sleeping habits to be displayed to the entire world on the 42nd floor of a casino slash hotel. Repulsive. I don't know what kind of sick pervert this James Taylor was, but damn it to hell if it didn't make me want to barf all over these aurora marble and pearl glass tile floors.

Looking around at the expensive room, I knew I was in the wrong line of business. These musicians were getting money for nothing. And their chicks for free. I should've gone into the music business instead. Maybe like a singer. I had a decent voice, at least for in-the-shower standards. Yeah, I should've become a singing detective. Probably make a lot more money. This was such a good idea, I decided to tell Marvin it.

"I'm in the wrong line of business, Marv. I should've become a singing detective."

He ignored me. "What're we looking for?" Marvin asked, rifling through the drawers of an end table. He upended all the contents onto the floor—Chinese takeout menus, an irresponsible amount of guitar picks, and some knee-high socks. It was like James Taylor's unpacking system was just random and haphazard.

"What're we—what? We're not looking for—this was your idea!" I said. "And Sshhh! This place might be bugged! You don't know."

"Bugged? Why would James Taylor bug his own hotel room? He's only staying one night before he has to be in Philly."

"You know these celebrities. Documenting their entire lives," I said. "Look, if he's not bugging his place, then what's this?" I asked, holding up a weird mechanical contraption with a ton of buttons on it.

"That's...that's the remote for the bed. It's one of those ones that can raise the upper body part to make you more comfortable."

I looked at the remote in my hand, unconvinced. "What? Like in a hospital? Gross. These people make me sick." I threw the remote down onto a coffee table. It rattled some loose change. "Hey, Marv, turn that radio on. It's an old detective trick I know. If we are being bugged, it'll drown out our conversation."

"We're not—ugh, fine. Anything's better than this conversation." Marvin said, flipping on the radio next to James Taylor's bed.

"You're So Vain" started playing at the very second he hit the power button. No surprise there.

"No, no, leave it on," I said, seeing Marvin reaching for the on/off button. "Might as well get it out of the way."

The two of us stood in silence, staring down at our feet, for the entire four minute and nineteen second runtime of the track. As the song faded out, Marvin turned the radio off. His blank stare betrayed his inner despondency, though I was impressed with his skin care routine—no bags under his eyes. For someone as discouraged as he was because of the song, his skin was surprisingly smooth. Almost too smooth, like silicone smooth. I wanted to reach out and feel his face to see how silky soft it was. I almost asked Marvin what lotion he used but thought better.

"So, uh, now what?" I asked.

"Now what? You're the detective!"

"Yeah, but need I remind you that this was your plan? As a matter of fact." That was such a useful phrase for us detectives. *As a matter of fact* implied that not only did you know what was going on, but that whatever you just said was 100% truth, so help you God, with a big G.

"My plan was only to let James Taylor come to us. Give him a surprise of a lifetime. You're the one that should have the experience to make a plan now."

"Yeah, well concerts take a couple of hours, you know. We could've enjoyed his music right up until the encore before coming up here," I said.

"No way was that going to happen. I can't stand James Taylor. 'Fire and Rain?' Ugh. Give me a break."

"You're a weird guy, Marv. You know that? Fine. Let's hide in the closet then, and we'll wait for him to show up."

Although the hotel's closet was bigger than any other closet I had ever seen beforehand, it was still a cramped two and a half hours with Marvin's heavy breathing driving me crazy. The sleeve of a brown tweed jacket with elbow patches kept flopping onto my forehead from its hanger. It smelled faintly of sandalwood and shoe polish.

Even crouching on my haunches, I kept bashing my head against the metal railing in the closet. Craning my neck was the only way to get around it, and I knew I'd have back problems galore the next day because of it. I needed a stiff drink and a stretch, but I'd have to make do with Marvin's cologne.

After an eternity of kneeling down like a catcher in the world's longest baseball inning, we heard the doorknob to the room jiggling. A creak of the door. A flick of the light switch. A clunk of a guitar case on the floor.

I jumped out of the closet. "Surprise!" I yelled, swinging my arms in James Taylor's face.

Marvin stepped out behind me. "This isn't a birthday party, Spence."

"Who are you guys?" James said, clutching his chest like he was on the brink of a heart attack.

"Sorry, sir, let me introduce myself. I'm Tracer Spence, private eye, and this is my client, Marvin."

"What are you guys doing here? Why are you here?"

I said, "We're here to interrogate you about—"

Marvin interrupted me. "We're here to murder you," he said, pulling out a gun.

"We are NOT on the same page, Marvin."

"You're going to kill me?" folk legend James Taylor asked.

"No," I replied. "No, we're not here to kill you. I don't know why he said that."

Marvin ignored me. "Yes, we're going to murder you."

"Marv, buddy, what the hell are you going on about? Want to let me in on the insane plan you hatched?"

"Look, maybe if he's who the song's about, and he no longer exists, then it'll stop. It'll all stop. And we won't be tormented every single day anymore."

"What're you even talking about?" I asked. Marvin was clearly more desperate than I had imagined. "Marv, put down the gun. That doesn't make any sense."

"Damnit, is this about Carly's song?" James asked. His long face relaxed slightly as he began to understand why two random people had showed up in his room. "Look, whoever you are, this is crazy. First off, I'm James Taylor. I can't just be murdered without consequence. And second, the song's not about me. It can't be. She wrote it before we were even married."

"He's got a point, Marv," I said, gently patting his arm, trying to get him to stop pointing the gun at the singer. "And why would killing him stop the song?"

The question hung in the air like a Get Well Soon balloon slowly deflating in a hospital room.

It seemed like I had everyone in control at that moment, so I stepped between Marvin and James. "Jimmy, look, please just tell us what you know about the song, and we'll be on our way. Me and my friend don't want to hurt you. No matter what he's threatened. Or if he's holding a gun—"

"And a poisoned blow dart," Marvin said.

"And a poisoned blow dart," I repeated to James Taylor. I turned to Marvin. "And a poisoned blow dart? Really?"

"Just in case, you know?" Marvin said, pulling a long, thin wooden reed out of his coat. He dropped it on the floor, and both James Taylor and I jumped at the CLANK sound. We were both on edge.

"Now, Jimmy, come on. Let's just have it all out, okay? What do you know about the song?"

James Taylor sighed. "Time was, people used to ask me about 'Sweet Baby James' or 'You've Got a Friend.' People used to care about the songs I wrote. It don't seem that way no more."

"Didn't you just play to a sold-out show? Like, five minutes ago?" Marvin asked from behind me.

"Just answer the question, Jimmy," I said. I tried putting on my best *you better talk to me about this soft rock hit from the '70s or else* face in order to intimidate Mr. Taylor. This involved squinting, so I couldn't see James Taylor and therefore couldn't tell if he was properly intimidated. Nonetheless, he started squealing like he was a hog under oath.

"She never told me who it was about. Honest. I never thought it was about me, and I'm not sure why that rumor got started. Just because we were married? Like I said, 'You're So Vain' was released before we ever got together."

"Keep talking."

"She refused to tell me who it was about, but the only thing I know for sure is that she told me…what she told me…it's not about Warren Beatty."

"Lies!" Marvin Hartley yelled.

I flinched, not expecting the sudden outburst.

"You're becoming really unhinged, Marv," I said. "I'm getting a real Nic Cage vibe from you. Ever see the movie *Face/Off*? Him and John Travolta do a whole *Freaky Friday* thing but with a lot less comedy and a lot more implied incest. I'm off topic. Watch it, if you haven't seen it. You'll know exactly what kind of feeling you're giving off right now."

"He's lying, though."

"Why would I lie about that?" James Taylor asked. I turned back around to face him, waiting for him to talk more. "When we were married, she refused to tell me who the song was actually about; I think that's what drove us apart in the end. But I think she wanted to compromise with me, to make something work with us. So, she told me that. She specifically said it wasn't about Warren. She said it made her so happy that he'd probably think it was about him, but that she wrote it with someone else in mind. With his ego, I just as soon believ—"

BLAM.

The bullet hurtled right past my ear, like an Olympic sprinter hurdling past someone's ear. James Taylor stood, holding his abdomen, blood leaking through his interlocked fingers. He fell to his knees, gasping for breath.

"How sweet that is," Marvin said, the revolver still held in his outstretched hand just like it was an actual extension of his arm.

"You wanted to shoot him just to use that one-liner, didn't you?" I asked.

James Taylor started coughing, blood spurting out of his mouth like a defective pond fountain. I ran over to him and cradled him in my arms. He started to fade.

"It's okay," I said. "You can close your eyes."

James Taylor looked at me with contempt in that moment, and I heard Marvin say, "And you chastise me for my one liner? Linda Ronstadt's version was better anyway."

Thirty seconds passed, the breaths from James Taylor raspy and short. Taylor's eyes flashed over toward Marvin. With his last breaths, he said, "Warren, you bastard."

Then he died.

I looked up to where Marvin Hartley stood. Or who I thought was Marvin Hartley. The man was pulling off his face, rubber strands stuck to his skin, clumps of glue hanging from his cheeks.

"Of course I've seen *Face/Off,* you idiot. Where do you think I got the idea?" Warren Beatty said.

23

I held the corpse of James Taylor, limp like a wet noodle. A pool of his blood blotted out around us, contrasting against the tile floor. His life had been extinguished, with a single ounce of lead. It's funny how a small thing, so simple, can take a man's everything. I mean, it's not *ha ha* funny, but more of an ironic type of funny. I guess you had to be there.

I looked up. There Warren Beatty stood, right in front of me. Instead of the nervous, geeky-looking fellow who I knew as Marvin Hartley, this older, handsome man was now in his place, blotches of make-up and synthesized mask parts still stuck on his face. Where Marvin had a full mop of hair; Warren's receding hairline inched itself up his forehead in his old age.

I was dumbfounded.

That's when I realized I was still cradling a dead man, and I leapt with a high-pitched "EEK!" because death is gross.

Beatty was still holding his revolver, but now it was dropped to his side, limp like a bare tree branch weighed down by fresh snow. After a few moments, he said, "So, gumshoe, you just going to stand there like a mute, or did you have anything in mind?"

"You just killed James Taylor."

"You're damn right I did. Let's see if my money's been worth it, though. Got any theories on what's going on?"

I knew he was setting me up for a Detective Poirot-style culmination where Agatha Christie's character sums up a convoluted plot in front of a room full of suspects. I didn't want to let Beatty down, but I'd never read any Agatha Christie, so I was going to take a shot in the dark.

"Alright, I can try to work it out. Marvin Hartley, our poor old Marvin Hartley, went crazy with that song stuck in his head non-stop. He hired me to find out the origins, of course. But then he forgot that he did so, as he was prone to do, his addled mind under too much stress. So he blackmailed you, famed and critically acclaimed actor Warren Beatty." I paced the room, hands behind my back. "He wanted you to impersonate him and to kill James Taylor. Because Taylor knew the truth. The truth that Marvin Hartley was having an affair with Carly Simon. It was all right there, plain as the day is long. The way Hartley walked with a spring in his step, the way his voice lilted when first hiring me. Yeah, Hartley was in love alright, and couldn't stand to live in a world where Simon had been married to anyone else before. This was to be a murder suicide, with you offing yourself after offing Taylor."

Beatty looked at me with a blank expression. "What in God's name are you talking about? You're not even close. It's like you don't even pay attention to your own life, you idiot. No. No. No, literally every single thing you said was entirely wrong."

"Well, you put me on the spot, Warren. How am I supposed to work like that?"

"You've been working on the case for about two weeks now. And that's the best you've come up with?"

"I dunno. I'd read it if it was a book." I paused. "Okay, I'd wait 'til it became a movie. Or an HBO miniseries."

Warren Beatty raised his gun, pointing it at my chest. I'll tell you this: you don't know what's most important to you until you're looking down the cold, steel barrel of a gun. And what was most important to me at that moment? Tacos. My tummy rumbled. I hadn't eaten all day.

"At least you got the murder suicide bit right. Only it'll be your suicide. And if you don't get what I'm saying—which I'm sure you don't—I'm telling you that I'm setting you up and framing you for the murder of James Taylor."

"Look, Marv—I mean, Warren, before you pull the trigger, just answer me this. What did you do with Marvin Hartley?"

"What did I do—are you kidding me? There never was any Marvin Hartley. It was me in disguise the whole time. I thought it was pretty obvious too. That first meeting in your office, my mask had a zipper down the back."

"I thought it was just a scar. I didn't want to call out your deformity."

"After that though, I used my Hollywood connections to get better masks made."

I nodded, coming full circle to the realization that I still wasn't following along. "So, you reveal yourself Scooby-Doo style, and that's all well and good, but why hire me at all?"

"I never was lying about my motivation. It was still there. I hear that damn song every single day. Every day. It haunts me. It torments me. Her voice grates on the essence of my very soul. I wasn't lying about that. I was hoping you could find out the origin of the song and tell me it WAS about me for sure. It has to be about me. It NEEDS to be about me. That's the only way it makes any sense why I would hear it day in and day out."

He paused for a moment. "Why do you think I had you kidnapped? I was trying to get information any way that I could."

It all clicked for me. "It" being my teeth, which were nervously chattering. But at the same time, the connections started making sense in my head.

"W.B. Warren Beatty. The Animaniacs were working for you…"

"I'm going to assume you're talking about the three college kids I hired, because I don't know who the *Animaniacs* are. But yes, they were working for me. I never did find out what happened with them. I suppose they took my money and ran. I'm rich though. I can afford a little wasted cash. What I can't afford is loose ends. You."

I felt a pang of guilt knowing the fates of those college kids.

"But…why do you need the song to be about you?" I asked. "Like what do you really want to know? Simon's on record as saying that it's at least partially inspired about you, no matter what Taylor just said now. Isn't that good enough?"

"No!" he screamed. His voice cracked. "No," Beatty repeated, more of a whisper. "No, it's not…it doesn't make sense. I never…I never did any of those things."

"What things?"

"The things. In the song. I never went to a horse race in Saratoga. I've never been to Nova Scotia. I've never worn an apricot-colored scarf. Nothing. When I was with her, she used to always talk about doing things like that, but it wasn't with me. But if she says the song is inspired by me, then it needs to fit in somehow! Don't you see it?"

Winning a horse race in Saratoga, seeing a total eclipse in Nova Scotia, parties, yachts…girls dreaming they were your partner while dancing.

Those images from the song lyrics echoed in my mind, and the combinations started to link. *Ellie,* I thought. *Ellie Dayton. I saw some of those things in her apartment. She had heard the song for thirteen years. Crazy. If I had heard the song every day for that long, what would I do? Maybe I would try to act out the song. Play it out in real life. Make it about me.*

Make it about me.

If I could get out of this situation with Warren Beatty, Ellie's apartment would be my next stop. Find those clues again. Put everything together for sure.

I needed to buy some time, much like a professional chef needs to buy some thyme. "And you killed James Taylor because…"

"Because he was lying! He said the song wasn't about me! You heard him!"

"Oh, okay, I got it. You ARE bonkers crazy."

"Alright, Tracer, let's see who's crazy after I frame your corpse for murder."

"You. You'd still be the crazy one."

At that moment, the "Inspector Gadget Theme Song" started playing, muffled from my pocket. My phone's screen was lighting up which was faintly seen through my jeans.

"What is that?"

"Someone's calling me," I said. "That's my ringtone."

"You don't keep your phone on vibrate? We were hiding out here for two hours. What if someone called you?"

"Hazards of the trade, I suppose."

"Ugh, fine. Let's just get this over with. Do you have any last requests?" Warren Beatty asked.

The theme song started over again. Whoever was calling me really wanted to talk. "Yeah, do you mind if I answer that?"

"No," Warren said.

I reached for the phone in my pocket. He screamed at me. He was becoming more and more untethered, a hot-air balloon losing the sandbags hanging over the side.

"What do you think you're doing?" he asked.

"You said I could answer it."

"No, I said you couldn't."

"You specifically said that you didn't mind if I answered my phone. You should be more clear next time you're in this situation, Warren. Communication is a good skill to have. As an actor, I thought you'd know that."

"You're getting on my last nerve, Spence."

"Me? Why I'd never." I was doing my best to delay the inevitable. Funny thing about the inevitable though, at some point it had to stop being evitable. My mind was working overtime to find some way out of this dire predicament. However, my mind seemed to have the same work ethic as I did. It seemed to be asleep, feet up on the desk, hat over its eyes, catching those Z's. It learned from the best. That's why I had a pillow hidden under my desk. That, and I enjoyed something soft for my feetsies to rest on. I always said it's best to take breaks on the job so it feels like you're getting paid for 'em. Sleeping on the job was my way of sticking it to the man, even if that man was me.

I cursed under my breath.

"Alright, flatfoot, time to face oblivion." Warren Beatty pulled the hammer back on his revolver. The CLICK thundered through the room, all-encompassing.

This is when I noticed it. The darkness. The shadows. Behind him, it spread out. A tidal wave enveloping the lone figure that his silhouette cast. Tendrils of black clouds twisted and slivered, the pall reaching toward him. Contours of the unseeable. They inched around him, silently, the limbs a penumbra on the edge of insanity. With a swift motion, they grabbed him. Pulled him. He flew backwards, off his feet. He went with a scream, the only victim to do so. If this were a movie, that stock audio of the Wilhelm Scream would be perfectly inserted here.

And he was gone. Disappeared.

I breathed out.

A moment passed. From the darkness, bones haphazardly were spit out, replacing his body where it once stood. They clinked down to the marble tile floor in a random mess of a pile. I kicked one of the bones away from me. Gross. I didn't want any part of them touching me.

"Great," I said aloud. "Now who's going to pay for my investigation?"

Just as Warren Beatty's bones came out of the darkness, so too did a paper check. It drifted to the floor in front of me, wafting in upside-down arcs. It landed on the floor. I picked it up. Written in fresh ink was a very hefty sum of money; it was signed by Beatty with me as the recipient. In the MEMO section, a scrawled note read "for the continuing of your services."

I pocketed the check, while also pulling out my phone. "Thank you, whoever—whatever you are," I directed into the shadows. "Maybe I'll find out. But, don't worry, I'm not in any hurry. Plus, I've got this other case to solve, so, you know, you do you."

My ringtone started up again. I bobbed my head along with the '80s cartoon song and looked at the screen. Unknown number. That meant it was a fifty-fifty chance of the caller being a debt collector, a solar panel salesman, or any random person I had never met out of the 7.53 billion currently on Earth.

I let it go to voicemail. If it was that important, they'd leave a message. Besides, I had to get to Ellie Dayton's apartment.

24

On my way back to New York, I called Serena. She answered with the world-weary voice that only those awakened in the middle of the night had.

"What time is it?" She yawned into the phone. "Tracer, why are you—you keep some strange business hours."

"Funny. I find I can never sleep after looking down the barrel of a gun. Guess I'm just not wired that way."

"Looking down the barrel of a gun? What? What are you talking a—"

"Shush. Nothing. Don't worry about it. It's a long story, and I don't have the patience or liquor to tell it right now." For as tired as she was, her mood was outclassed by mine. "I'm on my way to Ellie's apartment right now. Break in the case. How much have you cleaned up since I was there last?"

"None. I haven't been able to bring myself to go back there yet. But the cops were there today. I'm not sure if they took anything or not."

"Okay, good," I said, hanging up.

I quickly hit re-dial. Serena picked up again.

"Sorry," I said. "I meant to say goodbye before I hung up. Never liked it how in movies and stuff people hang up without saying bye. Always seemed kind of rude to—"

No surprise, Serena had hung up on her end.

The bus ride back was lonely. Lonely is nice if you like staring at the back of people's heads. My fellow late-night passengers averted their eyes from me more than normal—probably because of all the dried blood I had on my sweatshirt. I spent the ride looking out the window, counting the mile markers on the highway, reflected in the dark by way of the bus's headlights.

When I got to Ellie's apartment building, I made my way upstairs, forgoing the elevator. This was a mistake as I severely overestimated how tired I was. By the first flight, I was winded. By the second, I felt like I could fall over and die. I gave up when I reached the third floor, as I was hacking up phlegm. I made a mental note to start going to the gym, but even I knew if I followed through with that, I'd still wind up skipping leg day. Nonetheless, I walked out into the hallway on the third floor and took the elevator up to the fourth floor.

Ellie's doorway was covered in bright yellow crime scene tape, telling me not to cross. I tore it down. It would be a sad day on the planet when I listened to inanimate objects telling me what to do.

I still had the key to the apartment with me, so I slipped it in to the lock and opened the door.

Other than white powder scattered around the place where the police had looked for fingerprints, it didn't look like the cops had taken much of anything. The apartment was still in shambles, with trash lying around.

But it was this trash that I needed to focus on, this time around.

First stop was the oak table in the hallway, with the mirror above it. I thumbed through the junk mail, scattering it to the floor, looking for something specifically. An airline ticket that I couldn't remember where I put it down last time I was here. I thought the police may have found it and packed it up as evidence when I looked into the mirror to chastise myself. That's when I noticed the picture of Ellie and Serena shoved in between the glass and the mirror's frame, with the ticket behind it. July 31, 2008, a flight to Nova Scotia. Pulling out my cell phone, I searched the internet for "solar eclipse 2008." Sure enough, the first search result showed a total eclipse of the sun on August 1, 2008. A little less than thirteen years ago, Ellie Dayton had taken a trip to Nova Scotia to see a solar eclipse.

One clue down. In the same verse of Simon's song, the siren sings about a horse race in Saratoga. Last time I was in Ellie's apartment, I knew I saw a ticket for a horse race. Now the trick was to find it.

I ventured over to her kitchen. Utensils, pans, and those damn zip ties were still strewn about the counters. After searching for ten minutes through the different cupboards and drawers, I gave up and headed across the apartment to Ellie Dayton's living room. Right away, I found what I was looking for; in the open drawer of an end table, the 2017 ticket was placed on top of a recipe book. The Diana Stakes race, with $400 bet on Lady Eli to win. After another cursory internet search on my phone, I confirmed Lady Eli the winner of the race.

Ellie's horse won. Naturally.

I sat on the arm rest of Ellie's corduroy sofa, the cushion sinking half an inch beneath my weight. However, I felt an uneven bulge under my butt. I reached under and pulled out an apricot-colored scarf that was bunched up on the arm rest. I tossed it across the room.

My hunch seemed clearer and clearer. I shivered with goose pimples, since it was so rare that I had a hunch that turned out correct. The last time was maybe when I claimed that Mrs. Calloway was going to give our American History class a pop quiz in twelfth grade, and then she did. Though that may not even count, since I made that claim every day, hedging my bets. But I was certain of it…Ellie Dayton had spent years emulating the lyrics in "You're So Vain," tailoring the subject of the tune to herself.

This still didn't answer why she was kidnapped, though. Why she was murdered. Why her apartment was ransacked.

I pulled out my flask and took a sip. The warm scotch hit my tongue, and I let the oaky liquor sit in my mouth for a minute before it burned down my throat.

So what if Ellie had been acting out the song, I thought. *So what? Who would kidnap her—kill her—over that?*

I only had half the story. I needed to snoop some more.

In Ellie's bedroom, I investigated every nook and cranny I could, coming up empty on any new clues. I was too in my head. There was nothing around that related to the song—unless I was forgetting the lyrics.

Ellie's laptop was still in the room, placed on her nightstand now. I flipped open the screen, typed in the password of *YachtLover84*—this made sense to me now, compared to the song lyrics—and started typing "you're so vain song lyrics" into the internet's search bar.

But I only got so far as the first three letters, "y-o-u," when a search history entry popped up, in the drop-down box: *YouTube how to dance the gavotte.*

I clicked on the entry, which brought me to a video. A video I had seen before. Some young women doing a step-by-step analysis of how this Baroque dance was supposed to go, tap dancing and playing violin in between shots.

After the video was over, I finished my search for the lyrics to "You're So Vain." The search results confirmed what I knew, and the song's narcissistic subject watched themselves gavotte in the mirror.

I got that tingling feeling of a hunch again. Or it was the air conditioner powering on, with the cool breeze hitting my spine. There was only one way to be sure.

I hit play on Ellie's answering machine and skipped to the last message. While it played, I pulled out Ellie's secret diary from my hoodie pocket.

The familiar hushed voice enveloped the room, only now I was able to put a face to it. "Ellie, this is Sadie Marie. I haven't stopped thinking about what you did the other day. To me. How could you...how could you do this? How could we do this? I'm going to end this one way or another. One way...I've made up my mind. I'm going to take you out. Soon."

In the meantime, I flipped to one of the most recent entries in Ellie's journal.

Day 3541: Meeting with S.O. later tonight. I'm ashamed. I shouldn't be doing this but I have no other options. I NEED to end this—and this is the ONLY way.

S.O. Sadie Marie Olivierri. The message on the answering machine wasn't a threat, like I had originally thought. It was the tormented voice of someone having an affair, asking for a date. Sadie Marie and Ellie were going behind Serena's back, and Ellie felt ashamed for doing so.

My eyes darted back to the song lyrics on the laptop screen. If Ellie was copying the song, making it about herself, the last act…the last tormented, over-the-line, harrowing act she would have had to accomplish…was to be with the wife of a close friend.

I stared at the lyrics until the screen saver popped up. 3D Pipes of different colors, traversing a black vacuum. Classic. I stared at that for five minutes, my imagination lost in the void of this magical pipe land, connecting my thoughts to my case.

My reverie was broke when three loud knocks banged on the door to the apartment.

25

The knocks rapped on the door louder this time. Whoever was at the front door was being rude and impatient. I mean, this was the house of a dead woman, couldn't they give her some damn privacy?

I tiptoed through Ellie's apartment, moving as silent as a jellyfish wearing slippers. Those soft, fuzzy ones that you can slide on wooden floors with. When I got to the front door, I eyed up the peephole to see who was making such a ruckus on the other side. However, an errant piece of crime scene tape was fastened to the glass on the other side, so I couldn't see anything.

KNOCK KNOCK KNOCK KNOCK-KNOCK.

"Pizza delivery!" A high-pitched voice called from the hallway.

I decided to take my chances with the art of deception. "I didn't order a pizza," I said.

"Well…it's, uh, free pizza? You…you're our lucky winner for a free pizza?"

I hesitated. They even didn't seem so sure of the bull that they were slinging. It had to be a trap. There was no way it wasn't a clever ruse to get me to open the door and ambush me.

Still, though, how could I say no to free pizza, on the off-chance that such a contest did exist?

I opened the door. I was right—I wasn't greeted by a guy with a pizza delivery. Instead, I was greeted by some goon with a knife delivery. I backed away as soon as I opened the door, barely inching out of the way of a quick slash.

The baddie attached to the knife had a slender build. I couldn't see much more of them, however, as they wore a trench coat which hid their body and a black balaclava which hid their face. The blade of the knife glinted for just one moment, and I could make out their blue eyes.

They stabbed their knife forward, at groin level. My least favorite elevation when it came to knife-pointed-at-me altitude.

I've been in lots of knock-down drag-outs in my time—a healthy heaping within the past week even. And so, when faced with a knife stabbing in my direction, my instincts kicked it. I moved forward, giving them the chance to stab me.

This threw the assailant off, since most people try to dodge knife attacks. They overcorrected their angle, and grazed the side of my hamstring, their face planting into my thigh.

I took this moment to cry out in pain. Let's face it—a graze with a sharp knife still hurts like hell, and I'd probably need stitches.

I took the next moment to knee my attacker in the face. Their nose started bleeding. It was heavy enough to seep through their mask, the blood gushing onto my pant legs.

"Damnit! These were my good chinos," I said.

They backed up a bit, regaining their composure while holding their nose. The knife was still in their other hand, pointed at me. Their trench coat was twisted around their legs, and the assailant awkwardly spread their thighs, like a chicken getting ready to sit, so they could untangle the leather wedge back vent.

"Had enough yet?" I asked, looking around for a make-shift weapon to defend myself with. The only things in the hallway were half-empty water bottles and coins on the small table. I put my dukes up like a 1920s boxer, the international symbol for "I'm ready whenever you are, pal."

"I'm only getting started," they said. They were making their voice deeper than it was, disguising it.

"Well then, I guess you better—"

I was interrupted when they started running at me, full speed. They whirled their knife around, like an aggressive windmill. Backing up, I found myself in the opening between the kitchen and living room. I had a choice to make: the kitchen with its heavy cast-iron pans that could be used as shielding and its own knives to be used as weapons or the living room, where I could maneuver the large sofa between me and my attacker.

My choice was made for me, as I tripped over my own shoes. I went down on my ass, like the Titanic if the Titanic was going to need a good chiropractor after its collision.

Between the pain in my tailbone and the searing agony from the cut in my leg, my body throbbed with every aching move of my muscles. The last time I felt this much pain was when I went on vacation with my father to Tijuana when I was 13. One morning I woke up in an ice bath in some Mexican hotel, stitches sewn into the side of my abdomen, my kidney missing. It turned out to just be a lesson from my dad. He summed it up by saying, "If you can't take care of your internal organs, how're you going to take care of a dog, Tracer? Huh? Answer me that."

The bushwacker jumped on top of me, both hands gripping the hilt of their knife, pointed down at my face. I grabbed their wrists with my own hands, trying to stop the dagger from giving me an unwanted kiss.

By this point, their mask had been soaked with their blood. The woolen balaclava had reached its saturation point, and their blood dripped onto my face, into my open mouth.

"EW EW EW EW EWWWW," I said, spitting the coppery taste out.

On my back, being attacked by a crazy person on top of me, knife slowly inching down towards my beautiful, beautiful face…this was the worst position to find yourself in. At least according to *Fight Like the Wolf Inside You: A Semi-Erotic List of Combat Styles,* the critically acclaimed book I kept on my nightstand and skimmed through when I got bored looking at my phone. At this point, I wished I had finished reading the entry from the book which probably explained how to get yourself out of the situation.

But, I had to improvise. So, I wiggled. I wiggled my entire body, while still keeping my arms tight around their wrists. I wiggled and wiggled, hoping it would create some space that I could then wiggle out of.

"What the…what the hell are you going?" my assailant asked, breathing heavily, still putting all their weight towards the knife.

"Wiggling."

"Well, stop it. It's very distracting."

"No. No, I don't think I will." I wiggled some more.

"It feels so weird, though," they said. "Like I'm trying to murder a tub of Jell-O. Or a bag filled with worms."

"You're just going to have to deal with that."

I breathed in, summoning all the strength I could. With a heart full of resolve, I pushed, my hands and feet working in conjunction. I broke free. The attacker was launched away from me, hitting into the corner of a wall, the back of their head connecting first. Unconscious, they dropped their knife.

I kicked the blade away from their hands. It was heavy, heavy from the weight of the world, and I stubbed my toe.

I dragged my nemesis across Ellie's apartment into her bedroom. From there, I collected some of the zip ties from her kitchen, to restrain the mystery person to the leg of Ellie's bed.

I zip tied the assailant's arms with a few of the plastic bands. From there, I zip tied their legs together, and then from the wraps around their wrists, I connected them to the legs of the bed. Still, I wasn't sure just how many were appropriate strength.

"How many of these do you think I should use on you?" I asked. The unconscious body didn't respond. "More?" Still no response. "Okay. If you say so." I wrapped more zip ties around their limbs, in order to be sure. I learned enough from movies that the moment you turn your back on someone you think is down and out, well, that's the moment they attack you from behind.

Sure that they were knocked out and not going anywhere, it was time to unmask this fiend, Scooby-Doo-style.

I grabbed the bottom of the balaclava and pulled. At the same time, I exclaimed, "Why, it's Old Man Jenkins!" Only…it wasn't Old Man

Jenkins, the stereotypical Scooby-Doo villain. It wasn't Old Man Jenkins at all.

It was Serena Dayton. Her nose had swollen up and a purple bruise already appeared around her left eye, down her cheek. The light above us glinted off her blue iris, and she looked at peace.

Five minutes had passed, and she still hadn't woken up. And yes, I made sure Serena wasn't dead. She definitely still had a pulse. I was growing bored. I thought that maybe I should try to awaken her. To do so, I filled a pot from the kitchen with water. Apologizing beforehand, I splashed the cold water onto her face, which dripped down on to her body, soaking into her shirt. She still didn't rouse. Why was this such a trope in movies and TV shows if it didn't work? Damn Hollywood liars.

I waited, resting on Ellie's bed, for Serena to come to.

Finally, she stirred.

"Ow," she said. "Ow."

"How's your head?" I asked.

"Ow," she repeated.

"That covers that, I guess."

"Why…am I wet?"

"My bad. I poured water on you. Thought it would help," I said. "It didn't."

"So," Serena said, shaking her restraints, "what's the plan? We just going to sit here?"

"The plan is that I'll ask you some questions, turn you over to the police, and finish this damn case once and for all."

Serena smiled. It unnerved me. Her grin was evidence alone to throw her behind bars. It was the expression of a woman who knew she was beat, who was glad she was beat.

"Go ahead, Tracer. I'm done. What do you got?"

"When did you learn Ellie and Sadie Marie were going behind your back?"

"I can't believe you figured that out."

"I get lucky every now and then. You can call it a curse if you like."

"A few weeks ago. I...I didn't mind all the weird things Ellie did over the years, her obsession with that damned song. But sleeping with the wife of a close friend? When that close friend is your sister?" Serena paused, tears coming down from her eyes. Or was that still the water I dumped on her? "I couldn't let that go. I couldn't let that slide."

"What did you do?"

"I had her kidnapped. It was me."

"Your own sister? You had her kidnapped and murdered?"

"Just kidnapped! I didn't...I couldn't believe they killed her. Those bastards. I just wanted to scare her. To have her stop seducing my wife! I wanted my sister back! I didn't..." Serena got quiet. "I didn't want them to kill her. She was my sister. Ellie...I loved her." She looked me in the eyes, her unwavering look piercing me more than her knife could. "She wouldn't stop going after Sade. And Sade, she fell for it, for her. Do you have any idea how it is to be so...isolated from the people you care about?"

"There was that time in fourth grade my father told my class I had lice so all my friends would keep their distance from me. And then when they called his bluff, he did actually give me lice. Did it feel like that?"

"All I know is I had to do something rash, something drastic."

"Drastic? Drastic is getting a new hairstyle, not having your sister murdered."

"I didn't...I didn't mean for that to happen, Tracer. You have to believe me. I don't know why they killed her."

"I don't understand though...if you were the one to have her kidnapped, why get a P.I.? Why hire me?"

"You? You're a hack. A nobody. I needed to get Sade off my back, when Ellie was actually kidnapped. She was so worried about Ellie, worried when Ellie stopped responding to her. So I needed to pretend to do something. I needed to hire a detective who wouldn't find anything. I needed to hire the worst of the worst.

I needed you."

"You wound me," I said, placing my hands over my heart in a sarcastic gesture. Truth is, I was used to people calling me the worst. Someone's got to be the worst, so why shouldn't it be me? "Speaking of…why are you here? Why try to kill me?"

"Because my horoscope said to." She spit blood out on to the floor. "Why the hell do you think? Once the police got involved, I knew it was only time until they figured out I had Ellie kidnapped. Unless I could tie up loose ends. You were a loose end." She wriggled on the floor, repositioning herself more comfortably. Her trench coat opened up, showing her t-shirt clinging to her form. She had a full-body like a cup of espresso and was just as bitter.

"That's the nicest thing anyone's said to me. One more question. You seem like an upstanding member of society. How'd you find someone to kidnap your sister? Who did you hire?"

"I knew a guy at my garage, fixed his car a couple times. He knew a guy who knew another guy. I never actually spoke to anyone from the organization, but all I was told was that they're called the Hidden Star Hill gang."

"Stuart," I said. That proved how he was connected to the case, but I still didn't know why he had killed the Mick Jagger look-alike. How was he connected to my other case? There were too many threads connecting this case and the other one to just be a coincidence.

"Sit tight," I said. "I've got to make a call."

I dialed Detective Hardholm. Like a puppy greeting its owner at the door, he was happy to hear from me.

"What the hell do you want? Can't you ever call when I'm not sleeping? Or better yet, just not call?"

"And miss out on our repartee?" I massaged my right temple, my calloused fingers trying to provide enough pressure to make the headache I was developing go away. "Look, I got someone who you'll want to talk to. I don't want to say that I solved your case, but I solved your case."

"What are you talking about?"

"Mrs. Serena Dayton, sister of the deceased. She had Ellie kidnapped. Then she tried to kill me. Sweet kid otherwise, if you can past that kind of thing." I glanced over at Serena. She was staring blankly at the wall. "We're over at Ellie's apartment. You may want to come with an ambulance too, just in case. She hit her head pretty hard."

"I told you to stay away from that case, Tracer. You could be in real deep, you know."

"I always did have a problem listening to authority," I said. "Though my pediatrician found it was an eraser that got stuck in my ear, muffling sound. What kind of teacher just lets a kid stick a pencil in their ear during math class? That's what I want to know."

"She's there with you now, you said?"

"Yeah, I've got her zip-tied to the bed. She's restrained."

"Alright, you stay right there, Tracer. I'll be over, ASAP."

"Oh, one last thing, Hardholm. She didn't kill Ellie. I want that to be clear. She just wanted to scare her. I'm still working on the murder aspect."

"I thought you said you solved my case."

"I'm almost there."

"Whatever. Just stay there. Be right over." He hung up the phone on his end.

I knelt down next to Serena. Her countenance was still empty with resignation. In this moment, her expression looked soft; for the first time since I'd known her, her secret was out and wasn't caustically eating her up inside.

"I appreciate you telling Detective Hardholm I didn't kill Ellie," she said.

"Sure."

"Do you...do you think it'll matter?" she asked. "Like, in court? Or do you think they'll throw the book at me?"

"Well, I'm not a lawyer," I said, "but I have watched *My Cousin Vinny,* so I think I know a thing or two about how law works. And I'd say you have a decent chance of—"

"Never mind. Forget I asked."

"Fair enough. I fell asleep during it anyway."

From my pocket, my phone started vibrating, the ring tone starting half a second later. I pulled it out, looking at the screen. It was the same number that tried getting through earlier when I was in Atlantic City. How long ago that felt. It was only about three hours ago, but it felt like three and a half. I answered the call this time, being in a good mood.

I spoke in a high-pitched voice, "Tracer Spence Private Detective Industries. Your disgrace is our case. This is Mr. Spence's receptionist speaking." I didn't currently have a secretary after the last one left over a paycheck dispute—mainly that she was expecting one—but it's best to keep up appearances, so I always tried to answer my phone like this.

"Shut up, Tracer," a familiar voice on the other end of the line said. "We have your girl. Kidnapped. And if you want her back, you're going to need to meet our demands."

"Mom?" I asked.

"What? No. This is Stuart."

"You cretin. What do you want?"

"We have Vanessa."

My heart jumped. I didn't know it could do that. Always thought it was an overwrought cliché. Same with having a frog caught in your throat, which I was also feeling now, the lump of anxiety making it hard to speak. I was well-used to the feeling. It reminded me of the time my father caught me smoking cigarettes, so he made me swallow a whole frog as punishment.

My Vanessa. Kidnapped. Even with our previous argument, how could I get her mixed in all of this without thinking of the danger? Love had blinded me, just like Justice. Which is what Stuart was going to get. A big ol' heaping of some blindfolded justice.

Stuart continued, "We demand you stop your incessant prying. And we want the arm bracelet back. Come meet us and get your girl back."

That damned arm bracelet. Serena had given it to me, under the impression that whoever kidnapped her sister must've left the piece of jewelry behind. Stuart and his hired guns had come after me, tortured me just to get it back. Whoever it belonged to must be calling the shots. If I found the owner, I'd find the murderer. I was sure of it.

"I just have one question," I said. "Why do you keep using plural pronouns to refer to yourself? Is it the royal 'we' thing you're doing?"

"Sort of. That, and it really conveys that sense of authority that being part of a shadowy organization can give you."

"You know nothing of shadows," I said, thinking back to the pile of bones that used to be Warren Beatty. A shiver ran down my spine.

"So you want the girl or not?"

"How do I know she's alive? Put her on, so I know. Now."

"Ugh, fine," Stuart said. And then muffled, I heard "Alright, take the duct tape off her mouth, but I swear to God, you better be ready with some more, because if I have to listen to her ramble again, I'm going to lose it."

I heard clunking sounds as the phone was passed around, and then I heard Vanessa's voice, tinny through my phone's speakers. "Tracer? Tracer? It's me. I'm kidnapped, I guess you could say. But don't worry, I don't feel like I'm in that much danger. I've been in worse situations before. Like there was this time my family took a vacation to Memphis. Lots of country music out there. It was really awesome to just experience as a teen. And my mom and dad loved seeing how I was developing as a musician back then, really supported me in every way they could. Anyway, we're in Memphis, and my dad came from the office supply world. Cutthroat. Sticky notes and three-ringed binders were his jam, but he was always on the look-out for some up-and-coming would-be superstar who thought they had the office supply world figured out and would backstab anyone they could to move up the corporate ladder. But so, my dad, he was always interested in office supplies and paper, and I remember he took us to some paper and pulp company's headquarters and factory out in Memphis for a tour. I remember the tour guide made everything sound fascinating, honestly. But one thing led to another and bam! I got a paper cut. AND THAT WAS WAY MORE DANGEROUS THAN HOW I'M FEELING RIGHT NOW."

I had a feeling that last line was a subtle, passive aggressive dig directed towards Stuart and her captors more so than at me. Either way, I couldn't ask her if that's what she meant or not as the phone was pulled away at that moment. I no longer heard Vanessa's sweet voice.

I realized because she had dominated 100% of the conversation, I hadn't said anything to her and therefore couldn't verify that it wasn't a recording of her. Damn.

"Got it, Tracer?" Stuart's gruff voice shook me back to our conversation.

"I got it. Where am I meeting you?"

"Martha's Vineyard, Massachusetts. Be there tomorrow."

"Tomorrow tomorrow? Like another day from now? Or since it's past midnight, do you mean, like, today tomorrow?"

"What?"

"Do you want me there today, but later today? Or do you actually mean tomorrow?"

I heard him confer with his associates for ten seconds or so, as he explained the confusion. A lot of muffled voices argued back and forth over the intricacies of the English language and how time worked. Finally, Stuart returned to the phone and spoke. "Just get here as soon as you can. We'll be expecting you." He then told me the address to travel to and hung up on me.

I fist pumped. Every great detective has a way of tracing mysterious phone calls. Police do it with those machines and computers that seemed difficult to understand. Those chumps. It appeared I was so great that I had done it inadvertently when he told me the address. Nailed it.

Looking at Serena, still tied to the leg of the bed, I realized I wouldn't wait around for Detective Hardholm to get here. Not when Vanessa was in trouble.

"Think you'll be okay here without me?" I asked Serena.

"What? You're leaving? You're just going to leave me here tied up to the bed?"

I waited five seconds, unsure if Serena meant that as a rhetorical question or not. When I saw her waiting expectantly for my answer, I replied, "Y…yes? I mean, you don't have anywhere you have to be right? You're not going anywhere. And Hardholm will be here any minute. Besides, I have to go rescue the love of my life! And get those that killed Ellie. That too."

"Fine, whatever."

"Oh wait, I've got an idea."

I didn't want to be *that* rude and go without leaving Hardholm a note. I found a few pieces of paper—the backs of envelopes from Ellie's hallway—and began writing a quick explanation.

I did it. -Tracer

Placing this on the driest part of Serena's chest, I thought Detective Hardholm would see it and read it as if it was referring to Serena in the first person, and he would also know that I was the one to write the note.

On my way out the door, I realized that didn't make sense and that the message could be misconstrued as if it was a signed confession from me, Tracer Spence.

So, I wrote another note, placing it under the first one.

I mean to say Serena Dayton did it. "It" referring to the kidnapping of her sister, Ellie Dayton. Well, not physically doing the kidnapping. But hiring someone to do the physical act of kidnapping. Sorry I couldn't wait around to tell you this in person, but I had to go. This time "I" refers to me, Tracer Spence, Private Detective Extraordinaire. K Bye.

Again, on the way out of the apartment I thought that this second message might be too confusing. So, I wrote a third one, placing it under the other two.

If the other two notes are too confusing, just remember what I told you over the phone. That's what happened.

"Don't, uhhh, don't knock these off your body, okay? They're very important, Serena."

With that, I was out the door, on my way to Martha's Vineyard.

26

I made the seven-hour ride from New York City to Martha's Vineyard. My Uber driver was already upset that he was driving for that long straight through, but apparently, he was also incensed by my "snoring so loud it could shift the tectonic plates back into Eurasia." I thought that was quite rude of him to leave on my Passenger Rating, for all the internet to see. And after I suggested popping in my *Summer Jamz '99* mixtape for our road trip. I spent a whole night back before the turn of the century curating the perfect playlist. Yeah, I have Smash Mouth's "All Star" three times in a row on the CD, but it's that great of a track.

The Uber dropped me off at the coordinates I gave him, somewhere in Lambert's Cove. It's better for us detectives to say "coordinates" rather than "address." Makes us sound like we can figure out the longitude and latitude of a place. In real life, I'm not even certain which way is the longitude or latitude. One of them's on the Y-axis, right?

I said goodbye to him, and he sped off with only a four-letter word. A goodbye I was used to, honestly.

It was a sprawling estate. A tennis court on one end. A barn on another. Swimming pool in between. A wooden swing hung on a tree across from the fenced-in tennis court, swaying in the wind. It was a single wooden plank, tied to a thick branch with two ropes. The manicured grass of the estate crept right up to the dirt road. How do people get grass that neat? Is it a special lawnmower? Do they hire laborers with tiny scissors?

I saw a weather-beaten sign, hanging from a post, that read "Hidden Star Hill." The insignia—Stuart's tattoo—was also imprinted below to the words. A five-pointed star resting underneath a downward-facing crescent.

I knew I was walking into a den of thieves. The quaintness gave it away. Why else would thieves call their hiding holes "dens" if they weren't attracted to old-world charm?

The main house was all boxy and triangular, very house-like. Two stories. Lots of windows. A roof. You know, all the house stuff that comes along with houses. There was a second-story deck. I imagined the grifters and hoodlums that stayed here would spend warm nights playing cards on it, protected from the elements and mosquitoes by the screen surrounding the deck. Below that, welcoming all of us visitors, was an enclosed entrance jutting out from the front like an outie belly button.

As pleasant as the house was, I didn't feel welcome.

Stuart stood next to a simple wooden porch swing, towering over it, his shadow splayed out on the rock patio. This late in the afternoon, his shadow grew long and imposing, crooked and broken into segments as it scattered down the front steps. He had one hand placed on the back of a wicker chair, the other placed on his gun holster. That scar on his cheek I gave him ran pure white down his mug.

I strode up to him, my gait confident. Self-assured. I had swag. Mainly because my foot was asleep from the long car ride up here, and the pins and needles running down my leg were making me walk all funny.

He glowered at me, and I fully understood the term "shooting daggers." If his eyes were guns that used blades as ammo, he'd definitely be shooting them my way. If not daggers, then certainly Swiss Army Knives—which may hurt worse, if you unfurl each prong. I'd hate to get stabbed by one of them twisty can openers hurtling through the air at 1000 miles per hour.

"Let's go, sleuth," he said, grabbing the upper part of my bicep and leading me around the back of the house. His fingers dug into my muscle like a claw-machine in the lobby of a movie theater.

"Not gonna give me the house tour?"

"If it were up to me, only thing I'd give you is a slow death."

"But it's not up to you is it? You're just some flunky. Taking orders from the Big Man. So who is it? Who's your Big Bad Boss?"

"Play your cards just right and maybe you'll find out."

"As long as it's Go Fish. I never got the hang of poker. Can never remember what beats what. Is it a flush after a straight?"

Stuart ignored me, which was a real shame because I was hoping for an answer. For some reason, no one wanted to explain the rules of poker to a thirty-something detective. Just because someone should know something doesn't mean that they do. The silver lining was that I had an unreadable poker face due to never knowing if I had a good hand or not.

We had crossed over to the back of the house, Stuart still leading me by holding my arm. He pushed me forward, and I felt the strength behind his shove, a tiger coiled and ready to pounce. Stuart grabbed the handle of a steel Bilco door, discolored from storms past, and opened.

"Get in," he said, nodding in the basement's direction.

I never liked basements. Or crawl spaces. Or cellars. Or when your blanket is tucked too tight under the mattress. Too similar to catacombs for me, filled with ancient mummies and skeletons. They brought to mind serial killer lairs: skulls hung from water pipes, skin outstretched and flayed on the walls, moldy boxes filled with old National Geographic magazines. I shivered at the thought.

I made my way down the cement stairs, feeling the wall to sturdy myself since there was no banister. I made a mental note to call OSHA and report them. Secret hideouts count as businesses in my mind, and that would surely fall under federal jurisdiction for safety standards, right? I'd take these guys down in any way I could.

However, the basement surprised me. I was expecting a dark dungeon, dank and pungent. But instead, it was finished with wall-to-wall carpeting, thick synthetic fibers indenting underneath my shoes. Halogen lights were installed in recessed cans overhead, and though they made me squint with their brightness, I couldn't find fault with how dark the place was. Even the walls were painted off-white, making the room feel bigger and brighter than it actually was. Whoever these baddies had for their interior designer was worth the surely stolen money.

There was one main problem with the basement though. Namely, Vanessa was tied to a chair in the middle of it. Sure, it seemed like a comfy chair—she was sitting on a fluffy, green cushion—but the whole her being kidnapped thing really put a damper on me admiring the Feng Shui.

I ran over to her, ignoring the two guards behind her who were standing in front of some carpeted stairs leading up into the main house. Her face was bruised, deep purple marks smattered across her right cheek. She wore a sleeveless blouse, white with a floral print, and a bright red skirt—both slightly ripped and tattered from her manhandling. The ropes dug into her wrists and ankles, the skin red with irritation. Whoever tied her up must've been a Boy Scout, understanding knots like this. How far that goon had fallen—from America's beloved treasure of a Boy Scout to underworld rope handler.

She was gagged and couldn't talk, but I still asked if she was okay, cradling her head. She nodded. Then she winked at me. That foxy minx, flirting with me even in her tormented state.

I wondered what kind of torture Stuart and his goons had put her through. Chinese bamboo torture? Waterboarding? Iron Maiden? The Geriatric Handbag? That last one was especially evil as a form of psychological horror having to stick your fingers into a grandmother's purse, maneuver around all the sticky, unwrapped caramels, and find the last penny so they could hand exact change to a teenage cashier at a convenience store.

It looked like Vanessa hadn't been put through anything that horrific, though. However, there were various forms of torture that didn't leave bloody scrapes and punctures on a person. I would know—

with years of detective experience under my belt, you don't leave this business without knowing the different types of abuse inflicted on people. Hell, in my case, I didn't enter the business without knowing some types of torment. Just around my 14th birthday, my father would strap me up to something, some device he used to call "The Maker Taller," which I subsequently learned was The Rack, from Medieval times. I'd get on willingly—any time with my father was quality time—and he'd wind the ratchet, stretching my body out to its limits. As he used to always say, "No one respects shorties, Tracer. How are you going to get through life the size of a troll? If your own pa can't respect you, you think strangers are going to? Now suck it up, boy, and elongate them vertebral columns."

I looked over at Stuart. His arms were folded, interlocked like a soft pretzel.

"Stu," I asked. "What're we doing here? Why'd you bring Vanessa into this?"

"I told you, shamus, you've been sniffing up the wrong fire hydrant. You couldn't leave well enough alone, and you just kept up trying to solve your case. Never giving back what ain't rightfully yours, either. Well, my boss ain't liking that. As for your little caged bird here, she kinda fell right into our lap. You'll have to ask her, though."

I glanced back at Vanessa. She seemed to be smiling, underneath the gag in her mouth.

"Alright, I will," I replied to Stuart. I nodded towards the two other guards and pointed at the rope around Vanessa's face, indicating that I wanted to untie her mouth to speak to her. Stuart grunted. I took that as an A-Okay.

When her mouth was free, I said, "Hey, Stu, mind giving us a little privacy, huh? Just for a moment."

"I ain't leaving you two alone, Spence, if that's what you're thinking."

"No, no, that's fine. Just, you know, maybe don't listen. Pleeeeeaaaaaasssssseee?" I flashed my best puppy dog eyes at the big lug, hoping he had a heart somewhere underneath that black pit in his chest.

"Ugh, fine," he said. "Just don't—don't make that face again." He nodded at his two underlings. The three of them cupped their hands over their ears, earmuffing themselves, and proceeded to sing quietly. All three of them chose "The Piña Colada Song" and somehow harmonized with each other. They must've had practice doing this in their downtime. Stuart had a surprisingly lovely voice, a tenor, higher-pitched than I'd expected it to be.

"What's he talking about, Vanessa?" I asked.

"Shhh," she said, "come here first."

I leaned in and got a full-on blast of some smooches from her. She kissed like a tire swing: her lips gripped me like a durable rubber wheel, I felt weightless like I was suspended by a chain link, and I could totally imagine three or more children fitting on the length of her tongue.

Vanessa pulled away and smiled. I loved that smile just as much as the kiss, her teeth lined up like the crayons in a Crayola 64 box.

"How'd they get you?" I asked.

"I let them do it. I essentially kidnapped myself."

"What?"

"Yeah. I thought it would help you in your case. I figured they'd bring me to their base of operations, thinking they'd lure you here. Sure, they roughed me up a bit, but I'm a woman in a relatively successful cover band, playing shows most nights—I can handle it."

I paused. She really had an innate talent for this detective stuff.

I said to Vanessa, "How bad did they rough you up?" The three bad guys sang in the background about how much they enjoyed being caught in the rain, and the feel of the ocean, and the taste of champagne.

"Well, they sort of roughed me up. Sort of. It was my idea. I wanted the, uh, ambience to be right for your big showdown. So, I talked them into it. They were really half-hearted about beating me and seemed pretty uncomfortable. Most of this I did myself to be honest. Their hearts just weren't in it. I guess they don't have the same love of theatrics as I do."

"You've gotta have the theatrics. That's the main part of being a private eye. You think I enjoy walking around with a trench coat on most of the time? It's so heavy and hot. But, it looks cool!"

"I know! That's what I tried telling 'em!"

At this point, Stuart and his two goons finished up with their song. He took his palms off of his ears. "Alright, dick, time's up. You and your plaything shut up now."

"Call her my 'plaything' one more time." I shook my fist at him, like I was in some high school musical play.

"You're lucky the boss said not to harm you. Yet. As for later, I hope you're enjoying the ability to walk…"

I didn't like this line of conversation, so I changed it. "Just what's the plan here, Stu? What're you gonna do with me and my—wait a second, hold on." I turned to my love, sitting still tied up. "Vanessa, I'm so sorry about the other night. I've had some time to think about it, and I never should've left you alone on our date. I'm truly, truly sorry. And I know because of that I'm anxious about the answer to what I'm about to ask, but…what, uh, what are we? Like, are we going steady? Boyfriend slash girlfriend? Or are you…" I dreaded finishing the question. "…still seeing other people?"

"I can't believe you'd even ask that." She frowned, and I swore to myself that I'd never upset her again.

"I just mean, we haven't had the conversation yet. We never had the conversation and its implications and stuff."

"Are you seeing other people, Tracer?" she asked.

"No."

"Neither am I."

"So that means…?"

"That means that we're together, dummy. You're my boyfriend, Tracer. I already switched you over as my emergency medical contact."

I beamed like a Lite-Brite picture of a sailboat, with those shiny pegs glowing in different colors. "You're not mad about the other night?"

"Of course, I was. But I just needed a little time to cool off is all."

"So Stuart, that comes back and begs the question, what're you gonna do with me and my girlfriend?"

A look of disgust drifted across his face like a tumbleweed. "Wouldn't you like to know?"

"I would," I said. I was earnest. Always best to be up front in situations like this. Honesty is the best policy, with a return for store credit policy as a runner-up. If you think about it, it's a great compromise—the customer gets to return their defective product and the store gets to keep some business.

His silence was so palpable you could throw a blanket on it, neck with it in a movie theater, and it might even get a little handsy back with you. I guess it was a rhetorical question. I should've known he was a trickster, playing me like a sap.

The halogen lights flickered, the recessed can lighting emanating like the wick of a candle. It had grown slightly darker in the basement, and I wondered if anyone else had noticed. Behind Stuart, the shadow he cast along the wall floated off-kilter, almost as if it didn't belong to him. Maybe it was a trick of the light, but I could've sworn his silhouette inched closer and closer to his physical body.

"So, what's the deal, Tracer," Stuart said. "You gonna go your merry way with your plaything and leave your case behind?"

"That's a 'no can do,' kiddo. Gotta see this through to the end. You made this case personal," I said.

"What a damn shame," he said. Like he was slipping into a *something more comfortable* nightie, he slipped on some brass knuckles. "Guess we gotta teach you a lesson, now."

"I hope it's precalculus. I never got the hang of it. The square root of negative one? If it's not real, then who cares? I just don't get it."

THUD.

The two lugs tipped Vanessa and her chair onto its side, her head whiplashing against the carpet. At the same time, Stuart lunged at me.

Round two. Fight.

27

Stuart hit me like a ton of Lego bricks. You might think Legos aren't as bad as actual brick bricks, but let me tell you, a literal ton of anything is going to have a mighty force behind it. And have you ever stepped on a Lego brick barefooted? There's nothing more excruciating.

Down I went. His entire bulk tackled me to the floor. He may have had the upper hand, but little did he know I was used to this position. You don't get to be a great private eye without practice at hard drinking, and I had my fair share of nights plastered on the floor. It was a posture I was familiar with.

I let him hit me a few times. You know, give him a false sense of security. That and his hulking, monstrous body had me pinned down. The brass knuckles connected with my abdomen in a way that I could only describe as "a big ouchie."

They say the best defense is a good offense. So I went into my fool-proof plan of complete panic. It's never failed me before.

I flailed. I flailed wildly. Limbs akimbo, I let chaos reign supreme. My elbows connected with parts of his body he didn't even know existed. My feet kicked like a kangaroo throwing a temper tantrum.

The two of us rolled across the floor, intertwined, until we hit a wall. Finally, I was on top, and I jumped into a standing position. Well, really a crouching position, with me holding my abdomen. I was pretty sure I was internally bleeding, but you know what—as long as the blood stays on the inside, I suppose I was fine.

Stuart leapt up too. His luminous eyes displayed an animalistic hatred for me. His nostrils flared. His brows furrowed. His jaw clenched. His forehead did, uh, angry forehead stuff.

In that brief pause, the entire universe felt the tension between us. The fury we experienced was enough to start a blood feud that would last among our families for centuries, Montague and Capulet style, until long after we were both dead when one of my descendants fell in love with one of his, in spite of family history and social pressure. Yeah, we were about to go no-holds barred. It was on.

We pushed forward towards each other and had the most feral slap-fight. My head tilted back, I could barely see where I was throwing my open palms. His approach was more defensive, using one arm to try to hold me back while the other arm windmilled, clobbering and slapping my forearms and body. We thrashed. My arms lashed like Indiana Jones' whip, flagellating randomly.

After a few moments, we broke apart. Both of us were breathing heavy, our hands on our knees, backs arched. I was so tired, I dry heaved. Stuart panted. We were both covered in sweat and blood—who knew whose body fluids were whose?

I looked over at Vanessa. Somehow, she had gotten out of her binds. She was standing there, next to the two guards. All three of them were slack-jawed, staring at Stuart and me.

THWACK.

Stuart's fist, and the brass knuckles on it, connected with my jaw. A textbook example of a sucker-punch. The impact knocked me backwards. The back of my head connected with some mechanical contraption hanging and jutting from the wall. I clamped down reflexively and bit the tip of my tongue off. I spit it out, the crimson streaks of blood and saliva staining the carpet. I hoped they wouldn't be able to scrub the stain out, therefore reducing the resell value of the estate.

I was spent. My body gave out, and I just rested against the wall. Stuart was back on his feet, lumbering over me. He was bruised and scratched to hell, ripped off skin flapping off his bloody brass knuckles.

He grinned. A tooth was missing. What kind of dental insurance do henchmen have?

I relented to my fate.

"WHAT IS ALL THAT RACKET DOWN THERE?" A female voice caterwauled from upstairs. Apparently in the din and clatter, the mystery woman had opened the door and was standing in the threshold. All I could see was her elongated shadow drifting down the steps.

"Sorry, ma'am. We'll keep it down," Stuart said, wheezing.

"Stuart? Is that you? What are you still doing here? I'm not paying for your overtime. Get out of here already," the voice said. "And you other two boys, bring our guests up here. I'd like to talk to them." She closed the door, and a burst of cool air pushed into the basement.

"Yes ma'am, sorry ma'am," Stuart called after her.

He continued walking over to me. I flinched. He reached out. Grabbed a thin piece of yellowish cardboard above me. Placed it in the punch clock that I hit my head on. Thunked down the button.

"Alright fellas, I'm off the clock now. You can take care of them."

He walked toward the stairs leading upwards to the Bilco doors and outside. The other two henchmen helped me up, their fingers pinching the skin of my triceps.

Stuart looked back at me, almost longingly. "Tracer, this ain't over between us. You'll never know when I'm coming for you. Watch your back."

"And you watch your waistline. You're getting to that age when snacks go right to your hips."

He left. Vanessa and I were escorted upstairs to the main house.

28

The walk up the stairs was no longer than a minute or so, but it felt like an eternity. We may have been ascending, but the atmosphere felt like we were descending into a fatal trap, being lured. My legs, exhausted from my pummeling, felt like two beef sacks. My tongue had stopped bleeding, but was now numb, flapping stupidly between my cheeks. I only wanted to protect Vanessa, but I barely felt I could protect myself. It was an arduous journey up these godforsaken stairs, and I don't think I'm exaggerating when I say it was worse than the Donner Party's expedition across the Oregon Trail.

A decorative cloth and foam draft blocker kept the door at the top of the stairs ajar. The flower-printed cloth, slid onto the bottom of the door, had gotten stuck. When the lead guard pushed the door further open, the strong scent of incense wafted into my nostrils. I gagged. The aromatic fragrant smoke was too much in my state, and I immediately got lightheaded. Still, I trudged on.

We were led into a cluttered living room. Knickknacks adorned every surface they could. Vases of flowers were placed haphazardly on the floor, shoved against the walls. Little rows of ceramic cats and unicorns lined a table, next to a pile of half-opened mail. Tiny, fake tea kettles had their own hidey-holes in a wooden display case, mounted next to a clock on the wall. The clock itself was one of those ironic ones where the numbers went backwards.

Surely this place was home to an egotistical lunatic.

Speaking of, she sat on a worn corduroy couch, absentmindedly strumming an acoustic guitar. Her long, straight hair was covered by a floppy, straw sun hat. Her devilish eyes peeked through transition glasses, the lenses partially opaque at the moment. She was still attractive in her older age, and her black blouse accentuated that, even with the metallic belt styled with random shapes hanging loosely from her abdomen. She had multiple long necklaces, drifting down towards her chest, drawing my eyes like the focal point of a painting. Her tan was even over all her revealed skin—she must have been working on it for weeks. She smiled and lit up the room like the sun—obviously, she was used to everything revolving around her.

"Welcome to my lair," Carly Simon said.

Her smirk was strong enough to pull a semi up a small hill with a raise of her dimple.

"Why don't you two have a seat? Tracer, is it?" Carly reached out, palm up, indicating a stool for me to sit on across from a coffee table strewn with miniature elephant statues. "And honey, you can come sit next to me." She placed her acoustic guitar down, the neck resting on the outside armrest of the couch and then patted the cushion on her right side.

Vanessa sat down, inching as far away from the singer songwriter as possible, like a mouse trying to pry open a serpent's jaws. I took my place on the plastic stool, black with a back and four legs. In trying to get comfortable, the silver silicone leg caps squeaked across the wooden floor. A black scuff mark appeared.

Carly laughed, a staccato snigger, like the feet of a lizard moving across a desert. "A hard back chair for a hard-boiled detective."

"Ah, that's the clever wit we're so used to in your lyrics," I said.

The singer leaned back on her couch. "Now, I don't really want this to be an unfriendly conversation with you both, but I do think this is going to be a stern talking-to."

"My experience with stern talking-tos usually winds up with the business end of an electric cattle prod facing my way. Let me tell you, no matter how many times you tell your father he's got the voltage setting too high, the shock still sends your teeth a-chattering." I paused, rubbing the bruises on my sternum. "But I guess that's what you get when he catches you playing with Barbie dolls instead of the Stretch Armstrong he bought you."

Both Carly Simon and Vanessa stared at me, mouths agape.

The silence was broken by "You're So Vain" emanating from Simon's pocket, muffled. She pulled her cell phone out, and the ringtone became louder now that it wasn't muted by her denim jeans.

"I'm so sorry," she said, answering the phone. "Hello?"

"How rude can someone be?" I whispered to Vanessa. "You know you're in a meeting, right? Put your phone on silent, like a normal person. Even vibrate."

"She has her own song as her ringtone?" Vanessa pointed out in response. She raised her eyebrows.

"No, Stuart, no. I haven't got rid of them yet. Let me take care of this side of things, and you go on home," Simon said into her phone. "Leave work at work, for once. This stress is going to give you an ulcer and kill you one day. No, of course I don't want that. I just think you're too much of a perfectionist. And a workaholic. I appreciate the level of effort, but you need to learn to relax. Take a vacation day once in a while. I can't send you off on hits if work-induced anxiety has you holed up in some hospital bed. Yes, I'm well aware of Tracer and his reputation. No, I don't need you to come back. It's like you're not even listening to what I'm saying, Stuart. Go home. Get your mind off your work. Alright? Alright. Yes. Thanks. Bye."

"Now, where were we?" She asked, tossing the phone onto the coffee table. It hit the polished wood and slid into a white elephant, making the figurine rock back and forth. Its trunk, raised way above its head, mocked me with the swaying motion. "Oh, you know what—I don't mean for this meeting to be so formal. Tracer, my dear, why don't you get up and mix us some drinks?" She pointed behind me to a small bar with liquor bottles and glasses neatly organized.

I hobbled over, passing the guards that led us into the room. They hung back by the door still, I suppose as protection. The one that led us into this hoarder's Elysium of a room made eye contact with me but refused to say anything. Seems the rudeness of the boss rubs off on the henchman. It's like the saying—rot runs down. Except for tomatoes. And apples. They kind of rot from the outside in. Bread too. Was "rot runs down" even an idiom? Maybe I was confusing it with something else. Either way, I made a mental note to clean out my fridge when I got back to the city.

The bar in the back of the room was stocked full of top-shelf liquors. I knew this because I couldn't pronounce any of the names on the labels as they were all unfamiliar to me. I grabbed an 18-year-old Lagavulin, poured myself a shot, and let it race down the back of my throat like it was trying to win the Triple Crown. I know scotch is a sipping drink, but in this predicament, you take whatever clears your mind fastest.

"Tracer, honey, I'm in the mood for some tequila," Carly called out. She looked at me with a coquettish glance, trying to be seductive, enticing. Knowing what I did about Carly Simon, her expression came across as less *come hither* and more *come hit-her*. Luckily, I wasn't about violence towards women. Not for any real code of chivalry or anything though—I just found that in bar fights, women are quicker than me and tend to fight dirty.

I poured four glasses altogether: a tequila mockingbird for Carly Simon, a Manhattan for Vanessa (she requested extra cherries), and two more scotches—both for myself.

I realized I couldn't carry all four glasses back, so I downed one of my scotches at the bar. It burned. Maybe the Lagavulin would cauterize my tongue. At the very least, I could have one last taste before my execution—hell, maybe I'd succumb to alcohol poisoning before a bullet in the brain.

The walk back to the stool was more wobbly than I expected. I guess drinking hard combined with getting beat up really gets your head swimming.

"Thank you," Carly Simon said, taking her drink from me. As she reached out for her cocktail, her sleeve slipped towards her shoulder. At the top of her bicep, a pattern was revealed on her skin, her tan betraying her. More pale than the rest of her arm was an arc, running down into a star design, which then curved out in two more connecting arcs. I didn't have the arm bracelet with me, but I think I just found its owner.

I sat down and tried pointing as casually as possible at her arm. "So, Carly, did you happen to lose something? A bracelet of some sort?"

"Don't feign ignorance, dear. You know I lost my bracelet. I've been trying to get it back from you for a couple of days now. But now that you're here, maybe we can work out a deal. So, my friends, let's get down to it. What can I do, short of murder, to get you to stop trying to determine the genesis of the greatest song ever written?"

"Wait a second," Vanessa laughed. "You think 'You're So Vain' is the greatest song ever written? How could you ever be so…deluded?"

SLAP.

Carly Simon was quick. Like a rattlesnake on the spoiler of a Formula 1 car. I saw the red handprint on Vanessa's pale cheek before I realized what had happened.

"Don't you ever talk to me like that again." Simon held a finger inches from Vanessa's face, speaking to her like she was a dog who just had an accident on the carpet.

In that moment, I saw three things in Vanessa's eyes: pure contempt, welled-up tears, and my own reflection. My hair was a mess. I brushed it, using Vanessa's gorgeous irises as a mirror. All better.

"Got it, honey?" Simon asked, her voice losing the sharpness it had just moments ago. She patted Vanessa's thigh in feigned solidarity. "Don't make me do that again. I don't like being forced to do that sort of thing. It's beneath my station, but some people just need to be taught a lesson. You know what I mean, Tracer, right?"

I responded by sipping my scotch. And by then responding. "What makes you think that's what we're even trying to do? There's a handful of corpses piled up over the last few days, and you think 'You're So Vain' is the most important thing we're after right now?"

"Isn't it, though?" Carly Simon asked. "I know you were at the Rolling Stones concert the other night, hoping to glean some information off of Mick Jagger. And I know you were picking up where our poor, dearly departed Ellie Dayton had left off, weren't you? It all revolves around just one thing."

"I just don't get it though. Why did you kidnap Ellie? Just because her sister wanted her out of the way?"

"Tracer, I didn't just kidnap her. I saved her. I escorted her towards eternal salvation. She was…how should I put this? Her narcissism was driving her insane. Trying to make the song about herself. I just couldn't have that now, could I? In the end, she even thanked me, you know. She thanked me personally. Those were her last words."

"You're a monster," Vanessa said.

"By the way, Tracer, you didn't pocket a pile of zip ties while you were at Ellie's house, did you?" Simon asked. "Seems my boys misplaced them there on accident. Even after I told them not to leave any evidence behind. I would like them back. You can always reuse zip ties on others," she said, glancing at Vanessa.

I shook my head. "No, sorry. How rude of me. I should've thought ahead."

"Oh well. Now, please, what'll it take to get you to stop this madness?" Carly said to me, ignoring Vanessa. "Money? Women? Surely, Vanessa here can't satisfy a man with your…thirsts, am I right? I could get you any woman of your desires. Tell me, Spence, who's your perfect woman?"

"Lady Liberty," I answered without hesitation. It's a question I ponder quite frequently. When you're an underemployed detective, you have a lot of free time. And most of it is spent lost in your own thoughts, dreaming of Babylon so to speak. I had plenty of scrap papers with top ten lists and columns of pros and cons trying to reason my perfect woman. But any way I sliced it, that sultry woman welcoming the huddled masses into America always came out on top.

"Lady…Liberty?" Carly Simon repeated.

"Sure. She stands for the right thing. We know she enjoys reading, so she must be smart. And with the amount of time she holds that torch up, she's gotta be in shape. I can only imagine what her body looks like under that robe. Her figure must be statuesque."

"I've never hated anyone more than I do right now," Carly said. "And I knew Warren Beatty pretty well."

I turned to Vanessa, my inebriation clearly getting the best of me. "Vaness, I hope you know that's no reflection on how I feel about you. Out of all the real-life people, you're my number one, my perfect woman."

"Don't worry," Vanessa said. "I'll try not to get too jealous of the Statue of Liberty."

"Can we focus back on me?" Carly said. "I think we have more pressing matters to attend to than your weird fantasy crushes."

"Hey, when you're put in a life and death situation, you think about what matters most," I said.

"And you think the Statue of Liberty matters most to you?" Carly asked. "Fine, fine, forget it. I can't bribe you with a woman. But maybe, just maybe, I can bribe you with a bribe. How much to make this little problem go away, huh? Five hundred? A thousand? You can even keep the bracelet if you'd like, as long as it buys your silence."

"How much does sanity cost?" I replied.

"What do you mean?"

"I mean exactly that. The only thing that'll get me to stop is you shutting it off."

"Shutting what off?"

"Your song."

"What in God's name are you talking about? It's like I'm talking to a child with a tenuous grasp of language or reality."

I took another sip of my scotch, ignoring her offhand remark. "Like Ellie Dayton, every day for a year, I've heard your blasted song. Every single day." Another sip. "Vanessa here too. And same with my other client."

I held back the revelation that Warren Beatty was my client and that he was now in the big sleep. I imagined Beatty's wrinkled, old, dead face resting on an enormous pillow, arms crossed, laying in an oversized bed. Had to be even bigger than a California King. A California Emperor maybe? A Dictator sized bed? Typical Hollywood elites—can't be satisfied with even the biggest and best that reality has to offer; they have to imagine up new things even in death. I scoffed.

"You mean to tell me you've all been hearing 'You're So Vain' every single day?"

"It's been a living hell," I said. "Wait. You didn't know? That wasn't your plan?"

"Honey, I had no idea. But that brings up an interesting turn of events." Carly Simon crossed her legs. This was a typical femme fatale move that I learned in my time as a private eye, although normally the girls wore revealing skirts, as opposed to jeans. Still, Simon possessed a pair of thighs that could trap any man. You'd be happy to gnaw your own limbs off just to escape. And then you'd be walking around with no arms, bragging about the time you felt Carly Simon's denim against you. What kind of life was that?

"How so?" Vanessa asked.

"Seems that I shouldn't be the one bribing you and handing out money. Seems like you both owe me royalties."

"Royalties? Who says?" I asked.

"Simon says," Simon said.

This was a predicament I was used to. Reminded me of my father's regular policy of "reverse allowance." Every week I would have to give him an allotted sum of money for the chore that he called "putting up with your sorry existence."

Taught me money management techniques that I still used to this day.

"I'm…I'm not sure that's how royalties work, Carly," Vanessa said.

"Honey, don't try to use your smarts, it makes you unattractive. The music business is a complex beast. Trust me on this one; I've been in it for decades."

She really put the "bitch" in "ambitious."

"We're not giving you any money, you vamp," I said. "Just tell us who the song is about, and we'll be on our merry little way. You'll never have to see us again."

The singer songwriter paused and sipped her drink. After a moment, she placed her glass down on a white ceramic coaster patterned with a crow sitting on a vine of berries. She got up, walked over to a window. She opened the shades and stared out.

"Tracer, come here and join me."

"You're not my father!" I screamed. Orders from authority figures always bugged me. Even so, I wondered where that outburst came from. Ah, a mystery for another day.

"O...kay," she said. "Just come over here, will you? You too, Vanessa, darling."

I swirled the glass of scotch around in my hand, watching the legs of the Lagavulin run down the inside of the glass. Finally, I tipped the rest of the whisky into my mouth, holding it there, savoring its smoky flavor. I put the glass down on the coffee table, hard.

Balancing as best I could, I stood. I was lightheaded. More lightheaded than I should've been after the drinks I had. I shook my hands at my sides.

Although she opened the shade of one window—there was a second window next to Carly Simon that was still closed—it felt like the room had actually gone darker. I had the distinct feeling that we weren't alone. Call it a sixth sense. The sense of dread.

I walked over and stood next to Carly Simon, right in front of the window with the closed shades. Some cream-colored eyelet curtains bordered the tops of the windows and draped down about halfway. Vanessa stood on the opposite side of Simon. Carly gestured towards the opened window.

"What do you see?"

"It's a bit smudged. I can recommend you some better glass cleaner. Or if you use paper towels instead of a rag, it'll be less streaky."

"No, I mean, out there. Out there."

I looked out at the sprawling acres she called home. The pool, the tennis court, the pond—all ensconced in the nature surrounding everything. It all washed over me. I knew there was a specific answer she wanted, maybe one that would get me and Vanessa out of this mess. But for the life of me, I couldn't figure it out. I've never been able to understand the demented mind of the criminal element, and there was none more demented than Carly Simon.

"Well, there's that dog that's doing his business right at the base of your sign, if that's what—"

"I see a well-oiled machine," she interrupted, clearly annoyed at my answer. "A whole system devoted to me, and me alone. I see past the tree lines, past the city limits. All of this, all of you, just functioning cogs. Cogs with ears. Cogs with wallets. Cogs that my song is forced upon. And that you all have eaten up for years and years. Part of it is the music, sure. Part of it is my voice, angelic and glowing. But more than that, it's the mystery. The mystery of who the song is about. It's the perfect system. It ensnares everyone it comes across, like a bear trap. The snap of its jaws, melodious. And that's why I can't tell you. That's why I can never reveal my secret. It's all for me. Don't you see that?"

"And I thought I talked too much," Vanessa said.

"Ah, you certainly do, honey. We'll put a stop to that soon enough," Carly Simon said. She smiled. "So, Tracer, are you going to call it off?"

"No."

"That's too bad. Too bad. Looks like we're going to have to go to Plan B. Poison."

I stared at the glass of scotch still in my hand. How could I be betrayed like this by my favorite beverage? The horror!

"No, not that kind of poison, you idiot," Carly said. She trained a gun on me, one that seemed to appear out of thin air. Where was she keeping that? The two thugs still in the room aimed theirs at me too. "I mean *lead* poisoning."

With her back to my gal, Carly Simon didn't notice that Vanessa raised her own glass above the famous musician's head, ready to smash it down. However, Vanessa was too slow. Carly spun around, like the

Tasmanian Devil, and caught Vanessa's forearm. She bashed it into the window, forcing Vanessa to drop the glass. It shattered. A shard bounced off the wooden floor. It stuck in my calf. I dropped down to a kneel, wincing in pain.

When I finally looked up, Carly Simon was choking Vanessa, raising her off of the ground. Damn, I would've never pegged her to be that strong. Her gun was still aimed at me.

"How pedestrian of you both. To think you could defeat me."

"You know," I said, gaining more of Carly Simon's attention. "A man is like a car window. You can wind him tightly, cranking and cranking, until he's all closed up. Until you think you have him fastened and secure. But if you're not paying attention, and you keep winding? That's when the glass shatters under the pressure."

"What are you talking about? You mean those old hand cranks? They stopped making those years ago."

"I wouldn't know. I live in New York City and don't drive," I said.

She cocked her gun. Vanessa's cheeks turned blue.

"Guess you'll never learn now," Carly Simon said. "It's time for your *DIE-nouement.*"

"Actually, I think it's *curtains* for you," I said.

That's when I tugged on the lift cord of the shades next to me. I let my body pull them down as I fell to the ground. The shades sprung open, dashing the entire living room in blinding light.

We all saw the silhouettes of a couple of humanoid figures dash to get out of the brightness, towards the corners of the room.

"What the hell is that?" Carly Simon screamed, dropping and forgetting about Vanessa. "Shoot them! SHOOT THEM!"

Vanessa dove to the floor with me. She reached out for my hand. As we held on to each other, the sounds of a gun fight happened above us. It only lasted a few seconds, but it felt like an eternity.

Okay, that's a lie. It only felt like a few seconds.

Carly Simon, sliding against the window, slumped down. Her blood smeared on the glass pane. Looks like whoever cleaned that up later would really need my advice about the paper towels.

Her body fell between Vanessa and me. Carly's eyes were still open. Even though her corpse was riddled with bullets, she was still breathing. I didn't think she'd have long, though. Anywhere from a few minutes to a couple of days. Maybe a year, tops. What do I know? I'm not a doctor. I'm not qualified to give an accurate prognosis.

I army crawled over to her, my limbs tired. Aching.

"Stay with me. Stay with me, Carly. We'll get you help."

She coughed up blood. It hit me in the face and splattered onto my shirt.

"Ewwww," I said. Again, I am not a doctor—I'm not trained in bedside manner.

Carly Simon's eyelids were slowly closing. She was fading like the outro to one of her songs. I slapped her cheeks to wake her up, to keep her on this side.

"Come on, girl. I need to know. I need to know. Who's it about? What's it worth it anymore? Just give me a name. A name, Carly."

Her face lit up. She was energized again. Youthful. In that moment, she looked as beautiful as she ever had.

"I'll see you in Hell, Tracer."

And she died.

"No," I said.

She was still smirking. She had taken her secret to the grave. I had failed.

Shell-shocked and shamed, I grabbed her face. Sure, I was being selfish. But it hadn't sunk in yet. My fingers, spider-like, worked the muscles of her lips, opening and closing them like her corpse was a puppet.

"Okay, Tracer, okay," I said, through the side of my mouth, affecting a woman's voice, as if Simon's corpse was my ventriloquist dummy. But real ventriloquist dummies are still creepier, and I'll fight anyone who says otherwise. "I'll tell you. I'll tell you what the song's about and who I wrote it for. I'll tell you. I'll tell you! It's…" But nothing came out. I couldn't even trick my mind into making up a name.

Vanessa grabbed my shoulder, shaking me out of my strange reverie. I was embarrassed, but she just embraced me. Her hug felt like marshmallow soaked in hot cocoa.

We stood up. Cautious. The two thugs were also downed. Carly was both a good shot and a bad shot. Seems she missed her actual target but had gunned down her own men with ease. And her men had done the same to her.

It was a kind of poetry. In the way that I'd never understand it.

"Oh my god," Vanessa said. She placed her hand on her mouth.

"Looks like the femme fatale's fateful finale," I said.

I grabbed the gun out of Carly Simon's hand. I pointed it at the wall opposite of us, behind where the two goons had stood. I fired two shots. Splinters of drywall fell onto the hardwood. Vanessa ducked down again. I turned and shot the window behind us. The pane didn't shatter, but the bullet hole made a pretty dang cool breaking pattern.

"What are you doing?" Vanessa asked.

"We don't want the cops to know we were part of this. I'm making it look like Carly Simon and her thugs killed each other."

"But they DID kill each other."

"Don't worry. I saw it in a movie. *La Confidencial.* I think it's Spanish for 'The Confidential.'"

"You mean *L.A. Confidential?*"

"I don't think so."

"We should get out of here, Tracer."

The room was rapidly getting darker. Almost like the walls were closing in on us. Even the light from the windows behind us faded from our sight. The last vestiges of vision dwindled to a pinpoint.

"I think we're about to, Vaness." I reached out for her hand.

She took it.

Blackness blanketed us. It was as black as midnight on a moonless night. We were wrapped in darkness. Blind. Confusion. But I had Vanessa's hand in mine. I didn't let go. I wouldn't ever let go.

29

You know how when you close your eyes, you can still see some light beating on the back of your eyelids? You can still see patterns and those eye floaters that move around? People always talk about darkness in terms of having your eyes closed, but if you think about it, it's still light enough to see all these things. It's a nuanced distinction that I'm making here. And I only bring it up because until this point in the narrative I had never truly experienced complete and utter darkness.

I mean, it was black. Black-black. The complete absence of color. If I had a flashlight, it wouldn't have worked. All visible light was absolutely absorbed.

Time had ceased to have any meaning. Location too. I had no idea where we were or how long we had been in this state. I had once heard the phrase *time is a flat circle*. I hadn't understood what that idiom meant when I heard it the first time, and truth be told, I still don't understand it. I mean, what the hell is a flat circle? Like if you draw it on a piece of paper? How does that apply to what time is?

All this science-schmience stuff was above my head, but the phrase seemed apt now. I decided to say it out loud. Maybe it would reassure Vanessa, whose hand was still wrapped in mine.

"Time is a flat circle." I wasn't even sure if my voice or any sound would carry in whatever plane of existence we were in.

"What the hell does that mean, Tracer?"

"I don't know. Seemed like the right thing to say."

She squeezed my hand three times. I squeezed hers back four times, showing her I agreed with her sentiment.

"Have you ever been in an isolation tank, Tracer?" Vanessa asked. She continued without waiting for my answer. "One of those isolation tanks that you see in malls now? They're sort of the next big thing, like a really expensive fad, I guess. They only work if they're soundproofed and if the water you're floating in is the same temperature as your body. Some people use them to rest in. To be comfortable. Maybe for some therapy. I tried it once, stayed in for an hour. But it felt like it was only five minutes. Waste of time and money if you ask me. Give me a good bathtub, some lit candles, and Elvis Costello's 'Allison' playing low in the background. Much more relaxing any day of the week than one of those things."

My imagination ran wild with the image she placed in my head.

"My father made me try what he called an isolation tank, when I was a kid," I said. "It was before they started to be a thing though. He was on the cutting edge of technology, I guess. Ahead of his time. But it wasn't like the ones they have now. No water or laying down or black lights or anything. It was more just a cramped room under the stairs with a heavy-duty padlock on it. He'd leave me in there for days at a time. For *testing*, he always said. Whatever that means."

Talking was putting my nerves at ease. They've already been put through the wringer, put in their place, and put through the hoops. They deserved this brief moment of respite. My only hope was that whatever was coming wouldn't put them down.

"Tracer? How long do you think Simon's song has been plaguing people for? We can't be the only ones whose lives it's tortured."

"Well, it was released November 8, 1972. Which means…17,101 days it's been tormenting people for. I'd wager a guess that there's at least one unlucky soul who's heard it every day since then."

"How…how did you do that so quickly in your head?"

"Ness, in my line of work, you need to know math. Eight ounces to a shot, point 45 inches diameter bullet for my revolver, twelve days 'til rent is due with zero money. Carry the one. Still equals eviction."

"I know you're a lone wolf and all, but…have you ever considered adding another to your work? Your life? One plus one equals two."

"Me plus you, you mean? That could only equal trouble."

I couldn't see her face, but I could almost sense her frown.

"Trouble for anyone in our way," I said. I thought this teasing line was smooth. Chicks dig smooth lines.

"You're an idiot," she said and squeezed my hand again.

We waited in silence and darkness. An eternity of blackness, stretching on forever.

The eyes are a wondrous organ. They can adapt to almost anything. Except for people with glasses. Astigmatisms. Those weirdos who can't see colors. The completely blind.

What I'm trying to say is that in the void that Vanessa and I were in, I began to see shapes moving. Slightly more black humanoid shapes moving closer to us than the slightly less black background of the void. Their eyes, glowing like red eyes in terrible photos, were the only things not some shade of black. Otherwise, they were humanoid shapes with tentacle-like limbs and oversized heads. Almost like a come-to-life Funko Pop! toy of Cthulu.

Three of these Lovecraftian shadow creatures now stood in front of us. They spoke in unison, a creepy monotone. I wondered if they practiced this harmony speech pattern thing they had going on.

"TRACER OF SPENCE. YOU COME BEFORE US. IT IS TIME FOR YOU TO SPEAK OF THE RESULTS OF YOUR INVESTIGATION. JUDGEMENT SHALL BE SWIFT YET FAIR."

"I'm sorry, but what?" I asked.

"DO YOU NOT COMPREHEND THE LANGUAGE? SHALL WE SELECT ANOTHER TO CONVEY OUR THOUGHTS? WE BELIEVED COLLOQUIAL AMERICAN ENGLISH WOULD HAVE SUFFICED, BUT ANOTHER PREFERENCE CAN BE ADOPTED IF OPTIMAL FOR YOUR AUDITORY SYSTEM."

"No, no, English is fine. I just meant that I don't know what we're doing here. Or who you guys are. Or what you want with us. Or when lunchtime is. I'm starving. Even a glass of water would be nice."

"Look, whoever you are, we just want to know what's going on," Vanessa said.

Their eyes darted from me to Vanessa.

"INTERLOPER. INTERLOPER. INTERLOPER," they repeated. The pitch of their voices kept raising in harmonic triads, like a teenage boy running up stairs three at a time.

"Whoah, whoah, ease up there, big fellas. No need to panic. She's…she's my partner." I felt Vanessa's radiance permeate me like a stiff drink down my gullet.

"THIS PREVIOUSLY UNKNOWN INFORMATION HAS BEEN PROCESSED. WE SHALL PROCEED WITH THE CONVERSATION."

There was a pause. The three beings seemed unsure of how conversations normally went.

"So…you were going to tell us who you are…" Vanessa hinted for them.

"YES. OUR SOBRIQUET IS BEYOND THE GRASP OF YOUR HUMANISTIC MINDS. WE FEAR FOR THE SAFETY OF YOUR SANITY IF WE SPEAK THE NAME OF OUR BEING ALOUD."

"What? Really?" I asked. This was just like those Lovecraftian mysteries, where the main characters went crazy over the course of the story, winding up in some mental institution with Kermit the Frog as their roommate.

I had never finished reading a Lovecraft story before.

"NO. NOT REALLY. THIS WAS HUMORISTIC TO DISPERSE THE TENSION AMONG ALL OF US. OH, THE JOCULARITY."

The creatures made noises that could only be described as almost, but not quite, the exact opposite of laughter. Goose pimples raised on my flesh as the noise gritted into my ears.

"WE ARE ETERNAL. WE ARE UNENDING. WE ARE ALPHA AND OMEGA. WE ALLOW YOU TO CALL US THE SHADE."

"And you've been following me."

"WE DEEMED THIS ACTION NECESSARY FOR THE SURVIVAL OF OUR SPECIES."

"But you just said you were eternal," Vanessa said. "Unless you meant something else, I don't see what you mean about not surviving."

"THE INTERLOPER IS PERSPICACIOUS. WE HAVE SURVIVED FOR MILLENNIA. UNTIL THE PRESENT, WE HAVE NEVER BELIEVED OURSELVES TO BE OTHERWISE. THIS WAS UNFAMILIAR. WE HAVE ENCOUNTERED CATACLYSMIC ADVERSITY THAT WE HAVE NEVER ENCOUNTERED HERETOFORE. SOMETHING WHICH HAS CAUSED OUR SPECIES TO DREAD, AN EMOTION NEVER FELT UNTIL THIS MOMENT."

"Welcome to humanity, fellas," I said. "Existential suffering is such a part of daily life, that we joke about it constantly. You guys know Instagram? Try checking out a meme sometime."

"I think Tracer is getting off the point a little bit," Vanessa said. "What is it that caused your suffering? What changed? What made you stalk Tracer?"

"THE SONG." Their voices rang out in the ether. Reverberation hung off their voices like hand-me-downs on a child.

It all made sense to me now. These guys, The Shade, they were behind everything. Everything. My torture. Vanessa's torture. Warren Beatty's torture. Ellie Dayton's torture. My entire case.

"You," I said, anger dripping off of every word like water off of a stalactite. My words continued to tumble out, an Olympic acrobat across the gymnastic mat. "You did this. You caused that damned song to play over and over and over again. What have you done to me? What have you done to us? Do you even know what…what suffering and torment you've put us through? Every day. Every single day for the past year. Persecution. Carly Simon's voice ingrained in my mind like a brainwash victim. How dare you. How. Dare. You."

I couldn't be sure, but when The Shade spoke next, I sensed wavering in their voices.

"YOU MISUNDERSTAND. YOU DO NOT COGNISIZE. WE DID NOT IMPLEMENT THE SONG. WE DETERIORATE THE

SAME AS YOU. WE, TOO, LANGUISH AMONGST THE SIREN'S MELODY. WE WRITHE."

"What."

"Tracer, they didn't do this to us." Vanessa stroked my fingers, still holding my hand. "The Shade, they've had the same thing happen to them as what's happened to us. 'You're So Vain' has been repeating for them."

My mind raced. "So, what? What're you saying? They've been plagued with it every day too? This has all been a coincidence?"

"PRECISELY. EVENTS ARE CONTEMPORANEOUS. SYNCHRONICITOUS. THAT IS WHY WE HAVE SELECTED YOU AS OUR SAVIOR."

"Savior?"

"HAVE YOU NOT BEEN AS AFFLICTED AS OUR SPECIES? ARE YOU NOT A, AS YOU SAY, PRIVATE DETECTIVE WHO HAS BEEN DISENTANGLING THE PREDICAMENT? EXPOUND UPON US YOUR DIVINE WISDOM, TRACER OF SPENCE. THE SONG'S ORIGINS. THE PROVENANCE OF ITS INCEPTION. WE MUST ACQUIRE THIS INFORMATION BEFORE IT IS TOO LATE. THE ELEVENTH HOUR IS UPON OUR SPECIES. AND YOURS."

The darkness, the complete hopelessness and gloom of my surroundings and of my case hit me like a piano falling from a third-story window. I felt trapped, ensnared. A fox whose leg was caught in a hunter's metallic trap. And similar to the fox, I didn't have the opposable thumbs to undo the clasp. Metaphorically speaking. I did have actual opposable thumbs. They were quite helpful in opening bottom-shelf whiskey bottles and tying my shoelaces. But they couldn't help me here, in this void.

"But, I don't...I don't have the answer. She...Carly Simon...she died. She wouldn't tell me who the song was about. She's dead, and it's done."

I said all of this with the finality of a man who knew he was digging his own grave. I only hoped my grave would come with one of them soft pillows to rest my head upon. In life, I could never find one quite comfortable enough for me. How do normal people deal with these problems? How do normal people pick a pillow out at a store without really trying it? How do normal people know if a pillow is too soft or too firm before they take it home? And the stores I've been to—they don't accept returns, either. Those corporate bastard overlords, too good for strands of my hair in the fibers of uncomfortable pillows. I must've had a whole closet full of unbearable sacks of synthetic down and feathers.

"THIS OUTCOME IS DISHEARTENING BUT NOT UNFORESEEABLE. IT IS NOT CAPRICIOUS. AND, THE INTRINSIC OBSTACLE SHALL BE RECTIFIED."

"What?"

"THE EXPLICATION IS LOCATED WITHIN THE CONFINES OF YOUR BRAIN MATTER. IT WILL BE EXTRICATED. MANUALLY."

"What?" I felt like I was repeating this word like a mantra given to me by a Maharishi.

"ALTHOUGH YOU MAY NOT COMPREHEND THE ANSWER, WE ARE POSITIVE THAT YOUR LABORIOUS PERSEVERANCE HAS RESULTED IN THE ANSWER BECOMING LODGED IN YOUR INNER CONSCIOUSNESS. YOU MAY NOT BE AWARE OF THE ANSWER, BUT IT MUST BE DEEP WITHIN. AND WE POSSESS THE ABILITIES TO MANUALLY REMOVE IT FROM YOUR CEREBELLUM AND NERVOUS SYSTEM."

"Oh. Okay then. That sounds logical. And like a decent solution."

"WE ACCEPT YOUR STATEMENT AS CONSENT."

The Shade's tentacle limbs wrapped around my head. The suckers on their feelers felt clammy and damp. Deep pressure, like that of a diving submarine, suctioned onto my temples and around my forehead. Little pin pricks of needle-like appendages entered my skin. No pain, but I wouldn't say it was comforting to know these creatures were currently occupying some portion of my brain.

I may have made a mistake. A dire mistake.

"Wait!" Vanessa called out. "What are you going to do to him?"

"ONLY THAT WHICH HE HAS AGREED TO."

"Yeah, but, like, what specifically?"

"WE SHALL REMOVE THE EXPLANATION FROM HIS BRAIN. ALL SHALL BE RESTORED. HE SHALL BE VIEWED AS A GOD AMONGST OUR SPECIES. A MARTYR."

"A martyr?" I asked. "That sounds kind of cool, actually. I always looked up to Joan of Arc. What a babe. Whatever happened to her, anyway?"

"She was martyred, Tracer. You know, like to death."

"Oh."

"Yeah."

"WE SENSE HESITATION."

"You're damn right you sense hesitation," Vanessa said. "You can't kill him, just to find out this mystery that no other person's been able to solve in fifty years. It's not right. It's not right."

"AGAIN YOU MISUNDERSTAND. WE SHALL NOT LEAVE TRACER OF SPENCE LIFELESS. HIS ESSENCE SHALL NOT BE EXTINGUISHED."

"Oh. That's a relief."

"HE SHALL JUST BE A HUSK OF HIS SELF. A SKIN SACK WITHOUT THOUGHT. NEUROLOGICAL FUNCTIONS SHALL STILL BE INTACT. BUT NO COGNIZANCE WILL FLOW THROUGH HIM.

"NOW, IF THERE ARE NO FURTHER INTERRUPTIONS THAT YOU SEEK, WE SHALL BEGIN THE PROCESS."

Not a moment had elapsed before the suction had intensified. I wasn't dead, but a feeling like rigor mortis set in. They were siphoning something from my cerebrum, from my skull. I couldn't move or speak.

A tear traipsed down my cheek. In the total blackness, I was sure no one had seen it. I never felt more alone.

"No! Stop!" It was Vanessa again. Like every time she talked, she was relentless to get the last word in.

"I can figure out the answer," she said. "Just give me a minute, will you?"

The siphoning feeling stopped. I let out a breath.

"YOU SHALL HAVE EXACTLY SIXTY SECONDS IN HUMAN TIME. OTHERWISE, WE SHALL CONTINUE WITH OUR EXTRACTION PROCESS."

"Okay, okay. I got this," Vanessa said. "What do we know about Carly Simon? She was egotistical. Completely. More so than any other person I've ever met. And I dated quite a few men in my time. A lot of mistakes. Did I ever tell you about the guy who bordered his entire bedroom with mirrors? Making out with him was quite…awkward. He would keep his eyes open like a bat. Did you know they sleep with their eyes open? Maybe that's where we get that saying. Bats are gross. Flying rodents. Ugh. But yeah, and that guy, he lived with his parents too. Who does that? Why would they let him adorn his entire bedroom in mirrors? That must lower the value of the house. Watching yourself while sucking someone else's tonsils out is possibly the most egotistical thing I've ever been a part of."

"FORTY-FIVE SECONDS HAVE ELAPSED DURING THE COURSE OF YOUR MONOLOGUE."

"Ness, you might want to wrap this up," I said.

"That is," she continued, "until we met Carly Simon. Someone who viewed the entire world and everyone in it as revolving around herself. She was the sun, in her own mind. Gargantuan, bright, hot, the soul of the universe. Get it? Soul? Like Sol? The name for the Sun? Whatever. And she couldn't let someone, that poor girl Ellie you were investigating, Simon couldn't let her turn the song into being about someone else. Carly Simon, with her infinite narcissism, could only write that song about one person, and one person alone."

"Herself."

The tentacles of the creatures went slack.

"PROCESSING. PROCESSING." The Shade emanated noise akin to the old AOL dial-up tones.

"WE ACCEPT THIS AS FACT. VANESSA OF BUCKINGHAM, YOU EMANCIPATED THE SHADE. YOU HAVE DELIVERED US FROM AN UNKNOWABLE EVIL. WE SHALL WORSHIP YOUR

EXISTENCE FROM OUR HABITAT IN THE SHADOWS OF YOUR PERIPHERALS."

"Cool, cool," she said. "That's fine and all, but mind just letting me and my boyfriend go? We've had a long day, and I'd really just like to snuggle him now."

"YOUR COMMAND SHALL BE AUTHORIZED AND OBEYED. THANK YOU, WORSHIPFUL ONE. GO FORTH AND REVEL IN THE ACT OF SNUGGLING."

The Shade backed up and disappeared, not even their carmine eyes apparent in the void distance.

Just like that, the blackness dissolved around us. The darkness descended from my vision, pixelated like an old Nintendo system on an old cathode-ray tube television.

Replacing the obsidian of my perception was…apples? Pineapples? Crates of oranges, heads of lettuce, bags of spinach, vines of tomatoes, kiwis, grapes, avocados. As my eyes adjusted, I found myself in an unfamiliar grocery store. The produce aisle. But still with the love of my life, Vanessa, holding my hand.

30

This is it. This is the epilogue.

I know I shouldn't tell you that. That's not how these things are supposed to go. But I wanted to let you prepare yourself that this is the ending, the wrap-up.

It was two weeks later…

I know it was two weeks later, because Vanessa had just said that it's been two weeks.

"Tracer, it's been two weeks since everything went down. When are we getting another case?"

We were in my—our—office. Not much had changed, honestly. My desk was still there, crackers still in the drawers. My pet slug, Moby, was still there. My door, with my name and title etched in it, was still there and currently closed. There were two chairs now. Mine—behind my desk—and Vanessa's—next to my chair, also behind my—our—desk.

No, not much had changed, except for the *my* to *our* thingy.

I know, I know, you've got a lot of questions. And I'll get to them all, I promise. Let me start with the first and most pressing one. Where'd we get the other chair? Easy answer. I *re-appropriated* it from the accountant's office down the hall from me. He wouldn't miss it. He already had another chair. What accountant needs two chairs? It's just greed—pure, unadulterated greed. I only trust any accountant as far as I can throw them. They're heavier than one of those shot put balls, by at least a couple pounds. And I can barely throw one of those far at all.

Maybe fifteen, twentyish feet, on a good day. Therefore, I trust accountants less than I trust inanimate track and field equipment.

Vanessa was currently spinning on that second chair, her legs scooched in on top of the seat, arms wrapped around her knees. She looked like Da Vinci's aerial screw sketch. She had the physics of it down pat, possibly the first perpetual motion machine.

"Ness, that isn't how being a private eye works. We don't just get another case. It's like fishing. You have to bait the, uh, fishing thing. And send it out on the water, which, in this metaphor, is the crime-infested streets of New York. And then you have to wait until you get a bite. And only then can you, uh, do the fishing catching thing, and…pull on the string? The rope? The fishing rope? Then, and only then, will you be lucky if you've caught a case, instead of some seaweed or an old boot or whatever other gross things lurk in the Hudson River."

"I don't know enough about fishing to know if any of that made sense, Tracer."

"It did. Trust me. I'm a man. Men are born with intrinsic knowledge of fishing. It's in our DNA."

Vanessa sighed. Over the past two weeks, I got to know that breathy sigh very well. I smiled every time I heard it.

The grocery store we found ourselves in when The Shade dropped us off was a local one. Local to the small city of Gibraltar, Michigan, that is. When we appeared standing next to a display of bananas with a chalkboard sign that read, "I HAVE A PEELING YOUR DAY IS RIPE FOR PICKING UP THESE BANNANANAS. ONLY $14 A BUNCH," Vanessa and I were very confused. Fourteen dollars for a handful of bananas? That seemed exorbitant. But what do I know? I can't remember the last time I ate a banana, let alone bought one.

But that wasn't the only thing I was confused about. Like, how did the guy who wrote that sign still have a job? He misspelled "bananas." Terrible salesmanship.

However, the BIGGEST thing Vanessa and I were confused about was where we were and how we got there. Turns out, we weren't the only ones thinking that. We appeared right in front of a little old lady with blue-tinged hair. She looked like she had been eighty years old since the Carter administration. But what a set of lungs she had on her. The surprised scream that came out of her mouth literally said "AHHHHHHH!" But it figuratively said that she probably never touched a cigarette a day in her life, what with how clear the holler was. Good for her.

After the ambulance picked up the old lady and drove away—she had suffered a heart attack. But don't worry, the heart attack was unrelated to our sudden appearance. It was twenty minutes later in the frozen food section, next to the biggest variety of fish sticks I ever saw— Vanessa figured out that we were nearly 600 miles away from New York.

I suppose that's where The Shade live, or at least have their base of operations. Every good supernatural secret organization has to have a base of operations. And Gibraltar, Michigan just makes sense. Economically speaking, I bet they get tons of tax cuts from the city. The Gibraltar Community Center has karate classes for kids scheduled throughout the year. And every July, they have a Miss Gibraltar competition. As all things go, I bet The Shade are more than happy to call Gibraltar their home. Seems like a wholesome community.

Vanessa and I spent the time coming back to New York City as a sort of vacation get-away. Early on, something like that puts a lot of pressure on a relationship, but what choice did we really have? It's not like we've been that traditional until now, and I was ecstatic to have her company.

We learned so much about each other, cruising down the highways in our rental car. We opened up with all of our innermost secrets and desires. I found out that she hates Reese's Cups. The ridges on the edges are too sharp and pointy. And she has a delicate tongue. Just how delicate was something I was aching to find out. Meanwhile, I told her I wish all pants were made out of the same material as bathing suits. I like the way they cling to my thighs when they get wet. Makes me feel like that dude Michael Phelps. Why wouldn't you want to feel like an Olympic gold medalist all the time?

Yes, it was a sentimental soul swapping sabbatical.

When I say our trip back was heavenly and paradise and utter bliss, I'm obviously exaggerating for effect. Still, our trip back was heavenly and paradise and utter bliss.

I spent hours at a time watching the wind flow through Vanessa's hair like ribbons on an oscillating fan. We couldn't afford a rental convertible, and I don't like rolling the windows down, so it wasn't really "wind" blowing through her brunette hair. Instead, I just breathed deeply, puckered up, and blew onto her face. Same effect. Let me tell you, driving with a cricked neck towards your passenger isn't easy.

It was somewhere near Bloomsburg, Pennsylvania on I-80 where we decided Vanessa would join me as a private eye.

It made perfect sense. She showed throughout this insane "You're So Vain" case that she had what it took to solve the most heinous of crimes. From carrying the tools of the trade, to putting herself in danger for opportunity, to, you know, actually solving the case. Let's be honest—I also wanted to be around her as much as possible. Like a fly on the sticky side of duct tape.

It was also on that long stretch of road that I got the call from Mr. Beatty's banker.

"Hello, this is Carla calling from First Civil National Bank. Is this…Mr. Tracer Spence? Is that a name? Tracer? Really?" Her sonorous voice coming out of the phone's speakers hummed just louder than that of the car's engine.

"Yeah, that's me. It's a real name. And I happen to like it."

"Did your parents learn to read off the back of cereal boxes or something?"

"You're awfully flippant for a financial stoolie."

"I can afford to be. Unlike you at this moment," she said. The gal had gall. The broad had brass. The missy had moxie.

"What do you mean?"

"It appears that you were the recipient of the last check written by one Warren Beatty, who went missing on the same date that he quote unquote signed it to you." I could hear her making finger quotes over the phone. She was the type of person to watch movies with closed captioning on just so she could read faster than the actors were saying their lines.

"And that means…?"

"It means that a temporary freeze has been put on Mr. Beatty's account, and the transfer to your account will be put on hold until further notice. I'm sure that's hard for a man of your limited intellect to understand, so let me put it another way for you: money go bye bye."

"Hold up, hold up. Can you tell me this? Like legally?"

"Absolutely not. But who's going to stop me?"

I sorely needed a stiff drink and cursed the laws from stopping me from having one while driving. Ain't nothing like some bottom shelf whiskey to help shove bad news down your throat.

"You know your job can be done by an ATM machine, right?"

"I don't think it would be as cold, calculating, and unforgiving as me," she said. "Now, I'm going to hang up on you, Mr. Spence, to save you the trouble of having to search for the END button on your phone."

I knew I would never that money, like I would never see those self-tying shoes Michael J. Fox promised us in *Back to the Future II*. I was the only one who really knew what happened to Warren, and there was no coming back from having the skin slurped off your bones like beef goulash. Information was hard to come by, and I came by this information hard.

Still, I had the arm bracelet given to me by Serena to look forward to. For a little while, anyway. Until I looked up the tracking ID given to me by the United States Postal Service for the package I had mailed it in. After days of saying "IN TRANSIT" somewhere near Denver, Colorado, the post office's website switched to an error message of "TRACKING ID NOT FOUND." If I was ever going to see Carly Simon's jewelry again, it was going to be whatever she was wearing at her funeral.

Speaking of one Mrs. Serena Dayton, she wound up getting off with a light sentence of time served and fifty hours of community service. With mine and Detective Hardholm's testimony pointing the finger of murder at Stuart, the judge decided Serena wasn't completely at fault for her sister's murder. However, Sadie Marie Olivierri thought otherwise; she packed her bags and moved out of Serena's nice suburban home. Other than a hard-nosed chastisement from Hardholm and a negative Yelp review from Serena, I made it out of the case relatively unscathed.

As for Stuart, he had disappeared, slinking off, a silhouette into the night.

I was getting light-headed reminiscing on the dizzying series of events that had happened over the past fortnight. Watching Vanessa spin wildly in her chair also wasn't helping. I got up and stared out my office window.

Vanessa asked again, "Really, Tracer, how do we go about getting our next case? How do you solve a case? Teach me to be a private eye. I want to help"

"You know *Slylock Fox?*"

"The newspaper comic strip?"

"Right. It's sort of like that."

"What do you mean? We have to have an anthropomorphic fox give us clues?"

"No," I said. "I mean that I always read the newspaper upside down when working on a case, hoping to find the answers, just like in *Slylock Fox.* You never know, they may print something secretly like that and it'll break the case wide open."

"Has that ever worked?" she asked.

"Only when I can't figure out the mysteries in *Slylock Fox,*" I said. "Oh, and the crosswords too. They print their answers upside down on the back page."

Vanessa got up and touched my shoulder.

"Tracer, the next person that comes through that door, let's just take them on as a client. You never know where the journey will lead.

It's not like we have GPS in life. Your last case brought you to me. You can't just keep sending people away like you have been, like you're a bouncer at a nightclub whose list just reads 'no one.'"

"Come on, who have I turned away?"

"Yesterday. You turned down a client because you didn't like the cut of his jib. You even told him that." She affected a deep voice and said, *"Derp derp derp I'm Tracer Spence, and I don't like the cut of your jib, buddy.* That's what you sound like."

She rubbed my arm some more, and I was hoping she'd rub it right down to the bone.

"Well, did you see the cut of his jib? It was just gross."

"Do you even know what a jib is?" she asked.

"Yeah, it's that…it's that dangly thing that hangs in the deep pockets of your throat, right?"

"I think that's called a uvula."

"Eww, Ness, this isn't sex ed. No need to get clinical."

She ignored me, shaking her head. It messed her hair up, a dark strand of it hanging across her face. She blew at it out of the corner of her mouth, but it refused to move, like a stubborn mule scared of climbing up a steep mountain side. I brushed it back behind her ear.

"I think you're just afraid," she said. "Afraid of working your first case as part of a team. Afraid to let go and trust someone else."

She had read me like a book. A children's book. The only book I felt comfortable with because when I tried reading multiple syllabic words, I tended to move my lips along with them, sounding them out silently. High school was embarrassing for me.

"Listen here, there's only one thing I'm afraid of. And that's being left alone in a tanning bed for six hours while my dad tries to talk the receptionist into leaving me overnight. But the joke's on him, because they unplug the machines at closing to not run up the electricity bill. In the end, he wasted sixty bucks on that over-tanned receptionist chump."

I thought a moment more.

"Oh, and spiders. Also afraid of spiders. I can never tell which ones are poisonous or not," I said. "But I'm not afraid of us."

Vanessa planted a big ol' kiss, right on my smackers. That's what I call my lips because the sound they make while I'm eating mashed potatoes. I try not to eat mashed potatoes in public anymore.

"We're going to be great together," she said, right after she was done exploring my personal tonsil area.

"I wish we got the money from that check," I said. "Was gonna call my etching guy and get your name up on the door window with mine."

"Yours is just written in Sharpie on masking tape."

"I never said he was a very talented etching guy. That was the basic package. It was a good deal, too. He threw in the tape."

I tugged on my drawer and pulled out a sleeve of crackers. If I was going to stay in this business, I'd need to be as salty as this city was. And times like these, it seemed the city was made of 100% sodium.

"Vanessa, turn the radio on, will you? And I'll really start teaching you how to do this job."

I sat in my chair and leaned back, legs up on the desk. The cracker dust powdered my shirt. Vanessa reached over, flipped the ON/OFF switch to the radio, and then she too threw her legs up on the desk. Her high heels clunked into my sneakers. We were going to have to get another table or something if this was going to work.

"This is W.R.R.M., The WURM, coming at you all with another power block of soft rock," the radio hissed through its speakers. "Next up, one Carly Simon track for all you lovers out there!"

"No, no, leave it on," I said, stopping Vanessa as her arm reached for the dial. "Let's get it over with."

As a familiar track swelled from the radio, I pulled out my flask, my trusty sidekick. I took a pull of cheap whiskey and read the engraving on the stainless steel container.

To my son, the P.I.

Love, Dad

"First rule of private investigating," I said, tossing the flask to Vanessa, "is drink up."

She did, coughing as the swill hit the back of her throat. She tossed the flask back into my lap.

"Wait," she said. "I know this. This isn't 'You're So Vain.' This is—"

"'Let the River Run,'" I finished for her.

"Yeah. From 1988. It's a good song. Did you know it was written for the movie *Working Girl?* I never saw it but always wanted to. Can't beat some '80s movies, though I prefer the B-movie campiness to any of the…"

I let Vanessa go on, listening more to the timbre of her voice than the words. Her honey-drenched vocals are more song-like than conversational, and I let them wash over me. I take another pull from my flask. There's a lilting sweetness from the whiskey on the tip of my tongue, a warmth of bitterness as it swashes down my gullet.

As I drink myself into the sweet, sweet embrace of oblivion, there's only one thing I know for certain.

Carly Simon is—was—a cruel-hearted shrew.

END

ACKNOWLEDGEMENTS

This book is based off of a true story.

About 15 years ago, working at a place that rhymes with "Glunkin' Blownuts," I noticed I was hearing Carly Simon's song "You're So Vain" a lot. Like too much. At least once a day. Which we can all agree, is too much to hear one song for an entire year. At first, I chalked it up to the radio at Glunkin' being set to the same station, and as radio DJs are allowed limited creativity, it would be normal to hear the same song every single day. And then it kept happening. Even outside of work. At diners, on my college campus, in TV commercials, piped in to the space shuttle I tried sneaking into to get away from that damned song. And I realized the obvious—"You're So Vain" was *about* me. Why else would it be stalking me?

Anyway, the first person I need to thank is the amazingly talented Carly Simon. The Carly Simon in my book is not the same Carly Simon, as the real Carly Simon is, by all accounts, the sweetest person on the planet. She has gifted the world with an indelible song, one that has also kept a mystery on the public's mind for decades now. And I love a good mystery.

I am very grateful to Reagan Rothe and the Black Rose Writing team. They took a chance on a very stupid book, and for that, I'm glad to have them in my corner.

I could not have written an entire book without looking to a community of other authors out there, each one who looks to support others in the field. Authors like Tim Meyer and Jason A. Meuschke, whose advice on the future of this novel was indispensable. And thank you to authors Charles Austin Muir, Danger Slater, Sasha Lauren, Bill Schweitzer, Frank J Edler, J.C. Walsh, Chuck Buda, and Armand Rosamilia…whether any of them knew or not, they have been inspirations to me.

I am eternally thankful to my family. To my parents, for pushing me and for stoking my interests and creativity. To Lauren and Will, for being amazing friends who I can talk to about anything. To Cathy, Danny, and Brian for all your love and support. Marrying into your family was the smartest choice I've ever made.

To my friends and fambly. To Kristen, Nick, and Ben for reading my first rough drafts. This book wouldn't exist without them. To Nick and Ben again, along with Tom, for your advice. To Mike, Chris, Koray, Bill, Steve, Annalise, Chanel, Biz, Cody, Derek, Ed, Evan, MG, Nicole, Al, Matt, Maddy, Adam, James, Mike, Tommy, Ryan, and Danny. Each one of you has helped me through so many things over the years, even if you never realized it.

And, to my family. Thank you to my best friend, Tiberius. He is a once-in-a-lifetime dog, who marked me as his own the first time he met me. Hopefully the future will bring about a way for dogs to read books, and maybe Ty will laugh at this one. Thank you to my son, Wyatt. I hope you grow up, read this book, and realize your dad is a silly man. And thank you to my wife, Meg. If all that ever happened with *The Vain Curse* was that I would get to hear you laugh at all the dumb jokes I wrote, I would've been happy. The fact that other people may get to laugh at my dumb jokes is entirely because of you. Most of the good things in my life are entirely because of you.

ABOUT THE AUTHOR

Ryan Morgan Miller is a musician, podcaster, and author of the new novel, *The Vain Curse*—a book that will almost certainly not be up for any awards, prizes, or nominations of any kind. He has no qualifications for writing a comedy book about hardboiled detectives, except for the ability to ply himself with an inordinate amount of scotch. He can be found in the vulgar cesspool known as New Jersey with his wife Meg, his son Wyatt, and his best friend Tiberius.

Note from the Author

Word-of-mouth is crucial for any author to succeed. If you enjoyed *The Vain Curse*, please leave a review online—anywhere you are able. Even if it's just a sentence or two. It would make all the difference and would be very much appreciated.

Thanks!
Ryan Morgan Miller

We hope you enjoyed reading this title from:

BLACK ROSE
writing™

www.blackrosewriting.com

Subscribe to our mailing list – *The Rosevine* – and receive **FREE** books, daily
deals, and stay current with news about upcoming releases
and our hottest authors.
Scan the QR code below to sign up.

Already a subscriber? Please accept a sincere thank you for being a fan of
Black Rose Writing authors.

View other Black Rose Writing titles at
www.blackrosewriting.com/books and use promo code
PRINT to receive a **20% discount** when purchasing.

Ingram Content Group UK Ltd.
Milton Keynes UK
UKHW040753210723
425555UK00001B/105